Symona's Still Single

Lisa Bent

JACARANDA

This edition first published in Great Britain 2020
Jacaranda Books Art Music Ltd
27 Old Gloucester Street,
London WC1N 3AX
www.jacarandabooksartmusic.co.uk

A CIP catalogue record for this book is available from the British
Library

ISBN: 9781913090203
eISBN: 9781913090401

Cover Image: Uzo Njoku
Cover Design: Rodney Dive
Typeset by: Kamillah Brandes
Printed and bound by CPI Group (UK) Ltd,
Croydon, CR0 4YY

The unlocked door holds the answer.
You already have the key.

Chapter One

Reality

It's three am. Sunday has arrived and I have no business being awake right now, but I just can't sleep. I'm lying here fully alert staring at the bedroom wall, which is covered in white stripes of light that have beamed through my blinds from the street lamp outside. Some artists have sold artwork depicting the same thing for serious money. Ridiculous, when you think about it. I can appreciate art, but don't take the piss. Did you know there was an artist who sold his shit in a can for millions? I kid you not. He literally sold his shit for gold! If that isn't an alchemist, I don't know what is.

I need some of that transformative magic right now, because I don't understand how I'm in this position. If anyone, *in this spiritual hour,* is listening and cares to help, my name is Symona Brown, I'm thirty-seven years old and I'm a Public Relations and Communications Executive at a top media company. I love my job and I'm good at it, although I should be a director by now, with that director-level pay. This isn't even ego talking, it's fact. Work politics—aka institutionalized racism—is a block to progression and therefore lifestyle, which is a block to my ability to thrive. The ethnicity pay gap report needs to become mandatory ASAP so companies are made accountable to address those differences. This is 2016—yeah, it looks different, but there's still struggle.

I should also be married with children by now. Informed by society, family and my biological clock. To be fair, I'm also ready. I decided to be consciously single at thirty-two, and five years later, I'm still in the same position. How and why? A former Black male work colleague once gave me his thoughts, which I never asked for. He said, "Symona, the reason you are single is because you are opinionated and too educated." Shoved in my face like someone trying to force feed me. Please know, I didn't swallow that. It's not my truth. It's his, based on his own self-inadequacy. I just walked away, because that mindset isn't deserving of a response.

When you have been single for as long as I have, everyone who isn't tries to 'help' by telling you why you are. Everyone is a bloody guru. Apparently, the main reason is that I'm 'high maintenance' and 'too picky.' I'm not, I just have standards, which is imperative and a basic requirement. If that makes me picky, OK, I'm picky. In fact, I may need to be more specific in my affirmations, because what I'm calling for isn't coming and I know the type of man I want exists.

'When are the kids coming?' is the worst question at this age. There could be numerous reasons, which are no-one's business, but my case is simple—no man, no baby. I know there is love behind the intrusive question, usually asked by family members and friends my age with children, but it's too flippant and doesn't acknowledge the true rollercoaster ride of what I'm going through. Honestly, I'm battling with the fact that I now have less than twelve per cent of my eggs left, if research is to be believed. Even though technology surrounding pregnancy has advanced, pregnancies over the age of thirty-five are deemed risky. If... *when* I become pregnant, I would be referred to as a mother of 'advanced maternal age,' which is a lot nicer than the previous term, 'geriatric mother.' I don't feel old, I don't look old. *Black really don't crack.* And I'm *not* old—I'm fit, healthy and can pass for late twenties, but it's a different story internally, apparently.

At this ripe-but-nearly-expired old age (informed by the natural decline of my eggs), the real question is: do I still *want* children? If yes, do I have time for the man to come along or do I do it alone? I don't expect anyone to ask me this nor do I want them too, but this is the question playing on my mind right now and keeping me up at night. When people have what they once wanted, it's hard for them to remember what it was like when they didn't have it. Their lack of awareness and empathy silences me.

I love being in my own space, but I'm tired of coming home to an empty flat and cold bed. I'm bored of going out raving, because music isn't what it used to be and men don't approach anymore, plus I would rather be at home or doing something with my partner. I'm bored of going on holidays with the girls. I feel bad for saying that because they are great and we have had some good times, but I feel like I'm in a twenties loop and I'm ready for a new story, where they of course still feature, but not so centrally. The majority of us are in the same boat, so I do not doubt they feel the same. I'm bored of my plus-ones being a girlfriend or a male friend whom I have begged to come with me to a wedding. They don't even happen that often in my circle, and yet I always seem to still be single when the invitation arrives. *Shit! I'm triggered. Of course I'm triggered.*

I know this is because of Asta's call yesterday. I have known Asta since I was twenty-two years old. We met through a mutual friend and hit it off straight away. We did a lot together in our early twenties, from holidays and raving to spa days and dining out. We experienced so much together in our single days—less so as we headed into our late twenties and became more career focused. She's an investment banker now and she met James, a property developer when she was twenty-nine. She got engaged at thirty-two and Brianna, their first child arrived at thirty-three. She called me to tell me she is three-months pregnant with her second child, and that they have 29th June 2019 booked for their wedding day and she wants me to be one of her bridesmaids. We are the same age and our paths couldn't be more different. I'm so happy for her, but I feel sad and anxious for myself. I'm not comparing or mixing her life into mine, it's just that her brilliant news is a wake-up call. I'm far away from my family vision, and time is running out. '*What's for you, will not pass you*' is a saying I live by. But what if it already has?

2019 is a milestone year for both of us. As she heads towards chapter 40, she will be hoping the sun will be shining on her wedding day, whilst I will be hoping I have a partner accompanying me, on top of everything else. How dire is that? Did I miss the boat? Could I have done more to ensure I wouldn't be in this position now? I don't have the answers, but this cannot be my story. I rebuke it. No situation is permanent, *even though my single status seems to be.* A lot can change in three years, but I need to do something different. Question is… what?

*

I roll over to the other side of the bed and reach out to stop the irritating buzzing sound coming from the bedside table. *Thud.* Of course the phone falls because I am too tired to open my eyes. I swipe the floor searching for the device with my eyes still closed until my fingers come into contact with it. Through one squinted eye, I can see it's Chantel calling. If it were anyone else, I wouldn't have answered. I press the green button as I draw myself back up and place the duvet over my head. "Chan? Why are you calling so early?" My throat feels like sandpaper.

"Mornin, sis!" Chantel's loud, chirpy voice causes me to wince. "What do you mean early? It's ten am already, which is late for you." With judgment and concern Chan asks, "Why are you still in bed? Are you OK?"

"Ten? Really?" I feel as though I'd only just drifted back to sleep. I pull the duvet from over my head, open my eyes and sit up straight, using pillows to support my back. The sun is out and my heating is on, which is the best combination for December in the UK. "I woke up at silly o'clock and clearly managed to get back to sleep, but I feel exhausted." *And teary.*

"Did you have any mad dreams? I always do when I drink too much."

I laugh, because that comment isn't surprising coming from my sister. "I think I did. Hold on," I tell her as I close my eyes.

9

I tend to have vivid dreams, which I write down. Chantel knows this, which is why she's asking, however I didn't detect the usual mocking tone. I read somewhere that whilst you're asleep, your subconscious acts out what you need to pay attention to in your waking life, which I find fascinating. Remembering dreams is an art. If I think too hard or receive distractions, *like this call*, it can block the memory. I tend to close my eyes or stare at the ceiling as soon as I wake up and ask myself, what did I dream? Soon after, my memory serves me snapshots in colour that slowly unravel, in no particular order, like photographs being developed in a dark room.

I pay attention to the things I remember and any feelings that rise up and then I look up the meaning in dream dictionaries for explanations, which I reflect on.

"Erm... I dreamt that I missed my plane because I couldn't decide which door to go through." *Hmm, no interpretation required. It's crystal clear.* "Anyway. What's up?"

"I-went-on-a-date last-night...." Chan sings in excitement.

"Again? Wow he's keen."

"Nooo, you're thinking about Marvin who I saw on Thursday night. Last night I was with Seyi. I met him on a new dating app. I only signed up on Monday!"

"What? I cannot keep up. How do you do it? I'm having no luck and you're out here getting wined and dined on the regular."

"Well, you see, sis, the problem with you is that you're trying to find Nemo, but your Nemo is an expensive Bluefin tuna. Cod, salmon and tilapia are just as good, but you're overlooking them."

"Really? You are making me out to be a snob, which I'm not.

I just have standards. Why do I have to accept tilapia? I mean—"

Chantel interrupts. "For fuck's sake, can we lose the dramatics please? I have standards too. Lighten up and be more open, that's all I'm trying to say."

"I know, sorry. I've just been thinking about my single status a lot lately, and you're right. Listen, are you still on for lunch today at two pm? I can rustle up something, or we can go to our fave restaurant in Blackheath. What do you fancy?"

"Let's chill at yours, I'll bring Rocco since you haven't been licked by a dog in a while."

"You're such a cow. See you at two... Wait! Do you mind if I also invite the girls?"

"Of course not. See you all then. Love ya." As usual, she annoyingly hangs up before I can say bye too. I don't get what that's about but it's rude.

Morning Ladies,
Single Summit, today, 2pm at mine. Lunch will be provided.
It's short notice, but we need to talk about our single status.
Tash, come through if you can join.
Syms x

Fuck this single shit, and fuck hope. I'm not really a fan of swearing but sometimes you just need to include it to add weight to the level of fuckries. Hope is a waiting game, a dangerous one at this age. Why am I... *we*, still single? Something has to give. The girls let me know they are coming, thumbs up all round. Great!

"ALEXA, play India Arie!" Let's start this day.

*

There's something about listening to neo-soul whilst showering. The lyrics, melody and a smooth voice just help me ease into my day. *Love*. Even India's ready for it. Wanting it and being ready for it are two different things, though. I'm ready for love, but do I know what I need to do, to get it?

"Alexa, play *Mercy* by Okiem." I don't need any additional thoughts around love right now.

I end my shower early as I hate not feeling prepared when people are coming over. I quickly dry myself and slather my body in coconut oil—I *love* the stuff—before throwing on my beige, oversized dressing gown and heading to the kitchen.

"Fridge, please surprise me with goodies to save me from going out." I open the door and I'm greeted with orange juice, tomatoes, salad and Prosecco. If it was just my sis coming, I could definitely rustle up something with that and whatever is in the cupboards and freezer, but it's not gonna work for five people. The supermarket on a cold Sunday morning are two things that shouldn't go together.

Whilst I dislike winter with a passion, it provides a visual reminder that change does happen, even if I don't see it in my own life. The quiet road, lined with equally spaced trees, which were green, yellow then burgundy brown before their leaves started falling, know they will soon flourish again. Lose to gain, rest to restore. Death is also a re-birth. We can learn from nature.

It's a crisp day, the sun is shining and the sky is blanket blue, and everything looks clean and clear—including my face, which feels taut from being slapped by the wind. A free microdermabrasion? I'm not complaining. I also feel more grounded. I swear I had a mini mid-life crisis earlier this morning.

Whilst speed walking, I decide to make my *nothing can go wrong* dish—salmon with a medley of vegetables, mushrooms and sautéed potatoes, with green salad and coleslaw. My mission is to get in, grab bits and get out, fast. Chan and her sweet-tooth self will bring desserts when she comes by later, so I have one less thing to think about.

Bloody hell, the whole of South London appears to be here this morning. Is shopping on a Sunday morning now a thing? I pick up my basket, which becomes heavy in no time because I'm adding additional things, like vanilla-scented candles, that I want but don't need right now. By the time I arrive at aisle eight, it's really heavy. I put the basket down and throw in three packs of salmon, adding to its fullness. *Hang on a minute... Who is that?* He is at the opposite side of the aisle selecting meat, with his back turned to me. *Hmm.* Approximately six feet tall, broad shoulders, nice firm bum, solid looking thighs and calves, and his feet look neat in trainers. The fact that the tracksuit is grey is an added bonus. Grey, on an athletic looking body, is a turn on. Not sure why, but it just is.

I slowly angle my body hoping to catch a side view of him, but that presents no new information. *Well, I guess I eat meat today!* I make my way over to the other side of the aisle, pushing my heavy basket along with my foot. Standing not too far and not too close, I pretend to gaze over the selection of ribs before slyly looking to my right. Hair level one, rich brown skin tone, nice profile, full lips, strong beard game. *He is an alright looking guy!* I can't place his age from here, but I would guess between thirty-five and forty years old.

I snatch a look at his basket, which he is holding with his left hand. *Damn, that is a lot of meat. Surely that can't all be for him?* No ring. Nice bicep, look at that just popping through the hoodie...

"Hey, can I help you?" My thoughts are interrupted by the man I was meant to be looking at discreetly. I look at him and try not to give away my embarrassment in my voice.

"Hey!" *I sound too chirpy.* "Yeah, erm... I was just looking at your basket wondering if I should get lamb chops instead of ribs?" I say whilst holding up a pack. *Good comeback.* "I was in my own world there. I'm cooking for my girlfriends later so was just thinking if that might be better than salmon."

He responds, "I see. Well I would say go with the salmon..."

Nice tone, well spoken... I would guess he has always lived in South London. Nice brown eyes, smooth skin and really nice full lips...

"...It's simple and you can't really go wrong," he finishes, smiling.

"Yeah I think you're right. Thanks..."

Ask him a question to keep the conversation going! I'm racking my brains but nothing is coming. We are still looking at each other, and the moment is beginning to drag out awkwardly. *Think, Symona, think!* Feeling hot and embarrassed, I just want this three-second and counting painful silence to end.

"Have a good day," I eventually manage to say. I see a big red cross flash in front of my eyes. My spirit is disappointed. *I'm disappointed.* I was only meant to end the silence, not the whole damn conversation! *This is unacceptable.*

My mouth shut it down before my brain had a chance to process or edit. There is nowhere to go from here. *So, why am I still standing here?* I quickly wave goodbye, pick up the heavy basket with two hands, turn around and begin to walk away from him in a hopefully-normal manner. *Not too fast, not too slow, head up and shoulders back.* I attempt to make this heavy basket look effortless. As soon as I turn the corner and he's out of sight, I drop the basket on the floor, clenching both hands to relieve the pain. Feeling deflated, I stand for a few moments gathering my strength before reluctantly picking the basket back up and heading to the self-service checkout.

I have a cupboard full of bags at home that I save to use again, but never seem to remember to take them with me when I know I'm doing a food shop. I begin to scan items and look up to check if the machine has registered the coleslaw before I place it in my newly-purchased carrier bag. As I glance up, I see myself on the camera that ensures you aren't stealing—and it's only *then* I realise that I still have my leopard print headscarf on. I mean it isn't the end of the world—luckily I look cute in a headscarf—but regardless… Who knew fine men shopped on a Sunday morning? Mum always said *'Look your best, as you never know who you will meet.'* I continue to scan and pack whilst having an internal monologue. *Girl, this is why you're single! You have no game. You didn't even stay long enough to see if he liked you. You didn't even let him know that you may have been interested. Don't even get me started on the goodbye wave, what was that about? You looked like an awkward fourteen-year old!*

I finish packing and make my way to the exit. "The salmon is gonna be awesome," someone shouts. I look to my left, and it's the guy with the basket full of meat, now holding a second basket, just as full but looking like a perfectly balanced set of scales.

"Thank you," manages to leave my mouth, accompanied with a semi-smile as I step outside and head home, still feeling like a loser in a leopard print headscarf, struggling with bags.

Chapter Two

Single Summit

The doorbell rings and I don't even need to look through the spy hole. The ten-decibel, "Hey, I-AM-HEREEEE!" tells me—and the neighbours—that my sister has arrived. I open the door and I'm greeted by Chantel 's beaming smile—and snug under her arm is Rocco, her beautiful black King Charles Cocker Spaniel puppy. I gently stroke his head then hug my younger sis and kiss her on her cheek before inviting her in. I look down at the stiletto-heeled boots she is wearing and ask, "Louboutins on a Sunday? To chill at my house? You could have just come casual, sis!"

Chantel responds to the question by strutting through my hallway like a model, and then abruptly turning like she has come to the end of the runway. Facing me in a pose, she says "Excuse me, when boots cost this much, there is no best day or appropriate occasion to wear them. Every day is Louboutin day. Plus, it was your Mum who drummed into both of us that we should..."

I join Chantel to finish the motto that I have already acknowledged, "… Always look your best as you never know who you are going to meet."

"Exactly! So I'm work-ing-these… *boots*!" Chantel says with attitude as she spins back around and struts into the kitchen.

"Wait! Take those off before you come inside!" I shriek. *This girl has no respect.*

"Hold on!" Chantel shouts back. I hear her stiletto heels clicking across my kitchen floor boards before she quickly shuffles past me in the hallway again and back out the door. She returns with a shopping bag, dog bowl, Rocco's sleeping basket and treats, and then I watch her with love as she struggles to take off those dominatrix-looking boots. I want to laugh so badly but don't want to be accused of being bad mind.

People struggle to look good, and looking good can be a struggle. The proof is right here! Look at this twenty-nine-year-old, attractive, funny, kind, together (sometimes) woman. I don't understand why my sister doesn't work in fashion. She's always changing her style—braids this month, weave the next. I'm envious her workplace doesn't have a problem with it. She is an EA to the founder and CEO of a start-up tech company that are growing exponentially.

Chantel's boss is a thirty-four-year-old, forward-thinking white woman from Peckham who gets the importance of employing people from diverse backgrounds. Showing up and delivering is the only requirement. Chantel has shares, great benefits and gets paid very well because her boss believes, *'When people are happy with the money they earn, they feel valued and appreciated—and in turn, this brings greater contribution, performance and loyalty.'* I love her ethos and I wish every company would adopt it, because she is right.

Chantel lets out an orgasmic, "Ahh!" as she finally manages to get the boots off. She looks at me and states, "They're new, OK?" and proceeds to click her toes and gently rub the balls of both feet. She heads to the front room and I follow, watching her set up the doggy area in the corner of the room, to the side of the fireplace.

"This dog is treated better than you treat me," I express, laughing.

"Haha. Whatever! For dessert, I've brought chocolate eclairs because it's been a while since you have had something of a similar length in your mouth. I thought I would remind you of what you are missing out on."

"I literally cannot deal with you, you are too much," I say, laughing whilst shaking my head.

"I got your back, sis! I also brought prosecco, and white wine and lemonade so we can make white wine spritzers." I look at her, confused. "Why are you looking at me like that? Don't you remember how Zaara was at your last gathering when she drank prosecco?" Chantel raises her eyebrows and I look down in embarrassment. "Prosecco isn't for everyone and it's definitely not for her, so she'll be getting the lighter stuff instead. What's for lunch?" She walks over to the kitchen and lifts the lid off the pots and pans on the stove. "That's salmon, isn't it?" she asks, referring to the thing covered in foil in the oven. I nod and wait for the renk comment that always follows. "I knew it! Every single time, and the combinations don't even make sense. Where's the meat at?"

"Chan, you say *that* every single time and still leave a clean plate, so stop moaning. You're not gonna die because for one meal there isn't chicken on your plate. Although, earlier at the supermarket, I did pretend to eat meat to get closer to a good looking guy I saw…" I add whilst quickly turning down the heat on all the pots.

Chantel kisses her teeth. "The finest men eat meat," she says breaking out into a little two-step dance. "So you got his number, yeah?"

I shake my head, and then roll my eyes at Chan's disapproving glare. The doorbell rings, which saves me from a grilling. As I walk to the door, I smile to myself. She may be eight years younger and annoying at times, but I'm glad Chantel is in my life. She keeps me fresh and abreast of current trends… *Shit, you sound old Symona!*

I open the door and I'm greeted by Zaara, a former work colleague, now solid friend.

A five foot five inch pocket rocket with a signature style—big shades, voluptuous weave, hair done, nails done and a lover of anything shiny, which she pulls off with class. Bubbly, free-spirited and nuff, just like Chantel. *They would have been perfect sisters.* Zaara's parents are from Jamaica just like ours, and she too is first-born British.

She also enjoys the finer things in life, which includes men, who like her just as much. Her light brown, flawless skin and immaculate dress sense causes men to pay attention, whilst her cute dimples that appear on both of her cheeks when she smiles make them go doe-eyed. Throw in her personality and it's a wrap. Number and first date always lined up, just like that.

"Hey love, how are ya?" Zaara asks as she walks in and hugs me.

"I'm good, hun. Go grab a drink, Chan is in the kitchen and the others will be here soon. I'll be there in a sec."

"No probs, babes," she says, taking off her shoes before heading to the kitchen.

I walk into the bathroom counting in my head... *one, two, three, four*... There it is—the dramatic "OMG!" from down the hallway lets me know Zaara has seen Rocco. "He is adorable. Symona! Why didn't you tell me your sister had a dog?"

I don't bother responding because I know she is already engrossed with the puppy and Chan may not get him back.

I take off my headscarf and squirt olive oil into my hands, then gently rub them together before coating my whole head, giving my scalp the nourishing drink and my thick jet black hair some shine, before carefully unravelling each twisted plait. The doorbell rings again. "Can someone get the door, please?" I shout. There's no response, but my request must have been answered, as I can hear Tasha and Adisa's voices. "I'll be there in a minute," I yell. Grabbing my fist-pump Afro pick, I begin to stretch my hair from the root in different places across my head, instantly giving it more length and volume. I take a look and select a few individual twists, coiling them around my finger to give them more definition. I assess again and ruffle sections into the desired shape. *Why couldn't I have looked like this earlier at the supermarket?* I sigh, I wash my hands and head back to the kitchen.

"Hey ladies! So good to see you," I say embracing both Tasha and Adisa.

"No worries at all. But what exactly has prompted this 'Single Summit?'" asks Tasha.

I begin to respond, "Well, I've just been thinking—"

But then I'm interrupted by Chantel. "It was me. You see ladies, I had two dates this week and Symona is wondering *how?*" she says, smirking.

"Damn, I'm wondering how, too. I haven't had a date in…" Adisa looks up to the ceiling to find the answer and settles on "Agesss." The room erupts into laughter.

Zaara admits, "I'm not doing badly, but I'm happy to take notes from dating expert Chantel, cos even I haven't nabbed two dates in one week before. Girl got game!"

"Before the Dating Sermon begins, let me dish up." I suggest.

I begin to lay out the plates and cutlery on the table. Chan brings over the vegetables before going back for the salmon from the oven. I beckon everyone to the table, tapping my glass filled with prosecco, to remind the ladies to bring their drinks too.

Chantel brings the white wine and lemonade to the table and plonks it in front of a confused Zaara. "I'm good with the prosecco, hun."

Chantel looks at her and tilts her head to the side, as if to say, *'You sure, girl?'* Zaara mimics her, widens her eyes and through her pursed lips telepathically communicates to Chantel, *'I-am-good,'* which she hears loud and clear and backs off. My sister is renk but Zaara knows how to handle her.

"This looks lovely Symona, thank you," Tasha says as she pulls in her chair.

"Ah you're welcome, I'm glad you appreciate it," I say smiling, whilst side-eyeing Chantel.

She rolls her eyes and retorts back, "Surely you must have eaten this dish *many* times before? Anyway, let's eat." She begins to dig the serving spoon into the potatoes.

"No! Hold on, we have to say Grace first." Not waiting for a response, Adisa closes her eyes and bows her head. Everyone follows suit, including Chantel, whose hand is still holding the serving spoon.

Adisa is only one year older than me and has always seemed to know exactly who she is and what she wants. Born in Nigeria, she came to the UK with her parents and two younger siblings when she was eight-years old. She enjoys being a lawyer and loves the status it brings. She wants the whole package, husband, house and children, but wanted to reach her career goals first, so at thirty-two, she froze her eggs as a future investment. She is aware as I am that time is ticking, but she planned ahead…

A deeper shade of brown, Adisa's high cheekbones and big brown eyes are her stand-out features. She is the best person to tell you some home truths, but sometimes a slice of tact to wash down the bitter lemons she is serving would make it easier to take on board what she's saying. Now, though, she's just finishing Grace.

"For what we are about to receive may the Lord make us truly thankful, for Christ's sake. Amen!"

The ladies repeat in unison, and everyone begins to help themselves before tucking in. I take the opportunity to answer Tasha's question with no interruptions.

"So, I literally had a mini melt down last night." The girls in unison look up with concern. I tried to make that sentence as breezy as possible, but judging by their faces, I failed. I explain that I was triggered by Asta's double announcement, which turned the volume up on my own biological clock and man time-lines. "I have been consciously single for five years now, which I don't regret. After Stephen—" *Nice guy, just had no ambitions or drive* "—I wanted to ensure I wasn't just with someone for the sake of having a boyfriend. That's also a time waster, and I'm too old for that shit. But it's been a wake-up call, and it has me questioning whether I'm stuck in a comfort zone? I've had a date here and there, but no real change. I'm three years away from forty. Something needs to change from now, to ensure I'm not in the same position by the time I get there.

"Most of you lot are in the same boat for different reasons. I'm speaking frankly, to ensure we aren't all just sitting pretty, waiting for Mr Right to come riding in on a horse to save us. Cos he ain't coming that easily, and certainly not by that form of transport." Everyone laughs, which brings relief to what I'm saying, but this is serious. "When you do eventually see someone you like, do you even know how to flirt? And would you be prepared to approach him to get his number?"

"Yeah, I think my flirting game is alright and I'm confident enough to approach... but they may mistake my confidence for being full-on," says Zaara.

Adisa, meanwhile, had clearly come to a firm conclusion. "Boi, I don't know, you know. I think the man *should* approach. I'm old school. I don't think I'm asking for too much. It's the gentlemanly thing to do."

"Some men are shy though. So a guy not approaching doesn't mean he doesn't like you or that he isn't a gentleman," says Tasha.

"Who has time for a shy guy?" Adisa asks, scrunching her face up.

"Diana King does," offers Chantel with a semi-straight face. Tasha bursts out laughing and as a follow up pleads with Adisa to "*Have mercy, mercy, mercy,*" whilst bogling.

Adisa doesn't look impressed. "If you can't approach me, then already we don't have a future relationship. I like bold, confident men who can speak up, so he has just ruled himself out," she says matter-of-factly, whilst cutting into her salmon.

"He could be confident but due to rejection scars, he doesn't trust his approach?" offers Tasha.

"Is that my business? Look, I appreciate the life coach, deeper questioning, but I said what I said."

"Damn, I would hate to be cross-examined by you," Zaara says, looking at her in awe. "No-nonsense Adisa appeared real quick today!"

Everyone laughs, and Adisa's cracked smile shows she is also in agreement.

"Anyway, I'm asking because I saw someone at the super-market this morning," I say cringing at the memory of the encounter. "I pushed myself to get into his eye-line, he caught me looking and started a conversation. I couldn't give the signal that I was interested, and I missed a potential opportunity. How wotless is that?" I say, shaking my head. I'm still disappointed in myself. "We tend to focus on the last time we were approached by a man and acknowledge it as a distant memory and yet when the rare opportunity presents itself, like I said, do we even know how to flirt?" There is silence. "The nature of the game has changed, but have *we* changed to adapt to the times?" Confused faces stare back at me. "It's about the man, and *not* about the man. Regardless of whether he approaches or not we— Sorry, let me speak for myself: *I* need to develop some more skills, and do things differently, to get a different outcome."

"Hear, hear, sis!" Chantel says, whilst opening another bottle of prosecco. "Ladies, she is right. You have to be involved in the dance. Sitting on the sidelines will get you overlooked." "Dance? More like game," says Adisa.

"Either way, my point is you have to get involved. All my dates in the past two years have come via dating apps," Chantel retorts.

"Although I have cobwebs to clear, I'm not here for the wham-bam method," Adisa says. "Do you know who I am? I can't have someone I don't know up in this." She runs her hands up and down the curvy outline of her body.

"I'm so with you on that one," I reply whilst pointedly topping up everyone's glasses with the freshly opened bottle of prosecco that Chantel failed to share around.

"I don't see anything wrong with one-night stands. If two people want the same thing with no strings attached, then it is what it is, no?" Zaara replies, shrugging.

I disagree. "In the past, my sexual urges made me go back to exes even though I knew it wasn't the right thing to do. I felt good in the moment and crap afterwards. We broke up for a reason, and as soon as I realised it was my sexual memory taking me back, I stopped. Slightly different to one-night stands as I was going back to familiar ground, but for me, none of it is worth it. That is the reason I don't have fuck buddies, friends with benefits or anything like that."

"Sexual maintenance is important," Chantel says matter-of-factly.

"I get it, but I'm not sure how nourishing the experience is with various randoms. Whilst sexual maintenance is a thing, so is sexual memory and spiritual contamination. I'm busy, I don't have time to be cleansing my aura that frequently. Just my view," I say, piling salad onto my plate.

"Seriously, sex is an important stress reliever," Chantel presses on. "Massages and shopping ain't always gonna get to the route of the problem. I don't think we talk about this enough. Plus, there is nothing wrong with women tapping into their sexual needs and desires."

"I'm not saying there *is* anything wrong with it—my point is, we need to be mindful of the partners we allow into our intimate space and the purpose they are serving. Sex is a transference of energy and not every encounter gives you something."

This is going to become a tennis match if I don't stop. Not everyone sees sex in the way I do, so let me shut up before I'm accused of being judgmental. I shove salad into my mouth to restrain myself.

Adisa's confusion is evident by the lines that have appeared across her forehead, but they disappear as fast as they came when she begins to talk. "It's the safety element I worry about. You don't know them, these men on the apps. They are behind a screen and can say anything. If I was to have a one-night stand, I would rather be in my own space, but at the same time, I don't want a random in my place. In my bed is a bit too late to find out who they are. If I can't flirt to get a man, do I even have the courage to tell him to leave when we are done? What if he doesn't leave? It just sounds too awkward and risky."

Chantel is starting to get agitated. I can see it. She's avoiding eye contact and focusing way too hard on cutting the baby potatoes on her plate into smaller pieces, which she is now pushing into the mushrooms and surrounding sauce. Her plate is an unappealing mess, which I know she won't eat. I ignore her, instead revisiting my uninspiring online dating experiences.

"I joined a paid online dating site a few years ago because I thought people who paid would be more serious, remember? And I guess they were, but I found the majority to be just… *odd* and not my type at all. Just so many no-nos."

Tasha begins to laugh, shaking out her jet black dreads with uniform brown tips. "Symona, I cannot remember half these stories you've told over the years, you're gonna have to remind us."

She loves hearing my dating escapades and I love hearing about married life, a fair exchange I think. As a life coach, she is everything you would want from one. Grounded, considered and empathetic, whilst having the ability to kick you up the arse and help you get the change you said you wanted. Maybe it's by no accident that she's the only one of us who's married. At forty-one, she's only a handful of years ahead of me, but seems more well-rounded. She's just as assertive as Adisa, but Tasha's energy is softer, though not to be mistaken for weaker. You can feel her power and presence even when she's not talking. She's a true cheerleader and confidante.

Remembering Tasha's request, I begin to animatedly list the issues I've come across on the dating website on my fingers. "OK, so number one, the pictures. Men topless, posing in the shower, in the gym, near a bush, next to a car. Two, men standing, kneeling or stroking drugged tigers. Three, men being too forward and brash after two sentences are exchanged. Four? Men stating they want to call me to hear my voice because they are paranoid of 'transvestites'. I *literally* can't. Five, white guys with a fetish towards the darker hue of skin, proudly calling me 'Nubian Queen' in every sentence." I move on to my next hand. "Six, guys wanting to meet after they've said, 'Hi! My name is blank'. Seven? A few men stated I was 'out of their league' and were 'shocked I was single'. Every conversation featured the sentence, 'I can't believe you are talking to me.' *Painful*. Basically, I signed up for three months and gave up after a month. Waste of money *and* time."

Zaara and Adisa laugh, whilst Tasha shakes her head. "When I hear stuff like this, it makes me glad to be married. Ten years strong! Tevin and I have our moments, but I don't want to ever have to entertain this—"

"OMG! I have just remembered another site!" *I'm shrieking, time to lay off the prosecco.* "I joined a *free* online dating site, but I only lasted a couple of hours because all the men messaging me sounded like creeps and I just had this weird feeling that they were looking at my picture and wanking over it. I can't explain it. I just kept shuddering when I looked at their profile pictures."

Tasha and Zaara's eyes widen, Adisa looks disgusted, but Chantel clearly cannot contain herself anymore.

"Can everyone just calm down? Jheeze, how are you all going so left? There are so many free dating apps now that you don't even need to pay for an online service anymore—fact! You are always going to get cringe pictures, but guess what? Cringe to you is sexy to someone else—fact! I'm merely telling you all to *get-wit-the-times* or you *will* remain on the shelf, waiting and hoping for a good-looking dude to catch your eye in, let's say a supermarket, when all you actually have to do is join a dating app and do some online shopping from the comfort of your bed. Swipe left, swipe right! It really isn't that deep. In fact, sis, if you had this particular app, you could see if Supermarket Guy was on there and have a second chance to connect. Whether you believe in God, Source, the power of the universe or destiny, one thing I'm sure about is you also have to take *action*. The chances of meeting a kray bae is slim. And you don't have to have one-night stands, if you don't want to. Plus, I'm the *result* of a one-night stand remember? It's not all bad because I am here! Unless you all think I shouldn't be?"

Everyone is stunned into silence—except for Adisa, who manages, "God damn" under her breath, in awe of the speech full of shade and home truths. The mood has changed; no-one knows where to look or what to say. Everyone knows Chantel is my *half*-sister, but that doesn't stop the reference to the circumstances of how she came to be here from sending a dark, invisible cloud moving across the room, almost seeming to eclipse the sparkly chandelier above my dining room table. Chantel sighs and excuses herself, leaving the table to comfort-stroke Rocco in the living room.

I decide to give her space. These outbursts are not new, but it upsets me to see that she is still struggling. However, she needs to learn to control her emotions better. Eventually, I break the silence by starting to clear the table, since—based on the closed knives and forks—everyone appears to be done.

"Do you want a hand?" Tasha asks as I pick up the first plate.

"OK. Fancy helping me load the dishwasher?"

Tasha picks up some other plates whilst Adisa and Zaara are engrossed on their phones. For a while, the sound of crockery and pots being stacked in the dishwasher, and the whimpering sounds of Rocco in the front room, are the only noises filling my small flat. In the kitchen, Tasha rubs my back in wordless support, which I really appreciate. I'll cry if I look at her, so I nod my thanks before placing the leftover food in the fridge. I smile when I see the éclairs Chantel brought.

"Guess what we are having for dessert?" I shout, whilst whipping out the boxes from the fridge. Everyone looks up solemnly. "Chocolate éclairs! And not just any chocolate éclairs, but ones brought with love to remind us of what we are missing…" I tear open the box and carefully take one out, whilst suggestively raising my eyebrows and waving the chocolate topped, cream filled long bun for everyone to see "…Courtesy of Chan."

Adisa laughs and calls out to her, "Chan, get in here and explain yourself!"

There is a slight pause before Chantel walks back in and says with sass, "As I was saying, before the prosecco took over, I'm just trying to help y'all, cos ya'll be needing help." Everyone laughs and nods in agreement.

Although animated, I know Chan is still upset, so I go over to her and give her a hug. She murmurs that she loves me, and I respond softly, "I know, hun. I love you too, and I'm glad you're here. You know this."

Chantel kisses my cheek, moves out of the embrace and flicks the kettle on whilst announcing, "Prosecco and this type of dessert doesn't go, it's much better with a cup of tea. I know about combinations," she says laughing looking at me. *This girl is nuff.*

Tasha must have heard my thought, as she nods and smiles at me before we both return to the table, shortly followed by Chantel with several cups and a pot of tea. She exchanges smiles with Zaara when she notices that the white wine and lemonade is now placed directly in front of her. The cloud has dispersed and the jovial, light environment returns. I'm relieved, because we have bigger fish to fry.

"As I was saying... I think we need to do things differently to get a different outcome. What do you all think about that?" Suddenly I can feel a deep sadness rising within me from the pit of my stomach. *Don't cry, do not cry!* I can feel my eyes are about to spill the sadness and speak for me, which I don't want. I don't want another emotional outburst. *Pull yourself together, girl...*

"Look!" Adisa flashes her phone for everyone to see. "Whilst everyone was being glum just now, I researched the top five dating apps, chose this one, downloaded it, and boom! I'm activated and ready to hopefully swipe, like and match!" The room erupts into cheers.

I crack a smile, but I'm not present. "Chan, your mini prosecco meltdown showed me how rigid I can be, so fuck it. Here I am, trying to be more open, whilst still keeping my senses in check. I'm not about to lose my mind for the D."

"There is nothing wrong with being dickmatised," offers Zaara.

I'm annoyed we even have to have these conversations at this age. We should all be on a different chapter by now, talking about different things, like... Like marriage and parenting skills, instead of trying to figure out how to find a man. I'm thirty-seven and my growth feels stunted. I'm trying to hold on to the idea that having children is still a possibility, despite my age and no man. I don't want to start out as a single parent, and of course relationships aren't guaranteed. If we broke up, I would have no choice and I'd get on with it. It can be done. It *has* been done. I would like to make a baby from a place of love, which ideally we raise together and build a life together. I need to add that to my Man Requirements. There is so much to filter through, so many more things to discuss, and yet we have to start at stage one.

Chantel's smiling. "This is what I mean. Joining the dance, being involved, taking action! Proud of you, Adisa. Let me see your profile." She stretches out her hand for Adisa's phone, takes a look and acknowledges that Adisa has made a good start. "But here are some tips to make it better. Increase the number of pictures—two is not enough. The additional pictures are there to show your personality, so make sure the location and poses are different. Find your angles and catch the light. The three questions from your profile summary are there to give an insight into your personality, so when it says 'What is the worst drink you've tried?' don't just say 'a badly made Mojito'. Say something like, "Absinthe. It's green and lethal. I nearly died drinking a shot of that in Ibiza. I like breathing, thanks!" Do you see the difference? You are still being yourself, but your personality is coming through. Have a little play around with it, and if you need more help, I will add some gold-dust to it. OK?" She passes the phone back to Adisa, who nods in appreciation.

"Damn, I think I need to re-do my opening profile now," says Zaara, passing her phone to Chantel, who reads it out loud. "*I'm as extra in life as the extra 'a's in my name imply.*" She looks up and shakes her head. "Zaara, this is whack. Re-do that immediately," she says, laughing. "Listen, you guys are giving me a big head, but I'm no guru. It really isn't that difficult, but you need to put the time in like it's a CV. Looking for a job and looking for love are the same process."

"Destiny via dating apps?" asks Tasha as she circles her hands above her phone, acting like she is looking into an invisible crystal ball.

"Cupid and his arrow got an upgrade," says Zaara, laughing.

"I used to daydream about how I would meet my man, how big the diamond would be, and what the wedding dress would look like," I say. "However, I've realised that our whole idea of love is laced in fantasy, fuelled by romantic films. One of my faves is *Pretty Woman*—the rags to riches story, not the fact that

Richard Gere was old enough to be her dad. I'm not interested in a Sugar Daddy," I firmly state. "I also love *The Best Man*. Morris Chestnut? #Thatisall!" I add.

"There is something for everyone in that film," Chantel confirms, smiling.

"Yep, Shemar Moore is mine. Don't make me fight you," Zaara warns, pointing her éclair at everyone before taking a bite.

"Anyway," I say, refocusing. "I called this Single Summit because we all need to stop dreaming now. We need goals, strategy and action."

"You're making it sound like a business plan," says Zaara.

"Because it is, and I don't know how at this big old age I am just figuring that out. We know what we need to do to be strong candidates for jobs. We had a saving plan in order to purchase our homes, we have a fitness plan to keep fit—and yet we thought dreaming and hoping was enough to get a man! What the hell? Why isn't this discussed, or do we just not know? Is this a cultural thing?"

"Wow. Good point," Zaara says. "In terms of culture, I think my parents drummed into me too hard to keep my head in books and not on boys when I was younger, to the point that I'm so career-focused now. And now they are asking me about husband every minute. There was absolutely no discussion about how to *find and be* in a relationship with a man, though. Nothing!"

Although our parents are from different countries—Jamaica, Guyana and Nigeria—we all nod in agreement. Education and a successful career were paramount for all of us, with no distraction from boys. Mid- to late twenties, and the pressure to have a boyfriend, came from nowhere.

"Perhaps the idea is to just watch and learn, deciding the bits to take and discard? My parents have been together since they were twenty-two, that is a lifetime," Zaara adds.

"Adisa, you took action by finally joining a dating app, but what else?" I know it seems like I have ignored Zaara's great points, but I haven't. I just don't want to set Chantel off again.

"Prayer is powerful," says Adisa, as she pulls a chain from out of her top to reveal Jesus on the cross. She kisses it and tucks it back away. Chantel and Zaara look at each other and roll their eyes.

"Adisa, I don't disagree," I say tentatively, "but prayer without action is still hoping, wishing. No?" *Hmm, I could have said that with more tact.*

Tasha saves me by coming in with a barrage of questions. "What does your happy ending look like? What does love mean to you? What does it look like and feel like? How do you show it and how do you want to receive it? These are also important questions. Don't even get me started with expectations. The work doesn't stop when you bag a man…"

"OK, but can we bag a man first and think about the other bits later?" Adisa asks, laughing.

I slap my palms down on the table finally. "I've decided to do all that I can to get a man before I turn forty. That is my goal. I'm gonna analyse my past to figure out what worked and what didn't, to help inform me. Please note, this act of love is not from a place of desperation. I'm stepping up to be more courageous, whilst keeping my standards intact. Who's with me?" Not gonna lie, the silence surprises me. I channel Lisa Nichols to see if her style will land better. I clear my throat. "OK. I'm happy to do this self-imposed mission alone, but this time next week it's Christmas Day, and the New Year is following fast behind. Do you want 2017 to be the same as this year? Because I don't. Nothing new is learnt in the comfort zone. So I'll ask again—who's with me?"

"I'm with you!" pipes up Adisa. "I'm starting with this app, and I'm gonna try and be more engaging, and keep praying."

"Cool, but let's step it up a notch. You want a man who is religious—to be more specific, Christian—so how about you become more strategic in finding a man at church?" I say.

"Hmm, but there is no one in my church that I like," she says shrugging.

"Then you go to a different church. In fact, try lots of different churches," offers Tasha, going into solution mode. "You have a goal and you're just widening your catchment area, whilst still being faithful to God, who is watching your movements in his houses," she adds, smiling cheekily.

"OK, I can do that, cool. I'm gonna enrol Laura, she's my church friend. She can be my wing woman and I can be hers, as she's also single."

"Cool, you are sorted. Zaara, what say you?" I ask.

"Personally, I don't have time for that. My job takes me to different events and I meet different people already, they just happen to be in the same field as me."

"So, have you ever mixed business with pleasure, then?" asks Tasha with a serious face.

Zaara looks at me, clears her throat and pours out more tea.

Tasha, Adisa and Zaara catch the glances she makes in my direction and now *everyone* is looking at me.

Adisa raises an eyebrow. "Go on, spill!"

Whilst Zaara's head is down, focused on her tea cup, I discreetly shake my head and mouth "Shh" without the sound. The air is full of floating thoughts and intrigue, which are broken by Chantel.

"There's nothing wrong with seeing work colleagues," she says firmly. "But if you are going to do it, you have to do it with military precision." She takes a large gulp of her tea before continuing, "There's also nothing wrong with wanting a happy ending. As Black women, we deserve this, too."

We have now arrived to the scattered, about-to-go-left reactionary conversation, which I'm gonna try and steer back. "Hun, no-one is saying we don't. In fact, the whole point is to ensure we get what we deserve." She isn't looking at me and doesn't acknowledge what I'm saying, which is fine.

"OK, I'm going to stop going on dates for dates sake. I'm only going to go on dates with people that I really like and have built some rapport with. I was hoping quantity would eventually lead me to quality, but I think I should change tactics. Which also means I'm going to approach less. I wanna see what comes from that," Zaara says, with determination.

"Wow, Zaara. OK," I say, impressed with her ah-ha moment. "Chan?"

"I'm good you know. I'm happy with my dates and commitment-free life," she says, tapping away on her phone.

I nod to acknowledge what she has said and decide to

continue, rather than challenge the defensiveness that is oozing from her. "OK. So ladies, we have our mission. Tash, did you want to do something, too?"

"Erm, I'm just gonna buy some sexy lingerie and carve date nights into the diary."

"Eh-Eh, keeping-it-fresh. Yes, girl!" Zaara says, clicking her fingers.

Adisa announces she has to go as she has to prep ahead of her court appearance in the morning. Tasha and Zaara also decide to leave. They say their goodbyes, and promise to stay in action mode.

It was a good summit. The space is quiet, but I can feel a tense energy lingering. I open all the windows and decide to incense the flat. I light some charcoal on a spoon and place frank-incense resin on top, which I place in an open-top lantern. I then walk through the flat, gently swinging it back and forth, leaving a smoky trail behind me. I look like a makeshift priest.

"That smell is going to make Rocco ill," stresses Chantel.

"It won't, it's not harmful and the windows are open." Once I have walked around each room, I close all the windows, but I'm still not content. The flat hasn't returned to its light, airy and peaceful state. I head to the front room, where Chantel is now watching TV. I know she's not taking anything in because I can feel the cog-wheels in her brain turning. I pick up Rocco and place him in my lap, get comfy and gently stroke him. I can feel Chantel wants to say something, but I decide not to prompt. The silence is becoming unbearable, but I'm gonna stand my ground.

"Syms, can I ask you something?" she asks eventually.

I look up and nod. She seems nervous but I'm glad she is finally going to spit something out.

"Is there a part of you that kind of... hates me?" Chantel asks.

Chapter Three

Broken Pieces

There's a pause, because I'm winded by the question. I open my mouth to say something, even though I have no words, so I'm relieved when Chantel continues, "I wonder sometimes, because Dad's actions broke up the relationship with Betsy, and your relationship with him has never been the same since. You guys are hardly talking. You say everything is fine, but I am the reason for the break-up."

Triggered. My mind flashes back to the moment I was summoned home by mum. My flat mates were holding a dinner party and I had to leave just as it was getting started. Mum didn't say what it was about and I didn't question her because I felt a strong sense of dread. I got home as fast as I could. As soon as I opened the door, I was hit by an intense wave. I think love escaped through the door at that very moment and never returned. Mum and Dad were sitting at opposite ends of the table, and she asked me to sit down. For twenty three years I was an only child, but was now being told that I had a fifteen-year old sister. My mind was blown. Mum found a message accompanied by a picture of a teenager on Shaun's—my dad's—phone and questioned him about it, as the teenager bore a striking resemblance to me. He eventually told the truth, and Mum of course was devastated. He claimed it was a mistake, a one-night stand and he didn't intend to be a father to her, in fact he'd never seen her in person. Mum felt betrayed and heartbroken because she had wanted another child, but he'd firmly told her he didn't want any more children. She loved him and had came to accept his decision overtime, but this news was just too hard to swallow. An apology never left his mouth, She ended their relationship soon after, asked him to move out and served divorce papers.

I had always wanted a sibling and so when I found out, I had a rollercoaster of emotions but through the mix, knew I wanted to get to know my sister. Mum understood and supported my decision. She stood on the sidelines for months as she watched our relationship grow, and then fully embraced Chantel into her heart, because it wasn't her fault. The relationship with Chantel's mother, Leah, was also surprisingly healthy too, as Mum did not lay any blame at her door. Dad was the sole person to blame, and he refused to take responsibility for his actions due to his *wrong and strong* attitude.

Mum and I worked through our anger and various other emotions without waiting for an apology, because we wanted to move on. In spite of how she felt, Mum has always stressed that it's fine for me to have a relationship with my Dad, but as much as I love him, I just can't. How do you move forward with someone when they refuse to acknowledge what they have done? I learnt that day that it's up to us to set the bar on how we should be treated. My self-worth bar is high, because my mum's bar is high. I will walk away from any situation that doesn't positively serve me.

"Chan, you know I don't hate you," I answer at last. "Where is this coming from?" I ask, with genuine concern. Placing Rocco back in his dog bed, I go to sit closer to my sister.

"I just think what Dad did, changed your idea of men. You have trust issues, and I just think every time you look at me, you're reminded of that fact," she says, with tears beginning to fall. I put my arm around her shoulders and cuddle her. Chantel leans into the embrace, nestling her head into my chest and beginning to sob.

"Chan, listen to me. I'm glad mum stood up for herself and did what she felt was right. With the way he acted, I wouldn't have put up with that either. I love Dad and always will, but his refusal to acknowledge what he did to Mum makes it hard to be around him. His refusal to acknowledge and accept you, as we have, is just as bad. But my first disappointment with men came when I was twenty-one years old, with my first boyfriend. So the fantasy was shattered long before Dad's actions."

Chantel moves out of the embrace, wipes away her tears and adjusts her seating position. She faces me full on and asks, "What happened at twenty-one?" with slight concern.

"That's for another day. Just know, I love you dearly and I'm glad you are in my life. I don't want you to ever think I hate you, because I don't. So erase that thought from your brain immediately, OK?"

Chantel nods. There is a comfortable silence that I eventually decide to break because Chantel appears to be in a more listening place. "I've been meaning to say this for a while. Going on dates is great, but what are you looking for, hun? If we view that part of our lives in the same way as we would our careers, then what direction are you heading in? None of those dates have led to committed relationships. Why?" I ask as softly as possible, in the hope she doesn't just react.

"I have thought about it, too, believe it or not," she says, "and I think this way is easier. I'm having no-strings-attached fun. I'm doing me and not hurting anyone."

Red flags flash in front of my eyes at the words 'easier' and 'not hurting anyone', so decide to get straight to the point. "How has Dad affected you?"

There is a pause, before Chantel decides to get up and sit by Rocco. Whilst stroking him she says, "I don't feel men can be faithful. I know I am generalising, but I would rather not put myself in a position to feel rejected again."

I stay with the silence, a technique I learnt from my counsellor, because I know more is coming. After a few moments Chantel continues. "Dad didn't want me. I have never met him and I have never felt love from him in any capacity, so how do I expect another man to love me? How can I be expected to feel comfortable in love when I have never experienced it from my own dad?" She breaks down in tears. I begin to get up to go over and comfort her, but she puts her hand out as if to say 'Stop'. I remain where I am, giving her the physical and silent space she needs as she continues to cry. *It's so hard seeing her like this.* "So… this way is easier, I'm happy and I'm in control this way," Chantel says, wiping away her tears as the strength in her voice returns.

"It makes sense." I say tenderly. "Thanks for sharing. Your

outlook and what you attract can be positive even though you never saw it growing up."

"So a B in Psychology at A-Level qualifies you to come to this conclusion?" Chantel snaps.

Renk. My head tells me to respond thoughtfully, but my mouth goes into immediate-reaction mode. "Actually, it has been five years of counselling to work through my own shit that has enabled me to be able to see other people's so clearly. What I am saying to you is coming from a place of love and understanding, but it's landing in a different way in your ears and I'm not sure what that's about. Sometimes I think it's *you* that dislikes *me*, Chantel. You always seem to have some sort of snappy or sarcastic response." I get up. "I've been telling myself that it's just your personality, but I'm beginning to think differently now," I say, walking out and into the kitchen where I flick the switch on the kettle.

As I wait for it to boil, I slowly calm down. I notice yellow roses in a vase and for a split second question who bought them, before deciding it must have been Tasha as yellow is her favourite colour. I smile, close my eyes, and ask myself, '*What should I do?*' The solution arrives like a whisper that I just about catch: *Stand your ground. You have done nothing wrong.* I open my eyes in agreement, and proceed to unload the dishwasher. Once everything is packed away, I make a peppermint tea and sit at the table with a magazine.

Engrossed in the articles and I'm transfixed by one in particular which displays the bluest of blue sea, whiter than white sand, and golden sun lighting up the page to sell Barbados.

45

Fond memories awaken in me, fluttering around to the pit of my stomach. Only Chantel walking in looking sheepish reminds me that a mini argument had taken place. She takes a seat next to me and expresses how sorry she is. She knows there are things she needs to address, but is worried about opening up a can of old worms.

"The worms are already here love and they are wriggling around everywhere and onto me through your projections, which is why they need to be contained, addressed and thrown away. Oh, and you cannot wash them away with prosecco either, you know that right?"

"It's just so hard. You're so together, whilst I just spend a lot of time *looking* together. I just feel lost, and I'm thirty this year, and I'm worried that I will be alone if I don't sort my fears out."

I reach for her hand across the table, and tell her that even 'together'-looking people have dealt with—or are dealing with—things, and that believing they don't is a misconception that will only serve to make her feel even worse. Chantel's vulnerability makes me feel it's OK to share some more, too, so I decide to open up further with her...

"Chantel, I felt lost in my early twenties. I knew I needed something, but I didn't know what, other than not getting into another relationship for a while. On this particular day, I decided to go for a walk in central London. I was actively looking for answers, something that could help me. I wanted any kind of visual sign—for example, a white feather falling from the sky into my path to signal that angels were listening and were with me at that moment. Angels over God, because I left the church when

I was sixteen years old. God felt scary and judgmental, and the idea didn't resonate with me. And so I didn't reach out, because I disconnected that hotline years before. It took me a long time to realise I left *Christianity*, and not God. Anyway, I wanted a sign so badly that I was even willing to see one that just said *This is the sign you are looking for!*"

Chantel laughs.

"OK, so that would have pissed me off, but you get what I mean. I just needed to feel seen and heard. I wanted someone to know I was struggling but I didn't know who to turn to. My two amazing university friends were incredible, but I needed wisdom and guidance to get me through this. As they were the same age as me, they only knew as much as I did as a twenty-one-year old.

"I found myself in a bookshop. As you know, I love romance and psychological thrillers, but at this point I was heartbroken and felt like I was living my own nightmare, so didn't want to read about anything like that. My head was swirling with questions and feelings I couldn't connect to language, and here I was standing in front of an array of books hoping to find something with no idea what I was looking for. I stood back, took a deep breath and asked the angels and the universe to help me find what I needed. When you feel lost, you have nothing to lose right?"

Chantel shrugged and nodded, so I continued.

"It may sound crazy to your ears, but I just did this intuitively, and the book that jumped out to me had a vibrant orange spine. I pulled that book out, and it was called *In the Meantime: Finding Yourself and the Love You Want* by Iyanla Vanzant. I hoped somewhere beyond the vibrant cover, the words within would speak to me because the author was a black woman. I remember this day like it was yesterday, Chan." Beginning to feel sombre, I raise the vibration of my voice to disguise it. "I couldn't put the book down," I tell her. "Page after page brought guidance and confirmation and tears. I am a neat freak with books, you know this. I don't dog ear the pages, highlight or underline words, but this book was filled with red lines as I highlighted all the things that resonated with me. It helped me to process, heal and truly understand that no situation is permanent. I learnt and understood that I had the power to put myself back together again. I read books and went into counselling for the first time when I was twenty-two years old, because you don't have to do it alone. I raised the bar on how I should be treated, but it has taken nearly twenty years to look 'together', hun. That's all I'm saying. When you're able to look at your issues and own your own shit, you will not allow anyone to projectile vomit all over you. Like attracts like, so what and who are you attracting unconsciously?"

Very conscious of over-sharing—and of the fact that so much of what I was saying might still be stuff I need to work on—I finally decide to stop talking. Chantel looks at me and then gives me a hug. She is holding me for a while before she pulls back, looks at me and says, "Thank you." She promises to look at her 'cans of worms'. Eventually, she goes to gather up the doggy bits and asks me if she can borrow my sliders. "It's too dark now to bother putting my boots back on."

I roll my eyes and head to my bedroom, returning with the sliders, a tote bag to put her boots in, a new journal and a copy of *In The Meantime*. "I don't lend my books out, so here is a spare copy". I hand the items to Chan, who stands up and hugs me tightly again. She's silent now, but the hug says a thousand words. She picks up Rocco, and as she walks out, she says, "Can Fun Symona make an appearance soon? And I won't judge you if you gorge on those chocolate éclairs that are leftover. Love you!"

Feeling tired after our talk, I decide to run a bath. I like them hot and high. High enough to cover my whole body and spill over the sides if I move too much. I add Epsom Salts and lavender oil to the flowing water and light my candle—vanilla-scented ones are my favourite—placing it on my wooden cabinet below my large round, gold-rimmed mirror. I open the window slightly and shut the bathroom door with a sigh.

Sunday has always been my day to change bed sheets, and I would have done it earlier but making sure I had everything for the impromptu gathering took priority. After my bath, I smooth out fresh bedding and spray lavender onto my clean pillows to increase the chances of a good night's sleep, which I definitely need tonight. The summit and conversation with my sister was necessary, but tiring. I gather the crumpled sheets from off the floor, walk to the kitchen and stuff them into the washing machine. I hear a clunk, and fish around blindly inside the machine to try locate the thing that caused the sound. I give up and pull everything back out to take a better look, and eventually uncovering my pink dildo. *I don't even know why I have this. It does nothing for me.* I reload the machine and switch it on before heading back to the bedroom with the magazine and my pink, noisy fake dick.

The magazine I'd been reading earlier is still open on the same page, and once again I'm transfixed by the advert for Barbados. This time I notice a white couple in the background. I've never seen a person of colour advertising a luxury holiday. We travel too—so do people from Japan, Mexico and so on. Is there still an unspoken myth that we don't 'sell' lifestyle? *AKA white people won't buy it, if they don't see themselves in it?*

I look at the blue water and remember the first time I went jet skiing. I laugh at myself, remembering…

Chapter Four

Mr Bermuda

I'd always thought Barbados was a honeymoon destination or for big people who went on cruises, and therefore my twenty-three-year-old self didn't have any business going there. Asta, who had been twice before, convinced me Barbados was exactly where I needed to be to get the rest I needed. She said I would love the beautiful island, the beaches, the food, and people—especially the men. I wasn't interested in the latter, but I was sold by everything else. So there we were, on our way to what sounded like paradise.

Although we were travelling in economy, we told ourselves that we had to dress to impress because this was Virgin Atlantic, baby! We both wore heels, tight blue skinny jeans a white vest under a smart jumper to keep us warm on the flight, and Dolce and Gabbana sunglasses were in my bag, ready for the sun. I kicked back, watched numerous films and prayed that Barbados would be everything my friend said it would be.

As we were about to land, I noticed my left leg had swollen really badly. My mum gave me airplane socks to wear to help prevent deep vein thrombosis, but I hadn't worn them because I felt I was way too cute for those tight white hospital-looking socks that reached the top of my calves, plus my jeans were too tight to roll up, so I couldn't have put them on even if I wanted to. We were about to land and all I could think about was whether I had DVT—and if I did, whether my dibby dibby insurance would cover medical bills.

"Excuse me," I said discreetly to the stewardess as she passed. She stopped and smiled, waiting for me to say something. "I've noticed my leg has swollen really badly and I'm concerned about it." I pointed at my left leg. She looked down and saw the difference immediately. I looked at her face, trying to read the level of seriousness, but she gave nothing away. She calmly told me she'd be right back.

I looked at Asta and told her to start praying for me—*she's more religious than me, after all*—whilst I tried to remain calm, because I was scared that stress would make it worse.

I could see the stewardess talking to her colleague, and then they both looked in my direction. She picked up a phone and began saying something to someone on it. *Please let me be OK, please* I begged internally whilst still trying to remain calm. Asta still had her eyes closed and couldn't see my conflicting battle. I nudged her, and she opened them at last. "She's coming back," I whispered, and Asta squeezed my hand in half-hearted support in response.

"I have informed the paramedics, who will come on board when we land in thirty minutes. Please stay behind so they can check you out," the stewardess said. I nodded and mouthed thank you. On the outside I looked calm, but inside I was still in a battle. I kept pouring the water of hope onto the anxiety of doom, but every time I thought anxiety had been extinguished, it popped up again until we landed.

Being by the main exit had pros and cons. We would have been the first people off the plane, had I not had this annoying issue. Instead, everyone and his mother was passing us, looking at us with intrigue. We were the minority on this flight as it was, and being stared at in judgement and confusion was a lot to deal with on top of my internal anxiety. I tried not to care, but I did. I grabbed my phone, which hadn't switched over to the Barbadian network yet, to distract me.

It felt like a lifetime, but a paramedic eventually came on board. He took a look and confirmed what I already knew: the skinny jeans were too tight, and during the eight hours and thirty-minute flight I hadn't moved much. He instructed me to take half an aspirin once a day for the next couple of days and if the swelling didn't go down by the third day, I would have to go to the hospital. I was pleased with the outcome, and right away silently pleaded with my leg to go back to normal as soon as possible. In return, I promised to always wear the ugly socks on long haul flights. The paramedic disembarked the aircraft, and we began to gather our things.

OMG! I looked down and immediately also began to plead with my swollen feet. *How the hell was I gonna squeeze my feet back into those black, patent four inch heels?* I tried nonetheless, but both heels were hanging out of the shoe. *Mess!*

"How does Victoria Beckham do it?" I ask Asta, pointing at my problem.

She laughed her head off. "I'm not sure, but it looks like

53

we have the same problem." Her feet were slightly swollen too, but managed to fit back into her shoes fine. There was no way my feet were getting back in those heels, though. Thank God my common sense was around when I was packing my hand luggage. I slipped on my flip-flops, and we finally walked down the plane steps and into the gentle breeze. The blazing sun licked my skin with love, like it intuitively knew that was exactly what I needed. With sunglasses on my head, I walked through customs in comfort with a smudge of style and a whole heap of gratitude because it could have been so much worse.

As we were the last to leave the plane, we were able to breeze through customs without waiting in long queues, and our luggage was already off the carousel, standing upright beside it waiting for us. We headed for the exit and made our way out to wait for Asta's boyfriend. They kept in touch from South London to Barbados via regular long distance calls. *Commitment right there!* We came to a halt as we heard Asta's name being called, and we turned around to see a man walking with pace towards us. Asta greeted enthusiastically, and then she introduced me to him.

"This is Lyron!"

"Welcome, Symona!" he said. "I hope you like it here. Let's go." He looked exactly the same as he did in the pictures I'd seen. Coupled with the sing-song accent, I could see why Asta was attracted to this handsome man who looked nothing like the men back home in the UK.

Asta and Lyron caught up as I soaked in the sounds, colours and smells that wafted in through the open window, which all felt familiar. They roped me into their conversation every now and then, but I was happy to stay in my thoughts and observations. Although I'd just arrived, I was really happy to be there. We pulled up to a pale blue house which instantly reminded me of Grandma Cedella's pink house back in Jamaica due to the shape, size and veranda. Lyron carried our luggage into the house, showed me around and announced to both of us, "My house is your house. Take anything you want, and clean up after yourselves. You are both on holiday, I'm not, but I will try and chill with you guys when I can. Symona, I hope you love Barbados." *I love clear communication.*

We both immediately freshened up and exchanged our tight skinny jeans for short flowing dresses on top of bikinis, then headed downstairs, where we were surprised to see a guy who wasn't there when we first arrived. Approximately six feet tall, with golden brown skin and piercing green, warm eyes—which were looking in my direction. I looked behind me, there was no one there. *He's looking at me.* I matched his gaze and I felt as though he was intruding into my soul, but I couldn't look away.

"Asta and Symona, meet my boy Jaden…" *Why do good-looking guys always have nice sounding names?* I doubted very much he was single.

"Jaden, this is Symona, and Asta, my girlfriend. Symona hasn't been here before so we gotta show her what Barbados is all about."

Jaden smiled. "Hey ladies, nice to meet you both. You are on vacation so relax, no stress, OK?" We nodded and smiled. "I've gotta go back to work now, but I guess I will see you around." He spudded Lyron before walking out, jumping into his car and driving off.

"Guys, do you want a drink?" Asta asked as she walked into the kitchen. Lyron and I both shouted yes. "OK! Syms, come through so you can choose what you want," she said breezily. I got up and walked towards the kitchen, while Asta excitedly beckoned me to hurry up. I sped up my walk and she beamed at me. "Syms, he was *nice*. What do you think?" Asta whispers.

"Girl, he is fine. I have never seen a man like that in all my life. Looking like that he can't be single. Plus, I'm not here for man."

Asta opened the fridge door. "I can find out right now," she said, selecting a Fanta and beer from the shelf.

I grabbed a grape juice from the fridge and told her not to say anything to Lyron, even though I wanted to know everything about Jaden. I saw the mischievous look in her eyes and realised I'd have to plead a bit harder. "No, no, nooo. Shh! Don't say anything. Let's just see what the week brings."

Asta gave me a look, but agreed not to say anything. We both returned to the front room to relax, chat and listen to music for a bit. Lyron was a DJ at one of the local radio stations, where he presented the drive-time slot Monday-Friday, four 'til seven. He played us a mix of the Top 10 tunes that were blowing up in Barbados then, after which Asta played *Oi* by More Fire Crew. We were hyped! We showed off our Garage moves and sang the parts which we knew (which wasn't a lot), but we come together for the chorus. Lyron looked on in disgust.

"Ah wha di rasshole is this?" he exclaimed with confusion. We laughed our heads off at his reaction. "It's Garage, babes, come on, get with it!" Asta replied as she danced closer to him.

"You London girls have no taste," he said, turning off the music. "I gotta go to work soon, so how about I drop you to the beach, on the way?"

Our beach bags were already packed and ready to go, of course. Lyron dropped us off at Accra Beach fifteen minutes later and told us both to stay out of trouble. We looked around and decided on the best place to chill.

"Not too crowded, not too secluded," Asta began. "Near enough to the bathrooms but not too close, no screaming kids and no people in front of us—we want to have a clear view to the sea" she added, informing me of how to find the best spot. Once we found it, we helped each other lay our towels down onto the white sand and adjusted our bikinis before we took our dresses off and carefully lie down on our towels, facing the sun.

Soon my hands were behind my head and my knees were up and slightly parted. I took a deep breath in and a long sigh out, coming onto my elbows to look at the water in front of me. "If this isn't bliss, I don't know what is."

Asta looked at me, smiling. "Welcome to Barbados."

"I hope Barbados loves me, as much as I want to love it," I replied, before putting my sunglasses on, lying back down and closing my eyes.

I felt at peace for the first time in a long time, and was doing my best to stay in the moment. The sound of the waves, the gentle breeze and hot sun penetrating my skin all worked to begin my healing process. I could feel it. In the jet black behind my closed eyes, colours emerged like a paint brush washed in water. Red then purple travelled across my vision. This always happened when I meditated. Although I wasn't consciously meditating then, I was pleased to receive the sign that told me I was relaxed and my chakras were opening. I was going deeper and deeper, sinking further into a relaxed state. Through the swirling colours I saw those striking green cat eyes that belonged to Jaden. My empty mind began to fill up with clutter and the colours disappeared. *He is gorgeous, but guys like that don't look at girls like me. I'm not here for that. I don't want any drama. I don't want this holiday to be about him. I just want to feel OK...*

I tried my hardest to quieten my mind, but Jaden, and my dad, and Darren, my ex, started to take up space. Pricks of tears began to form in my eyes, and I took a book out of my bag to distract myself. After reading the same page three times, I put the book down. My mind wandered even when Asta was talking to me. She suggested something to me, and I just said yes. Her squeal and level of excitement told me I should have been paying more attention.

"OMG! Really? I thought you were going to say hell to the NO! Yes! I am so excited. Come on, Syms, let's go and find out how much the jet skis cost, then."

Before I could say anything, she was running towards the man in the florescent orange wet suit. I reluctantly followed, fear already setting in. In a flash, I was on the back of a jet ski with Asta speeding off away from the shore.

Now you have a distraction to distract from your original distraction. Suck it up! As Asta was laughing in excitement as she sped over the waves, I was screaming in hysterical fear, which may have landed as excitement to Asta's ears, because for some reason my screams sounded like I was laughing hysterically. The constant spray of salty water knocked my contact lenses out. *Can this get any worse?* Blurred vision coupled with fear was a horrible combination. People looked like dots, and dry land looked like a blurry mirage. The further out we went, the more uninviting the deep blue sea became. *Are there sharks in these waters? If I fall, will it be easy to get back on? Why are you thinking about that? You are NOT going to fall. It's not happening!* Panic was really setting in. I had no idea how long we'd been out there for, but I was done. I was searching in vain for a waving fluorescent orange figure in the distance, but I gave up to focus on looking forwards, because I don't want whiplash. The zig-zag, speed, and being slapped by sea water, was already making me feel queasy.

We both heard a whistle. "We have to go back now," Asta shouted to me, sounding disappointed. *OMG, YES!* A wave of relief washed over me, along with more salty water, but I didn't mind, because the shore was getting closer and closer. I contained my happiness because I didn't want to lose focus. The goal was still to get to shore without falling off that thing.

The sand was hot under my feet as I stumbled onto it, but I didn't care. I was safe, frazzled, a stone lighter and with hair that I was going to have to wash. *You should have braided it, but no, you wanted to look cute with your relaxed hair. KMT.*

"That was amazing! A real rush!" squealed Asta as we collected our valuables and headed back to our towels. I tried to hide my feelings, but my energy did not lie.

"I feel sick. Never again. I need to sit down." I flopped onto my towel. "I just need to get back to bliss," I added, knowing I looked traumatised.

Asta—AKA the adventure-junkie—laughed. "OK hun. I am gonna go grab some roti for us from the hut over there," she said, pointing to the triangle-roof hut to her far left. "Drink some water, I won't be long." She passed the litre bottle of water to me. I took a couple of mouthfuls before lying down on my front, resting the right side of my head on my bent arms. I saw Asta walking towards the hut and slowly closed my eyes to stop the sick feeling. I felt so wiped out that even my brain was tired. So I just lay there, allowing the sun to blast my vitamin D-deficient skin and turn it golden brown.

The sound of voices getting louder and louder stirred me out of my drowsy sleep. I opened my eyes and saw a girl walking with two beefy lifeguards. I blinked and blinked again, but my vision didn't become any clearer. *No contact lenses,* I remembered. But that was definitely Asta's laugh. I lay there for a few moments thinking *how the hell am I supposed to wipe the dribble from my mouth, sleep from my eyes, fix my hair and bikini bottoms and put lip gloss on without whoever she's with seeing me?* They were getting closer and closer. I elegantly moved into an upright position, quickly grabbed my Wet Wipes from my bag and swipe my face and mouth, then placed the used wipe back in my bag, feeling a bit fresher. I decided to leave my hair as it was a lost cause. Instead I placed my sunglasses on top of my head to act as a headband, making it look less wild.

"Hey Syms, sorry I took so long. I was talking to Dwayne and Simeon here," Asta said as she arrived.

"No worries, love. I fell asleep." I looked at the men—life-guards. "Hey guys, nice to meet you. So, have you saved any lives today?" I asked breezily, whilst acknowledging it was probably their most-asked question.

Low-level hair, dark skin, dark brown eyes, chiselled face, athletic body and thighs with every muscle on show, Dwayne looked good already—but even better in those blue shorts with the yellow strip at the waist.

"No, not today," he replied in that beautiful accent. "I prefer to keep it that way, but we are here if anyone gets into trouble," he added, like a true pro.

Simeon nodded in agreement. "So, I understand this is your first time in Barbados?" I nod, too. "Are you liking what you see so far?" he asked. I caught the potential trap.

"Yep, I'm liking the *island* so far."

Dwayne turned to look at the sea. "Well, enjoy your time. We gotta head back now. It was nice meeting you both." Simeon waved, and they both turn to walk off.

"Oh, quick question," Asta shouted after them. They both stopped. "Later on, can we get a picture in your lifeguard hut?" she asked cheekily.

"Yeah, sure. Swing by when you're ready," answered Simeon.

"OK!" she bellowed back.

"Babe, only you could go to get a roti and come back with two lifeguards. I cannot deal with you," I said, laughing.

"Listen, I was walking to get food to bring you back to life, minding my own business. They called out to *me*," Asta said as she sat down on her towel. "I'm sorry I took so long. Here you go." She handed me the chickpea roti. "This is exactly what you need to get back to 100 per cent."

"Thanks, hun. The little nap and the eye candy has already perked me up," I said as I bit into the food. "This is so good."

"I told you! And washed down with this, you are gonna be even better," Asta said, holding up a bottle of rum. I shook my head and smiled.

We ate in silence as we watched the people around us jogging, swimming, playing Frisbee, and children building sandcastles and crying as each wave dismantled their efforts. I devoured the roti in no time—I don't even think it hit the sides. "That was so good, I wish it was bigger!" I proclaimed. Still chewing, Asta nodded in agreement.

As I looked out to this picturesque view, a lump formed in my throat. I surrendered to it and tears began to fall. I had my sunglasses on, so Asta couldn't see. I took a moment and cleared my throat before speaking. "Asta, thank you for inviting me here. At first I was worried I would feel like a spare wheel with you and Lyron, but it's all good and… I am just happy to be here. I needed this without even knowing. Thank you."

Asta put her arm around me and hugged me. "I know you did. You have been through a lot in the past four months. Two years if you add all the stuff with Darren…"

Every time I heard his name, I could feel the anger in the pit of my stomach. He completely ignored me when he saw me at uni after we broke up. He blocked my texts and calls. He just handled it all wrong, and I never got to say what I wanted to say to him. I didn't deserve that treatment at all. And now, two years later, mum and dad have broken up and I suddenly have a fifteen-year old sister? What the hell is going on?

"…You needed this time out," Asta finished softly.

"I did," I said, wiping away my tears.

"Relax, chill and have fun. You deserve it, hun. Plus… is it time to get back out there?" she asked tentatively.

"Hmm, not sure if I'm ready for that, but I promise I will try and be more open."

Although I meant it, I felt apprehensive. The last two times I'd been intimate with someone after Darren, I had been so overwhelmed and emotional. I tried to control the feeling, but I just couldn't. I was there, but not there at the same time. I mean, my head went elsewhere, so I kind of checked out of the moment. Darren was my first—we'd been going out for six months, so I couldn't even say I've had a lot of good sex to compare it to. But I knew sex shouldn't involve crying afterwards. Not tears of pleasure, but tears of hurt, pain and guilt. Each time, I cried. They were patient. They held and comforted me, *which is what I wanted from Darren*, but I saw their distress and knew they wouldn't call again. Why would they want to put themselves through that again? It's safe to say, my confidence had been knocked and I hadn't been with anyone since. I decided to remain single for a while. It had been one and a half years actually, but I still felt somewhat broken and undesirable.

The way Jaden looked at me made me feel wanted though, and it had been a while since a man had looked at me like that, but I also felt nervous. Asta knew all of what happened, but she didn't know how I still felt.

"Come on, let's freshen up and get those Baywatch-esque shots at the lifeguard hut," she suggested, laughing. Dwayne and Simeon happily obliged in group shots, couple-looking shots, and shots of Asta and I together. Asta decided to re-create Pamela Anderson's famous pose and run with the yellow lifeguard rescue float in slow motion, which I happily tried to direct and capture, whilst howling with laughter. *I haven't laughed like this in a while*, I thought. As we headed back to our towels, I flicked through the pics and I stopped at the pictures of me and Dwayne. *We look good together… but I still don't think I'm ready to be in a relationship. I'm twenty-three, there is more than enough time.*

"Look!" Asta said, pointing at the horizon. "Let's have a drink and watch the sunset before we head back home. I have a key, so I will just text Lyron to let him know." I nodded in agreement. Asta took out the rum and Coke that she had tried her best to hide from the sun, and poured the liquid into red plastic cups. "Here's to a fabulous week's holiday in paradise," she said as she raised her cup.

I raised mine and added, "May we feel relaxed and rejuvenated."

We both said "cheers", and sipped the strong, lukewarm beverage. The heat of the alcohol hit my chest, which I could then feel spreading out. "It looks like we've started something," I said, pointing at the lifeguard station now surrounded by three girls waiting their turn to pose on the yellow steps.

"I bet they've wanted to do that all day," said Asta with a laugh. "Here's to us being trendsetters," she added, raising her cup again. I knocked her cup with mine in agreement, and we took another sip of our drinks.

We watched as the colours in the cloudless sky appeared to change every minute the sun lowered further down. Blue, orange, red, pink and finally a rich midnight blue blanketed the sky as the sun sank out of sight. *God exists, how could s/he, they, not? God paints each evening; I'm witnessing this right now.* Tears began to form again, which I did not allow to fall. I closed my eyes. *God or universe, if you are listening, please support me in my continuous healing and help me to trust again. I'm open and ready to receive your guidance and blessings. Please continue to watch over Asta and I, and place only good people in our path whilst here. Amen.* The air became cooler, and we made our way home.

*

I settled into Barbados really quickly. I loved chilling on the beach during the day, catching jokes with the lifeguards, reading *In the Meantime*, again eating Cheffette's and raving at night—Boat Yard, Reggae Lounge and Ship Inn. Everyone was so kind, and I loved the unspoken cultural rule of saying good morning, good evening and goodnight out of respect and courtesy to people who crossed your path. Men would look at us and nod, "hello" and keep it moving! It was a breath of fresh air, and I felt seen and connected for the first time in my life. We were so disconnected in London.

Asta and I walked through the market in Bridgetown to get to the bus stop, as we had decided to visit a different beach.

"Good afternoon, miss," a Rasta man who was selling

mangoes called out to me as we approached. We both stopped. "Good afternoon," I said, looking at him whilst getting ready to tell him in the warmest way possible that I didn't want any mangoes.

"Let me tell you something. When you go up those steps, look right and you will see a beautiful thing." *Not what I expected.* I nodded to acknowledge his instruction, followed by, "Have a good day." I walked up the steps and expected to see a statue or something, but as I looked right, I saw my reflection staring back at me. I smiled, and whilst it was only a glimpse, as we walked on, the moment was long enough for me to see my soul. *I know you. I recognise you.* Sadness was present behind my eyes, but I also saw my power, my beauty, and it felt good. That moment caused something in me to switch back on, and I felt hopeful again. *I was meant to meet that man, and I was meant to receive the message in that way.*

*

"Hey, hey, I'm home," Lyron shouted as he walked in. He saw we were in the kitchen and headed towards us. "That's what I like to see, my woman in the kitchen, cooking dinner for her King." Asta rolled her eyes. "What are you making?" he asked as he kissed Asta and gave me the usual high-five greeting.

"Macaroni pie," Asta proudly announced, before adding a caveat. "Trying to anyway, Bajan style."

"OK! And what else?" he asked expectantly.

"That's it. I'm trying to perfect the pie," Asta said forthrightly.

"Jesus Christ! You have already failed. We don't serve macaroni pie by itself, EVER! You English girls aren't being serious, man!" Lyron said, vexed. I tried hard not to laugh at his animated and over exaggerated complaint.

"Right! We're all going out tonight, and we are going to need food. So just stop. Imma take over so we can eat properly," he said, shoo-ing us both out of the kitchen.

"No, we can help," I plead.

Lyron paused. "OK, but you have to listen to my instructions. I'm already hungry and don't have time for back chat."

I scrunched up my face in disapproval.

"What I mean is," he corrected himself, "too many chefs in the kitchen creates a mess. Follow my instructions so we can work together and have a great meal. Yeah?"

"Hmm, you brought that back nicely," I acknowledged. "I will be happy to help," I added sarcastically.

"So the last requirement I have is that you have to say *Yes Chef* after each instruction," he said, laughing.

"You can piss right off!" Asta exclaimed, laughing, although clearly annoyed.

Lyron barked orders, swearing left right and centre as the power got to his head. He was in his element, and we decided not to give him any reason that would cause him to get even more animated. Both Asta and I rolled our eyes and got on with it for an easy life. We were also hungry, and the sooner the food was done, the sooner we could get ready.

Lyron dished up the food, and Asta and I were amazed at what he has rustled up with our help in under forty-five minutes.

Snapper and rice, with coleslaw and macaroni pie, which he'd saved, as sides. We sat down to eat, and with each mouthful Lyron took, he commented on his cooking skills.

"God damn, your boy is a bad ass in the kitchen," he said, shoving food into his mouth. "Shit, this macaroni pie has got to be my best yet!" he added, looking at it like it was a work of art, before demolishing it. "Don't even mess with my coleslaw!" There was a brief silence before he started again. "Jheezeeee, I would make an incredible chef. I should charge your arses. English girls, this is the standard, the bar is set. Don't disappoint me tomorrow.

The way to a man's heart is through his stomach, they say. Well, baby, I can already cook, so what else you got for me, Asta?" he said finally, laughing, before closing his knife and fork.

There was a pause before Asta responded, smiling. "Thank you, hun, for this marvellous meal. It is truly incredible. Symona and I are ever so grateful. Our bellies will be lined sufficiently because of you. Thank God you eat fast, because your self-applauding is a lot to stomach and we want to keep what we have just consumed down." We both laughed, whilst Lyron looked stern. He cracked a smile when Asta walked over, sat on his lap and kissed him sweetly on the lips. He responded, and they both engaged in a passionate exchange.

"Oh get a room," I said, laughing as I got up to go upstairs to get ready. I put music on and took a nice long shower. The soft water caressed and nourished my skin in ways South London water didn't seem able to do. Even my hair felt better with this water.

I walked into the bedroom after my shower to find Asta

grinning like a Cheshire cat. "Oh Lord! You two give me jokes. I don't want to know, just get in the shower," I said sternly with a smile. Asta did what she was told, and I finished getting ready and headed downstairs to wait for them.

*

We walked into Boatyard and scanned the room for a place to sit. I immediately noticed a man at the bar who looked a cross between Tank and Omari Hardwick. I nudged Asta's arm.

"What?" she asked, irritated at the unexpected prod. I remained staring ahead. "Look!" I said without my mouth moving—*skills*. Asta followed my gaze and saw the man sitting at the bar. "Bloody hell, Symona, you clocked that already? He is gorgeous." We went to the opposite end of the bar to where he was sitting and ordered two Bacardi and Cokes.

"So, are you going to talk to him? If you are, I think you should do it before Lyron gets back from the shop. If you think it's hard now, his big mouth will make it harder," Asta said, laughing.

"We've just got here. I need to assess the situation first. He may be with someone, and I'm not desperate. However, I agree—Lyron would love seeing me squirm," I agreed, feeling dread creep in.

"So, just do it now," Asta stressed.

"Noooo. I may be confident, but I'm shy around good-looking men, you know this. Plus, I don't want him to get the wrong idea."

"He won't. Let's have a shot of Bacardi together now," Asta

said encouragingly.

"Doing a shot, letting that seep in, and feeling confident all before Lyron comes back with his cigarettes is not enough time," I informed her.

"Lyron knows everyone. In the time it takes to walk from the shop to here, he will be stopped ten times, I bet you. So there isn't any real rush. Take your time, love," Asta, said, providing a good case.

"Haha. Thanks, Batman. I wouldn't even entertain this back home."

"I'm telling you. The sun and sea helps."

In that moment, I decided I needed to come out of my comfort zone, and that I shouldn't need alcohol to strengthen my courage.

"I am going over now," I said, climbing off the bar stool. Asta gave me an encouraging smile, as I smoothed down my burgundy, figure-hugging asymmetrical dress before walking over to the guy at the end of the bar, who was still sitting by himself.

I swept my fringe across my forehead and neatly tucked it behind my right ear as I approached.

"Hi. I saw you from over there and thought I would come over and say hello. I'm Symona," I said with confidence. He looked at me and smiled. *Shit, he is even better looking close up. His teeth are whiter than mine and his eyes sparkle…*

"Hello, Symona. I'm Aaron. Really nice to meet you. Take a seat," he said as he pulled out the stool next to him. He had an accent, but not Barbadian or American. I couldn't place it, so I asked as I climbed onto the stool.

"I'm from Bermuda."

"Bermuda! Wow, I have always been fascinated by that country because of the Bermuda Triangle," I said, with genuine intrigue.

"Yes, the Bermuda Triangle is also known as Devil's Triangle, did you know that? Fifty ships and twenty airplanes have mysteriously disappeared..." *This could have gone a different way, I'm sure he is asked this a lot.* He continued with his facts. "...The triangle is the area marked to highlight where these mysterious occurrences have happened. But you know, Bermuda is also known for its beautiful beaches, some of which have pink sand and crystal caves..."

"Really? I had no idea."

"Not many people know this. Would you like a drink?" he asked.

"Bermuda sounds beautiful and a country I hadn't considered going to. Erm, no. My drink is over there. Let me introduce you to my friend." I turned around and saw Lyron and Asta looking over discreetly. I smiled and beckoned them both over, whilst signalling to also bring my drink over.

As they walked over, I explained to Aaron that Asta was my friend, also from London, and that Lyron was Asta's boyfriend of nine months. I introduced everyone, and then Aaron got in another round of drinks. We settled on the stools and he explained that he was visiting his brother, who lives there. "You will meet him later," he explained. We all got on well and continued to chat, laughing and drinking. Aaron had a nice vibe about him. He was confident, quiet—which could have been mistaken as shy, but it really wasn't that. He was just quietly confident, with charming qualities. Two hours later, we decided to head to Ship Inn, as apparently it began to get live round 11pm.

It was only when we got up from our stools that I noticed he was shorter than me—in heels. *OK, so he is about five feet seven inches and I feel like I'm towering over him in my four-inch heels. I'm five feet six, so I'm really not. I need to stop my nonsense.* He informed me that the leather straps from my right strappy sandal had come undone, and before I could even acknowledge the situation, he was bending down and strapping the laces back up to the middle of my calf. *God damn.* I was even more attractive to Mr. Bermuda, now. I looked at Asta who looked back at me with impressed surprise. I caught her looking at Lyron as if to say, "*watch and learn.*" He looked down to see what she was referring to, and kissed his teeth as if to say, "*don't get your hopes up, love.*"

As we headed out, Aaron opened the door, placed his right hand on my lower back and gently glided me through. *This feels so nice.* At twenty-nine years old, he was six years older than me. As we walked to the open air club up the road in silence, I was feeling good. *Safe, secure, cared for and elegant.* His gestures made me feel like a lady. *Are all older men like this?*

As soon as we walked into Ship Inn, Asta and I searched for seats, whilst Aaron and Lyron went to the bar.

"He seems like such a gentleman," Asta said, grinning.

"I know, right?" I agreed. "It's a shame he's shorter than me, though."

"Seriously, don't even watch that, Symona. What is height in the grand scheme of things?"

"Hello, ladies!" a man said, interrupting our conversation. We both looked up and were greeted by three men, in fact, all wearing white, approximately in their mid-thirties. *Coincidence or planned?*

"So, what are your names?" asked the same guy.

"Shanice and Tia," Asta lied.

"Nice names. Are you from London?" asked guy number two.

The Barbadian men were nice enough, but I knew if we both engaged it would look like we were seriously entertaining the conversation. I decided to let Asta respond—she's great at small talk. Finally, I could see our men approaching with the drinks, but Aaron stopped walking and nudged Lyron to do the same. I looked at both of them, wondering why they had stopped.

"Symona!" Aaron called to me.

"Asta!" Lyron called to her. Asta looked up, past the men, who then also turned around. Mr Bermuda and Lyron put the drinks up as if to say, "We got the drinks, come on over." We got up and began to walk over to them.

"I thought your name was Shanice?" asked the guy who first began speaking to us.

"It was, for the moment," replied Asta cheekily as we walked over to our guys. Aaron kissed me on the cheek as he gave me my drink. *Talk about asserting your power. I love it.*

We talked and danced together as a group, whilst each 'couple' found alone time on the dance floor, too. I was surprised when Aaron first led me to the dance floor. He held me close and set the rhythm. I was doing really well to stay in the moment, until he started whispering in my ear.

"You are very attractive, and you look so good tonight," he said in a low voice, causing dormant parts of my body to awaken. His smell—the mix of chewing gum and alcohol on his breath accompanied by the sandalwood-musky cologne—was also a turn on. He pulled back from the close embrace to look at me. I looked back, and his eyes were just as enticing. He pulled me in again and said, "I would love you to come back to my hotel tonight. No pressure, only if you want to OK?"

I nodded my response, and my thoughts went into overdrive. *Stay on the beat, stay on the beat, stay in the beat. OK... It's been a while. Do you want to chance it? Do you really want to potentially go through that disappointment again?*

He gently kissed my neck. *Hmm. What will Lyron think of me if I go back? He doesn't really know me, and the last thing I want is him thinking I'm easy.* I could feel myself starting to panic. I moved away and told Aaron I'd be right back. He asked if everything was OK, and I reassured him that I was just going to check up on Asta. I threw him a sincere smile before I left and begin to search for her within the sea of people. After no luck, I decided to search the toilets.

"Asta, are you in here?"

"Yes, babe. I will be out in two mins!" she shouted back.

Relieved, I looked in the mirror, fixed my hair and applied more powdered foundation to matte my sweaty face. I looked at myself again, surprised. *Five days in Barbados and you're a golden girl now.* I put the now-mismatched foundation away and dabbed my face with a tissue instead. Asta came out of the cubicle and I updated her as she washed her hands.

"WHAT! Yes girl!" she shrieked.

I grabbed some more tissues from the side of the sink nearest to me and handed them to Asta.

"Hun, choosing to be with someone intimately doesn't make you a hoe," she said. *She knows me well.* "Who exactly are you worried about?"

"I don't want Lyron thinking bad of me, and I don't want to be classed as your hoe-ish friend."

"Are you OK, Syms? Serious question. Why do you care so much?" She paused. "OK, I get it, just a little bit. But hun, being intimate with a guy you connect with doesn't make you a hoe. I'm not judging you at all, and neither will Lyron, I promise."

"Thanks, hun. As I am staying in Lyron's house, I will speak to him now, just so he knows where I am."

Asta nodded. We linked arms and as we were about to walk out of the toilet, Asta broke into song —*"Ah you dat? Ah you dat? Ah you dat?"*—whilst doing the bogle. *This girl. She is a breath of fresh air, and I wish I could be as open as she is.* The support meant a lot, but I was still battling my thoughts and feelings. The line between nervousness and excitement was thin. We both laughed as we headed out to find Lyron, but I was all too aware that my nerves were suffocating the flickers of excitement.

The thing about men is that they are easy to find. They will only ever be in three places: at the bar, by the bar or on the outskirts of the dance floor. We headed to the corner of the bar and Aaron introduces us to Troy, his brother, who had arrived and looked nothing like him. After the greetings were exchanged,

I decided to speak to Lyron. We moved a couple of steps away from the group.

"So…erm… I'm thinking of…"

"Syms, I am not your dad. You don't have to ask me anything I get why you would want to, but you don't. Aaron is cool, I like him, you guys have a connection and if you want to continue the good time, then go ahead." *Huh*! I was surprised. I didn't expect it to be so easy. I didn't even get a sentence out. I smiled and I could feel my shoulders relax.

"Did you really think I was a cock blocker?" Lyron adds with a smile.

I wasn't prepared for the question! He must have seen the stress on my face because he started laughing.

"Lighten up girl, I'm joking." I cracked a smile and nudged his arm, before we both re-joined the others. I stood next to Mr Bermuda, leant in and said, "Ready when you are". *You caught some courage with that sun. I see. You sure, girl? OK, so I'm not ready, but I want to go. So for once, I'm not talking myself out of it…*

Aaron looked at me with serious eyes and walked over to Lyron, asking for his phone. He punched his number in and gave it back. He then went over to Asta, who was standing next to me, and said, "Lovely meeting you. Don't worry about your girl, imma take real good care of her. Your boyfriend has all my details, mobile number, the hotel I'm staying at and my room number, so don't worry. She will be back tomorrow at 10:00am, I'll make sure of it, OK?"

Asta seemed pleasantly taken back at the level of consideration. She raised one eyebrow and smiled before hugging him. She then turned to me and said quietly, "Just enjoy, and I will see you ten-ish. You have both of Lyron's numbers so just call if anything. The hotel he is staying in is P-L-U-S-H and it's about 20 minutes from us, so you aren't far, OK?"

I hugged and kissed her before saying goodbye to everyone.

Aaron locked his hand in mine and we walked out of the club and into a taxi.

I feel so good…

Chapter Five

Comfort within Discomfort

The air freshener was so strong in the cab and the driver was clearly pissed off that he wasn't out raving, because he had created a rave in his car. *The music is so loud.* My nostrils and head were under attack. *Please don't let me throw up, please don't let my first holiday fling end in an embarrassing way…* I looked at Aaron as I put my seat belt on. He smiled back and placed my hand in his. As we headed off, we both looked straight ahead and didn't say a word to each other for the entire journey. Even if we'd wanted to, the music would have drowned us out. *I wonder what he's thinking? Is he nervous? He doesn't look it. I can't believe I'm doing this, but I feel really proud of myself now that I'm here. This whole night has felt very surreal, movie-esque and I hope it continues to feel good and right.*

We entered into the hotel courtyard, and Aaron stepped out first and helped me out. We entered the hotel holding hands, and Aaron led the way. As we walked past the reception desk towards the lifts, the receptionist looked up and nodded his greeting to us both, then continued working. *Knowing my luck, the same receptionist will be there when I leave. Ugh. The walk of shame is something that I am not looking forward to.* I heard Asta's voice:

"*Stop caring so much*," and I did my best to banish my negative thoughts.

"This is a really nice hotel..." I said as we walked into the lifts. The doors closed and before I could finish my sentence, Aaron stood in front of me, placed his hands on my shoulders and slowly moved me backwards until my body pressed against the large mirror in the lift. I gasped at his spontaneity and the coldness on my back, which took me by surprise. He looked at me for a moment before he pressed his lips onto mine. I closed my eyes and responded. He moved in closer and I could feel his manhood pressing against my thigh. I tried to calm my thoughts down surrounding what might happen next. My body was tingling whilst my mind was stirring panic.

The lift pinged before coming to a standstill. We had arrived onto the fourth floor. Mr Bermuda stepped back, smiled and once again held my hand as he led me out of the lift and down the corridor to his room. Once inside, we both took our shoes off and placed them by the door. I turned around and smiled at the luxury before me. He stood beside me, laughed and said, "I told you I'm taller than you." *With shoes off, yes, but not with shoes on, that is the most important part...* I decided sharing my thoughts would be mean, so I didn't.

"Come in, Syms, take a seat," he said as he gestured to the cream couch. As I sat down, he asked if I wanted a drink. I opted for rum and Coke and a bottle of water. *One for continued courage and one for hydration...* He brought the drinks over, and placed them on the side table before sitting down, facing me. He was so easy to talk to, and we talked for a while on a range of topics.

Every now and then, as I was listening to him, I reflected on what I knew about him. He was a gentleman, intelligent, confident, funny and he made me feel at ease, effortlessly. His brown eyes said a lot, and I was kind of amazed that I was there. *Men that look like him, light-skinned and good looking, don't usually go for girls like me. I'm usually viewed as being too dark. From what I've seen, they tend to like long hair, not short hair like mine…*

Once again, he took control and leant in for a kiss. He cupped his hand on the back of my head and moved in closer towards me, kissing me passionately, *just like they do in the movies.*

"How do you feel about having a shower together?" he asked, pulling back to look at me.

Without hesitating I responded, "I would love to." He kissed my hand, pulled me from the comfy couch and led me to the opulent spacious bathroom that had a roll-top bath, walk in shower, toilet and two sinks, his and hers. He lit some candles, put on some R'n'B music and turned on the shower.

He placed my hands on the top button of his crisp white shirt. I took his non-verbal instruction and began to unbutton his shirt from the top down. I was nervous but didn't want to show it. Once his shirt was open, I placed my hands on his shoulders and slowly glided my hands down his arms, taking his shirt with me until it dropped to the floor. His caramel skin was soft and his body was perfectly sculptured, not one interruption by a blemish or tattoo. I moved in closer to him, looked at his lips and leant in as if to kiss him. I watched him close his eyes and open them again when it, the kiss didn't arrive. I looked at him teasingly as I unbuckled his belt and unzipped his shorts. He looked at me, and I looked back just as intensely, telepathically telling him *I can be in control, too.* His smile told me that he received the message. In spite of my nerves, I was enjoying the moment. I felt more like how I used to be.

I allowed his shorts to fall to the ground, and as I went to pull his boxer shorts down, he stopped me by holding my wrists, which took me by surprise. He moved in closer and gently kissed my neck and décolletage. "Hmm," I gently moaned. He slowly gathered the bottom of my asymmetrical dress in both his hands, raising it up towards my chest. I lifted my arms up and he pulled the dress over my head and dropped it onto the floor. He took me in, and I looked back in full confidence, glad that I wore those lace knickers and shaved my armpits and pussy, on top of loving my athletic body and perfect tits.

His lips touched my ear lobes, which sent a sensation to the middle of my back that I have never felt before. My back arched in response.

"Are you ok?" he whispered. *No, I'm here with you, you gorgeous specimen of a man. The hotel, this room, the music, everything is perfect and I need to calm down because I feel overwhelmed and tipsy.*

Although internally freaking out, I managed to whisper back a very calm and convincing, "Yes."

He worked his way down to my breasts, giving both equal attention before expressing how much he liked them. His hands moved down to my bottom and he rubbed both plump cheeks before he put his hands at the top of my lace knickers and slowly rolled them down my legs. They landed on the floor and his face landed in-between my legs, which I didn't expect. *WTF! He is not playing around.* I placed my hand on his shoulders to steady myself. *OMG! This feels so good.* I tried to regulate my breathing, which was becoming difficult in the steamy bathroom, on top of the alcohol I'd already consumed. *If he's gonna be down there, I would have preferred to shower first.* He had skills but now I couldn't concentrate. I gently tapped Aaron on the shoulder.

"Hmm?" he asked, sending vibrations to my clit causing me to moan harder.

I stuttered the words out. "I, I... Mr Ber... I mean, Aaron, this feels great but I would feel more comfortable if I showered first." I said as I gently cupped the side of his face.

He kissed my clit, stood up and said, "No problem, let's jump in the shower."

He took off his boxer shorts and I unapologetically looked at his package. I moved closer to him and touched his well-endowed, circumcised and hairless penis. I cupped his balls as I took a closer look, satisfied.

"So, now that your inspection is over, do you like what you see?" he asked.

"I like to inspect the goods before they come into my home," I said teasingly, but I was also being serious.

"You have a neat pussy. It looks good, smells good and tastes good, that's it for me."

I tried to hide my surprise. *That's your checking system. Hell no! Way too lax for me.*

The bathroom became really steamy, so he opened the windows, which I was grateful for. The breeze does wonders immediately. As I was about to step into the shower, I turned back. "By any chance do you have a headscarf or do-rag?" I looked at the waves in his hair, whilst praying.

"Hun, I just brush and the waves come, so don't need one. I'm sorry. Let's find something," he said encouragingly.

I should have got braids or even a weave. I wouldn't have this problem now if I did, but no, looking cute with my pixie hair cut took priority. I followed him to the bedroom, adamant a solution can be found. I spotted a pair of black silk boxers in his open suitcase and decided against asking for them, even though I was prepared to wear anything that ensured my hair wouldn't look too messy in the morning. In the end, I resorted to using a pillowcase, which he watched me transform into a decent-looking headscarf.

"You women are resourceful. I would never have thought of that," he expressed.

"We got skills," I said, smiling as I walked back into the bathroom and into the shower. He followed, closing the sliding door behind him.

We stood in a position for the water to rain down on both our bodies, but without wetting my headscarf. He guided me by the waist to move forward. Standing behind me, he lifted my arms up and without a word, instructed me to place them on the wall in front of me. *I love the gentle power he exudes.* He placed shower gel on the shower body puff, creating a thick, soapy lather, and began to slowly wash my skin from my neck all the way down, giving equal attention to both the front and back of my body ending at my feet. *This feels really sensual and loving.*

He rinsed the shower puff and placed more gel on to it before giving it to me. We swapped places and I began to wash his wide, muscly back, admiring his physique as I worked my way down. He turned around without being instructed and watched me stand up to wash his chest, arms, abs and thighs. I purposely missed out his genitals and headed to his legs and feet. "You can wash your own dick," I said as I stood up, handing the body puff back to him. He laughed as he confidently handled his business, watching me.

He turned off the shower once he had rinsed himself off, and I stepped out and begin to dry myself. I handed him his towel as I wrapped mine around my body.

"We can do better than that," he said, taking an oversized white dressing gown from the back of the bathroom door and helping me put it on. I felt like I had received a big hug. *I want to live in luxury all the time.* Once dry, he opened a discreet cabinet and took out another robe which he put on. We both headed to the living room, where he opened the balcony doors. I walked out, and the view was incredible. I watched the overlapping waves meet the start of the white sand again and again, as they twinkled under the beam of the big round moon and star-filled sky. *The sound of waves is so peaceful.* I breathed in as deeply as I could, because I want to take it all in. *I want it to fill the void within me.*

"Here you go," he said, I broke my gaze to look at him and took the bottle of water before sitting opposite him on the mosaic-patterned table and chairs. My nerves must have washed away in the shower, as I felt good. I looked at him, smiling, and pushed my hands into the pockets of the dressing gown as I reclined back to take in this glorious view. My right hand touched something in the pocket, which I pulled out. *WTF?* I raised it above the table so he could see what I was holding. "Is there something you want to tell me?"

His face dropped. I placed the gold band on the table and pushed it towards him.

My heart was pounding and the thoughts in my head were racing just as fast.

"Let me explain..." he began. *Triggered.* Red flags appeared. Anger at the pit of my stomach began to fire up. *Calm down. Calm down. Breathe Symona. Take in the air and calm down.* Feeling like a vulnerable idiot—*and already looking like one*—I removed the makeshift headscarf from my head and began to fix my sweated out hair in an attempt to regain control.

"I'm married, but things aren't good at the moment. I'm here because I needed to have a break from my family to clear my head."

"*Family?*"

"Yes, I have a one-year old son."

"Oh my God! How does this situation help you clear your mind?" I asked assertively.

"Let me finish," he said calmly, but with a firm bass in his voice. "This was not my intention when I arrived. I love my family and I want it to work out. I saw you when you walked in and thought you were beautiful. I was psyching myself up to talk to you, but I was hesitant. However, my intention was to talk to you," he said.

But you didn't have to because my fast self did the work for you. I laid all my cards on the table and you just took the opportunity. Why wouldn't you? Of course, I didn't say that to him. I said, "But you are married! By not wearing your ring, can't you see how you are lying to yourself and others?"

"I take it off before I shower, and I just forgot to put it back on. I'm being honest," he insisted with a slice of stress to his tone.

"Well, when were you going to tell me?"

"I have been wanting to tell you since we got into the taxi."

"The taxi! But that's even too late? Can't you see that?" I said in disbelief.

He opened his mouth to say something but no words came out. He exhaled deeply. Silence followed, broken by crashing waves which added more tension to the drama unfolding. *I didn't ask the right questions.* Just like that, guilt dropped in, even though it wasn't mine to wear in this scenario. I was so used to punishing myself that I was ready to marinade in it. *No Symona,* he *didn't tell you. It was* his *responsibility to tell you. This is not your fault.*

"Why get married if you're willing to cheat?" I tried to say that as calmly as possible. I genuinely wanted to hear the answer to the question, because my own dad refused to answer it or acknowledge what he had done. *Is this what I—and every woman—have to look forward to, even after we say our wedding vows? If so, just let me know now, so I can save myself from the hurt and lies. I'm twenty-three years old and already pent up with disappointment in men.* I looked at him intensely, waiting for an answer. He just looked uncomfortable.

"I have never considered cheating before now. It has been stressful the last couple of months for both of us and... and seeing you... I just want to be intimate, to feel... to—"

"To fuck it away?" I finished crassly.

"No, Symona, please. I have too much respect for you for that. I just want to feel…"

Of all the men I could meet on this small island, I attract someone who is no different to Darren or my dad. Like, really universe? Really?

Aaron didn't finish his sentence and I didn't push, because I didn't care. I wasn't religious but I respected commitment, and right then I felt men didn't follow the same rules. *I'm generalising and I don't care.*

"I know what it's like to be cheated on, and that's why I don't deal with married men or men who are in relationships. It's just not right," I told him calmly.

"I understand but, I'm the one in the situation and not you. I have someone to answer to, not you. I have to deal with my own guilt."

Did I hear that correctly? He is still up for this? I looked out to the landscape in front of me and I knew I was in trouble when my brain started assessing what had already occurred. *You already danced, kissed, touched and showered with him, so you have already been intimate. You have already crossed the line without knowing, and yet here you are still taking the moral high ground.* I thought for a moment. *You know what? I want to feel to. I want to be in someone's arms, to be held and cared for and desired, and as he says. I don't have someone to answer to, he does. So why am I about to carry guilt that isn't mine?*

"Symona… Syms." He interrupted my thoughts. "Are you OK?"

Not knowing how to answer, I remained quiet. He walked

over to me and held his hand out, which I took after a slight pause. He pulled me up and embraced me. *He smells so good.*

"It's late, just stay. We don't have to do anything," he said.

"*Else*. We don't have to do anything *else*," I corrected his sentence. He smiled, kissed my forehead and led me back inside. I saw the red flags and I chose to ignore them because I wanted to stay.

*

"Morning beautiful, breakfast is here," Aaron said, sticking his head out of the sliding doors. We'd slept on the balcony, after... I got up to walk inside, and all of a sudden I heard cars begin honking. I looked down and realised: if I could see the cars coming down the hill, the cars could see me. *Is this Karma for doing something I wasn't meant to?* The shame! I ducked down and crawled my naked body back into the living room. He laughed his head off before asking if I slept well, knowing full well that I didn't. He had been so attentive and giving, and it had been just what I'd needed. Of course I had felt emotional, but it wasn't as bad as it had been in the past. *I feel slightly relieved.*

Over breakfast, we both decided what happened was a one-off. He called it "a glitch in our moral compass." I happily agreed, whilst knowing it was a selfish get-out clause to make us feel better. *I'm a hypocrite.*

After my shower, I prayed before I took off my makeshift headscarf, which must have come off at least three times that night. My hair was going to be messy, it was inevitable, I was just hoping it would be fixable. *Oh No!* I looked like a troll doll. My hair was dry as hell and standing upwards. *I need this to lay flat ASAP.* I didn't want to bother Aaron with my hair problems again, so I just decided to use cocoa butter on my scalp—it was the only thing to hand. I wrapped my hair back up and hoped a miracle would happen before I left. Determined to honour his return-time promise, he called me a taxi. I wasn't ready to do the walk of shame—though to be fair there was never going to be a good time—but it was interesting that he wanted to keep his pledge to a man he barely knew over his wife, whom he'd made a commitment to in God's house. I'm just saying... but who am I to judge now? If I still went to Church, I would have been repenting my sins. I would even have drunk from that silver cup the priest never seemed to wipe properly before giving it to the next person in line. *Eww.*

The receptionist called to inform Aaron that the taxi has arrived. I checked myself over to ensure I looked the best I could. As we left his room and made our way down to the lobby, he said all the things I want to hear. "I really enjoyed spending time with you, Symona. I had a lovely time, and hope you did too." His words were matched by the way he looked at me.

"I really did too. Thank you for making me feel so comfortable," I said, smiling. *He has no idea how important last night was for me.* We walked past the reception desk, and I couldn't help but look to see if the same receptionist from last night was there. *He's not—yes!* I felt relieved, which made no sense as it was evident, based on my attire at nine thirty in the morning, that I clearly spent the night and this was my walk of shame. *Stop caring so much!*

We walked outside to the waiting taxi, and he kissed me tenderly goodbye. As he opened the car door, he said, "How about dinner tomorrow at 7pm?" A red cross flashed in my mind's eye. "Meet me here. You still have my number. Let me know." I looked at him and offered only a smile back as I got into the taxi. He was still standing there as we drove off, but I refused to look back.

The man was pushing my moral compass. *We just agreed this was a one-off and now you want to tempt me with your smooth voice and alluring eyes? REALLY? What do I do?* How was I even asking myself that question? *There is nothing to do, HE IS MARRIED. See the lesson and learning and keep it moving. Do not consciously choose this scenario again.* I planned to put it down to experience. It would be wrong to entertain another night... *I think.*

*

I told Asta everything as soon as I got back. "Oh boi," was her response to everything. She said that when she had no real words to express what she was thinking. But *oh boi* in different tones could mean 'wow!', 'oh dear' or 'are you for real?' Which was usually accompanied with wide eyes and shaking her head, or the use of expressive hands. She was disappointed with Aaron and lay the blame firmly at his door, however I still chose to take responsibility for my part, as I had intentionally crossed the line once I found out. She wasn't having any of it. Instead she chose to focus on the courage and spontaneity that led to me "finally getting laid."

"Girl you deserved it. I hope you feel good."

"I do," I said, smiling. Telling half-truths. I'd enjoyed being in his company and being intimate, and as Asta already knew, I wasn't proud of sleeping with a married man. However, I chose not to mention that I had cried. It's so embarrassing that sometimes talking to people makes it worse for me. After we'd finished having sex, which had been gentle and attentive and surprisingly loving, I went to the bathroom to freshen up—and then it happened. I'd burst into tears. I can't even express why. I was just grateful that I didn't cry in front of him—I didn't want to go through all of that again.

I really wanted to see Aaron again, because I felt at ease with him, but I also felt guilty about it. Surprised about my conflicting feelings and hypocritical actions, I also didn't want to be swayed into anything. Not because I was weak, but because I didn't want to be encouraged to do what I *think* deep down I wanted to do, even if I knew it was wrong.

The next day, Lyron decided to throw us a barbeque as our holiday was sadly coming to an end. Asta and I helped him prep—thankfully he wasn't as annoying that time. I was quiet, with Aaron still on my mind. His smell, his looks, how he touched me and made me feel… *I want more.* Flashbacks popped into my head, which I shook and blinked away every now and then, but the thoughts continued. *We already did what we did, so dinner is fine, right? OK, OK it's not, but after this trip I won't be seeing him again and…* Was I really trying to justify my decision?

I heard the internal question and I instantly felt under

pressure. I was searching for an answer as I carefully peeled potatoes, but my brain flooded with snapshots of Aaron's best features—his Hollywood smile, warm brown come-to-bed eyes and perfectly sculpted body. *Symona, your time with Aaron has served its purpose. Let it go and learn from your learnings.* Arriving like a whisper, I heard those words loud and clear, which I couldn't ignore. I succumbed to doing the right thing and decided not to meet him that night. The fresh sexual memories were harder to ignore. My body felt awakened again…

A hard knock at the door broke my concentration. As I was closer to it, I wiped my hands and went to answer it. I opened the door and was greeted by Jaden, the friend of Lyron's whom we'd met when we arrived, with the green eyes. *What the fuck?* I hadn't expected to see him again. Inside I was flapping around like a headless chicken, but on the outside I would like to believe he received me as a graceful swan.

"Hi," he said breezily. "Do you have a toothpick?"

I was baffled and I must have looked it, because he asked the question again.

"Hey, erm… I don't know, come in and take a seat while I have a look."

I headed into the kitchen and announced that Jaden was here, before searching for something I hadn't seen all week. I found a packet of chewing gum and offered that to him instead.

"I don't eat gum," he said very bluntly, landing as plain rude.

"Well, I don't have toothpicks, so…?" I snapped back.

"Thanks for trying to help," he said in a softer tone as he touched my elbow. I relaxed, smiled and offered him a drink.

Lyron greeted him with a beer and they chilled and talked whilst Asta and I finished prepping in the kitchen.

I could hear Jaden and Lyron talking in the living room, and Jaden definitely had a personality to match his looks. His voice was smooth and velvety, whilst his contagious laugh, with a slight huskiness revealed to me he was a smoker.

A moment ago I was debating whether I should see Mr Bermuda again, and then the hot guy I met on the first day knocks on the door. What is going on?

"Decisions, decisions, eh?" Asta said, smiling at me. "Aaron or Jaden? Go or stay?"

"There are no decisions. I'm not going to see Aaron and Jaden, I don't even know if he likes me or not or whether he's single."

"Well, he is single, and he likes you," Asta said, smiling and bogling. I looked at her, confused. "I asked Lyron," she added very matter of factly. "We are here for a week. Did you really think I was going to just wait and see?" She paused for effect. "And this is why I'm Batman."

"Why the hell did he wait the night before we leave to come back, then?" I say, surprised and pissed off. My morals could have remained intact if I'd known he was interested in me.

"Hun, we're on holiday, he isn't. Anyway, he's here now and that's all that matters. You can be really time-focused and rigid, you know."

"I just… I mean… potentially two different men in under twenty-four hours?" I was mortified at the prospect.

"See, this is what I'm talking about. Let it go. Embrace it

all. Live. As long as you are being careful, that is all that matters. Hold that thought, I'm just going to the bathroom," she said.

I finished off seasoning the chicken, and then washed my hands.

"Hey, can I help?" Jaden said, entering the kitchen. I turned around to look at him whilst wiping my hands.

"Hey, erm… I think we're done now," I replied, looking at the food covered in cling film and foil. "Thanks for asking, though," I added, looking at him and at the same time catching Asta behind him, giving me the thumbs up.

"What are you smiling at?" he asked. *Busted.* There was no point lying.

"My poker face is shit, I really must work on that," I said, laughing. "The truth is, you make me nervous."

"You make me nervous too, so we are in the same boat."

"What?" I said in shock.

"I asked you for a toothpick! Who does that?" he said, laughing too. "I didn't know what to say. I felt so stupid, and I know I pissed you off." We both laughed and the awkwardness disappeared.

*

Jaden and I were getting on so well. We were chilling upstairs and had been talking for hours, interrupted only by kisses that each time made my stomach flip. His lips were like soft pillows— each time they connected with mine, they sent electric sparks to my heart and stomach. *I have never felt this before.* He made me nervous every time he looked at me, because of how he made me feel but also because it took me a moment to register green eyes staring back at me. It was so rare to see within brown skin, and he was already just so stunning. It was like there was a magnetic pull that we were both responding to. The attraction was instant, mutual and intense. I wanted time to stand still because I wanted to remain in the presence of this gentle, attentive, funny, intelligent and attractive man...

I woke up smiling. Jaden was next to me. I couldn't believe we stayed up all night talking. I was going to be shattered later, but it was worth it,—plus, I could sleep on the plane.

He had to go to work, but it was clear he didn't want to go just as much as I didn't want him to. I felt like I'd always known him and we were meant to meet. Constant kisses replaced words, but nothing was lost. In fact, I felt there was more being said because it was unspoken. I understood his language. My lips tingled as fast as my heart beat, and I felt the loss when he left. *It sounds dramatic, I know.* I hadn't been looking, but I found him and lost him in the same breath. My last hours in Barbados were filled with sadness...

*

As soon as I took my seat on the plane, I selected the films I wanted to watch, knowing full well I would be conked out after I backed two glasses of wine with my dinner. It had to be done to ensure I had a good sleep.

"Thank you so much for suggesting this trip, hun," I said to

Asta with gratitude.

"You had an alright week, the cherry on the top, Jaden?"

"For sure. We just clicked, and I can't believe it. We swapped details, so I hope we keep in touch."

"I'm sure you will. And Aaron?"

"OMG! I literally forgot. Even though I decided not to see him, I really wanted to speak to him. Never mind."

As the plane sped up, Asta grabbed my hand and started praying. It was a ritual, and one that I loved and appreciated. As we ascended into the air, I put my headphones on and began to watch my first selected film. I couldn't concentrate though, because my mind kept throwing out flashbacks that my body reacts too. I closed my eyes and decided to give thanks.

Dear God /universe, thank you for allowing me to be open enough to have this experience. Thank you for putting into my path two men who allowed me to feel loved and cared for, if only for a short time. I hope you aren't judging me, and I promise to reset my morals and values. I feel hopeful again and for that I am grateful.

Chapter Six

Debbie

26th March 2002

"Here you go Symona, take this."

I looked up and Debbie, my counsellor, was leaning forward holding out a box of tissues. This was my sixth session—I missed last week's because I was on holiday. I was just starting to get over being embarrassed at crying in front of her, and sitting in silence. At first I'd wanted Debbie to save me, and when she didn't, I would talk about anything to break the silence, and fill the space, but I got it now. The space allowed me to say what came, and feel what rose up. There was just so much pain, and my tears were my only words right then.

My whole world had been rocked *again*. Finding out I had a sister, and Mum and Dad breaking up as a result, hit me hard. My mind felt like tangled spaghetti and I knew I needed additional support. I had gone private as the NHS waiting list was too long. I liked Debbie. She had kind eyes, and I felt she understood what I was saying. If she didn't, she'd ask for clarification. Debbie was a Black woman about my mum's age, which in a way was comforting as I couldn't talk to mum; she was going through her own stuff. However, because she was my mum's age, I worried that she might judge me, with what I told her... I mean, I didn't feel judgement from her, but the concern was there.

I pulled two tissues out of the box and wiped away my tears. I took a deep breath before continuing. "I knew he was married and I still slept with him. That makes me no different to what Dad has done to Mum."

"Do you really think what you experienced is the same?" she asked.

"No, but... Cheating is cheating."

"How do you feel?"

"Disappointed."

"In who?" she asked.

"I'm disappointed in men, and in myself."

"Tell me about the disappointment in yourself."

I stared at the picture on the wall of this medium-sized, cream room. My eyes were always drawn to it when she asked me questions that I didn't want to really answer. I was sure she had already noticed that was what I did. It was a large picture of a forest with different shades of green highlighted by shards of light from the sun above. It was beautiful, and gave me a sense of peace and hope that I could join the dots, see the woods for the trees and make sense of my own tangle of emotions.

"I let my strong need to be comforted affect my morals and values."

She looked at me, nodding. I knew another question wasn't coming, because she wanted me to elaborate on what I had just said.

"I just wanted to be held I guess and feel normal."

"Normal?" she asked.

"I've been—had been—celibate for two-ish years before I slept with Aaron. How many young adults are doing that? I wanted to *feel*, to be close to someone, to feel good about myself, but I don't. I can't." I could feel the lump in my throat forming. I drank the glass of water in front of me, hoping the liquid would wash away the building pain expanding in my throat. My eyes pricked and I allowed the tears to flow—they needed to come out. My surrender immediately dislodged the lump, allowing my words to travel out of my mouth. "I can't because... because my brain isn't allowing me to and so I don't always enjoy it. Sometimes sex just isn't worth the upset it causes me. That in itself is upsetting. Having sex won't fix my intimacy issues, and I'm glad I know that. It's my issue to solve. In the same breath, I'm disappointed in men because I don't trust them—they *can't* be trusted. Darren, my first boyfriend accused me of cheating on him, but he was cheating on *me*. And Dad? I'm still in shock. No 'sorry', no nothing. I'm just so angry, angry at dad, Darren and with myself. My celibacy has pushed men away, and that was my intention. I just don't want them anywhere near me."

"And yet you want to be held, be comforted and feel, feel 'normal', which refers to a sexual context," Debbie said, paraphrasing.

"Yes. But I... I feel empty and sex doesn't fill it. I want to feel normal."

"You feel empty?"

"Yes, I am and I feel empty."

Chapter Seven

Mr Barbados

Hello Mandy, I hope you are well. I'm not coming in today as I feel absolutely awful. I have been up all night with a temperature. The team know what they are doing today as tasks were set for this week on Friday. I'm totally switching off and hope to be in tomorrow, call me only if there is an emergency. Have a good day.

Syms

I re-read the text message and press send. I just lied and I feel OK about it. I rarely take sick days so Mandy, my boss, won't bat an eye. I'm not even ill, I'm just feeling a bit down, so I'm giving myself the day off. I have no plans but intend to lie here for as long as possible. My screaming bladder spoils that plan. I reluctantly shuffle to the bathroom and pee a river before heading to the kitchen. It's nine thirty am, *way too early for rum.* I settle for hot chocolate and a packet of chocolate biscuits and head back to bed. No sooner do I switch on the TV, I turn it back off again. *Daytime TV is actually depressing.* I've bunked off work and have no idea what to do with myself.

Through the cloud of various thoughts, Jaden pops in after

my reminiscences last night and brings with him a nostalgia that propels me to look through some past holiday albums. I reach for the box behind my mirrored sliding doors and instantly find what I am looking for, because I label my albums. ***Barbados— March and September 2003***. I crawl back into bed and start flicking through. *I wonder if Aaron sorted things out with his wife?*

I smile at one picture. *The leopard print sofa!* The most out of place thing in the mansion we stayed in, but somehow it worked… Jaden and I kept in touch after we first met. He consumed my thoughts and dreams after we got back from our first trip. I missed him, and Asta missed Lyron, so we took another trip six months later…

*

Once again, Lyron picked us up from the airport and we headed straight to the mansion. "People are going to think we're rich. Not only are we back in Barbados again, we are staying in a mansion." I failed to reduce the level of my excitable squeal.

"I know right? We got lucky with the cheap flights and a mansion for free. Thank you, baby," Asta said, caressing Lyron's face as he drove.

"You girls are lucky that I have great relationships with international friends. We are gonna have a blast."

This time round, both Lyron and Jaden were able to book time off work, so they were staying and relaxing with us for the first week. I could not contain my excitement and I couldn't wait to see Jaden when he finished work that evening.

The mansion was everything you would expect a mansion to be, complete with a maid, which was amazing but also made me feel weird. I didn't want to be served like this. Asta felt the same. Lyron didn't get it, but he was overruled, so he called his friend and it was agreed the maid could have the week off. Asta and I gave her two hundred pounds as a gesture of thanks, as we wanted to ensure she wasn't out of pocket just because we wanted to be with our 'boyfriends.' Far from rich, we just thought it was the right thing to do. She showed us where everything was in the house before she left, and she seemed happy.

The swimming pool was so inviting, but with my freshly glued-in weave, I had no intention of water touching my hair. I could have gone for braids, but I thought weave looked more desirable. I hoped Jaden liked it. Lyron hadn't said anything, which might have meant he didn't, but I didn't care about his opinion. I unpacked my suitcase and made myself feel at home, which was so easy to do there. Once done, I headed outside and sunbathed by the large swimming pool as Asta and Lyron caught up inside. I kept looking at the time on my phone, because I wanted seven pm to arrive as soon as possible. In an attempt to control my anxiety, I began to journal. I'd been doing it since I'd started counselling seven months ago, and found it really cathartic.

"Hey baby."

I was woken up by a smooth, distinctive voice, coupled with kisses my body remembered way before my brain was able to register who it was. I opened my eyes and he was *there*.

"Hey hun, it's so good to see you. How are you?" I said whilst adjusting to an upright position.

"I'm good, and happy to see you."

I melted under Jaden's gaze, and melted again when he helped me to stand up so he could embrace me. His smell, his lips, his tongue, his everything sent electricity sparking over my body. I could not get enough of him. We headed to the bedroom and made love for the first time. Fears and worry were nowhere to be found. *Is this due to the counselling, him or a combination of both?* I felt so good.

Both lying naked, I was in his arms. Jaden kissed my forehead and asked, "Are you OK?" I nodded my response and he continued, "Can I ask why you cried?"

I was annoyed at myself for not addressing it first, but I let it go. I wanted to tell him everything—my history, everything—but I chose to focus on how he made me feel.

"I can't explain it, but I'll try. I… I just felt loved, adored and cherished. The way you hold me, look at me and touch me, makes me feel full, and I cried because I was overwhelmed by the feeling." *This is the truth.*

He kissed me passionately as his response, which was enough, before slowly stroking my hair.

Oh God, he's gonna feel the tracks!

"You know I love your short hair," he said breezily. *Which translates to 'I don't like your new hair.'*

"I know. I just thought I'd try something different. Do you like it?"

"You can wear any hairstyle, hun, I just think short hair makes your features pop more, that's all," he said, adjusting his position to look at me. "Regardless, you are still beautiful to me," he added, before kissing me. *Wow, the clean-up is fast, even when there is nothing to clean up. I'm loving his awareness.*

We jumped in the shower and then headed downstairs for dinner as Lyron had shouted that it was ready. I had never met someone who wasn't a chef be so passionate about food. The table by itself was impressive, but more so with the amount of food that was laid out.

"Bloody hell, this looks like a feast!" I say, surprised.

"Fit for two Queens, of course," Lyron said in the direction of Asta, who rolled her eyes as we began to tuck in.

As the conversation flowed, I was present but couldn't help acknowledge that I could easily get used to it, all of it. Good conversations with good people, maybe even living there with Jaden. *This is the life. Please make this week just stretch out. Please.*

"Are you OK, babe?" Jaden asked, moving my long hair out of the way to touch my neck.

I nodded, and he leant forward to kiss me.

"Oh, get a room!" shouted Lyron, laughing. "You two are so soppy."

"Erm, hello! You can learn from them," stressed Asta, laughing. Lyron's expression showed us all he disagreed.

Although the sun had set, it was still warm outside. We headed out to the garden, solar spotlights guiding our path. With the gazebo at the bottom of the garden, it seemed a perfect place to have a wedding… We drank, chatted and chilled to a backdrop of reggae. I sat by the edge of the pool, both feet dipped into the lukewarm water, which felt so nice. The boys were cracking jokes, whilst I was talking to Asta over at the other side of the pool. She went to say something suddenly, but it was too late... I was in the pool. *One of these idiots pushed me in.*

I was wearing a weave and I wasn't a strong swimmer. *Like WTF!* My feet hit the bottom of the pool and I pushed myself up, gasping for air when I reached the surface. Luckily for me, I wasn't too far from the edge. I swam to the best of my intermediate ability. *I really need to be consistent with my adult classes. I like swimming but need to increase my confidence. I just panicked. I should be to save my own life.*

"Argh! Who did that? It's not even funny! Throwing a Black girl into any depth of water, will never be funny." *Unless you're an adventure junkie like Asta.* "This hair is fresh, it's glued and I have no idea about the damage this chlorine may cause. And now... And now I have to wash my hair. This is long!" I stormed off, heading straight to the bathroom to work out what to do. I may have come across as dramatic, but the whole point of having the weave was so I didn't need to stress about my hair. *A makeshift pillow headscarf issue is nothing in comparison to this!*

I washed the weave and my own hair as gently as possible, praying the glue didn't lift, before blow drying and straightening it all. I was so vex. If I had been a cartoon, steam would have been coming out of my ears. Jaden walked in tentatively, which told me he could sense the steam pouring out of me.

"I come in peace," he said, waving what I assumed was meant to be an invisible white flag. "I'm so sorry baby, I thought you would have found that funny..." My eyes throw daggers at him.

"…But I can now see it wasn't. Please forgive me." He knelt on the floor and hugged me from behind. I looked at him through the mirror in front of me, and just like that the vexation disappeared.

"You're forgiven, even though I've just wasted two hours of my time. And now I'm pissed that I can't be pissed off at you for long."

"I mean no harm, plus we're on holiday girl, no stress."

"No stress," I repeated, smiling.

*

The first week flew by, and the second week went even faster. Before I knew it, I was at the airport looking for souvenirs that I didn't want to buy, wasting time before we went through customs. Waking up to Jaden every day had given me an insight into how it could be. I didn't want it to end. Every time he left I felt sad, and as I was about to leave the country, I once again felt heartbroken. Asta was just as miserable as I was—then suddenly, she shouted Jaden's name. I looked at her, and she was frantically waving. I looked in the same direction—and he was there! He was actually there. My heart began to race, and my stomach fluttered with butterflies. I ran out and met him halfway, hugging him.

"Hey baby, I missed you already so I had to come." He held my face in his hands and kissed me slowly and passionately. *A thousand kisses from him would never be enough.*

"I'm so glad you came. I miss you so much, too."

"I borrowed my boss's car so I could get to the airport on time. I'm so glad I caught you."

Him showing up like that meant everything, even just to say goodbye.

*

Damn, we really had something, I think, looking at the photographs. All these years later, Jaden still pops into my head every so often. I've tried not to snoop, but Facebook tells me he is married, now living in Canada. At the time he couldn't see himself moving to the UK and in my early twenties, I couldn't really see a future in Barbados, so I guess I just saw this as an amazing romantic fluke encounter. I was grateful for it, grateful for the slice, because at the time I didn't think it was possible to have the whole cake. That magnetic pull was there for a reason. I felt it, *we* felt it and acted upon it, at least for a while. I shouldn't have let the reality of distance define our future, as it killed possibility and hope.

Is Jaden 'the One' that got away? *What is for you will not pass you.* He didn't pass me. We had our moment. Our time. Our season. And it was beautiful. Maybe that was all it was meant to be. I learnt how it feels to be loved unconditionally. I was reminded that I am deserving of love, and that good men exist. Perhaps that was it. I will never know because I wasn't brave enough to entertain a bigger story.

Chapter Eight

New Year, New Me

1ˢᵗ January 2017

The thought of dressing up in this cold weather, paying for extortionate rave tickets, overpriced drinks and overpriced taxis is no longer something I am willing to do to see in the start of the New Year. I know better now—which is why I'm in my bed. Chantel called me boring, which I'm not, although I am bored, not that I would ever admit that to her. I've done my time and now I would rather spend the first day of the New Year sober, clear-headed and ready to action my goals. I like to start as I mean to go on.

The countdown begins. *"Ten, Nine, eight, seven…"* and I have my good ole friend Baileys with me ready to cheer in the turn of the year. "… Three, two, one, HAPPY NEW YEAR!!" I raise my glass to the TV, take a sip and watch the amazing fireworks. I've never been kissed under the mistletoe at the strike of the New Year. Does that even happen, or is it another fake reality conjured up only in films? I'm sure it's some people's reality, just never been mine. *Is this something worth putting on a bucket list? Hmm. Nah.*

As people begin to sing *Auld Lang Syne* while overlooking the London Eye, I turn off the TV. I love the togetherness, excited faces and joy, but that song has got to be one of the most cele-brated non-celebratory songs I have ever heard in my life. It's dead. No beat, no soul, no nothing. I literally feel depressed when I hear it. I finish my drink and settle in bed to read the messages that are starting to come through on my mobile. I was planning to wait until the morning, but gave in. Back in the day I would have written so many messages in advance, lined them up and sent them at the strike of the New Year. Now? *Meh!* My WhatsApp is filled with "Happy New Year!" messages in the form of memes, gifs and text. A few are from men I haven't spoken to in ages. Their 'How are you?' at the end of their messages tells me they are either lonely at home too, wished they secured a winter bae months ago, or they're out with the boys drunk and reflective—or pissed that the night wasn't as hyped as they hoped.

This time of the year does strange things to people. It's a time of reflection, which can bring regret and the urge to rekindle. I ponder over my situation and instantly feel restless. I decide to change up the vibe. I'm feeling some old R'n'B, and select songs on Spotify that pop into my head. *Can't You See* by Total, *You Used to Love Me* by Faith Evans, *Grind With Me* by Pretty Ricky, *Soon As I Get Home* by Faith Evans and by the time I get to Keith Sweat's track *Twisted*, I'm done. *Why are you selecting these songs?* This is self-sabotage. Why? Because it gets me all lovey-dovey and yearning. I can feel nostalgia rising, helped along by Baileys, who may just get me into trouble if I don't catch myself. I have no business contacting anyone!

Instead, I decide to go onto my dating apps and prep for my challenge, and I'm surprised to see I have some messages.

Hey, you look great. Do you like me? Lets chat!
Really forward.

Hi sexy, you look good.
OK, but I need more than that as an opener.

Hey, reply back.
How is that even a message? And don't tell me what to do.

Can anyone effectively communicate online? If so, come find me! *Jheeze.* The second app is no better, so I give up and stare at the ceiling whilst trying to block out the awful song choices from the house party taking place three doors down: Little Mix followed by Lionel Richie and now N-Sync makes no sense to me.

I'm looking forward to new experiences, continued health, wealth, joy and love. From here on in, the word *hope* will not leave my mouth. I want—no, I *expect*—love this year, and it will show up as respect, commonality and pure awesomeness. Nothing for me will pass me, so rather than concentrating on what I don't have, I look forward to what is coming. It's already written. *I must remember that.* I know what I like and I like what I like, but liking what I like has meant that I'm still single. *Really? I may need to look a little deeper.* I'm open to the challenge, though. I let go of fear and look forward to seeing what openness brings, whilst continuing to learn from past experiences. This mission will not work within the comfort zone, or fear, so the only requirement I have is that I have to be attracted or intrigued by whoever's out there for me.

So here it goes: New Year, New Me.

Chapter Nine

Cupid Strikes?

There is no map, directions, estimated time of arrival or departure. It cannot be found in diamonds, pearls or any other consumer-led materialistic object that happens to be heart-shaped and in the colours of pink or red. The truest essence of love is free, simple, unexplainable, felt... Oh, unless it is Valentine's Day.

Today, is the day when refusing to buy into the bullshit could cause an argument with your partner. Although I'm (still) single, pressure is the one thing I have in common with those in relationships. My pressure, however, stems from myself. I refuse to feel depressed, upset, or bitter as I hear the squeals from work colleagues receiving flowers and chocolates. I'm being challenged right now as I sit in front of two massive, lovely bouquet of flowers, that thankfully are blocking out the stretched-out grins that I know are permanently fixed onto Sharon and Kerry's face—a blessing, I guess.

Everyone wants to be thought of, and I challenge you to find a person on this earth who doesn't like gifts. This essentially ties up Valentine's Day. Combining it with the guilt-laced undertone of *if you loved me, you would* cements the success of such a day for businesses. It has nothing to do with freedom of expression or choice, it's driven by external demands and pressure. There are 365 days of the year—more than enough time for loved ones to show you how much they care and love you. This day seems to be less about an individual experience and more about a collective experience of 'Look what I've got' or 'I'm loved because I've got something', whilst sitting on top of each other in restaurants with low lights and red roses on the table.

I've never received anything on Valentine's Day. The single red rose from Dwayne when I was nineteen years old doesn't count, because he gave one to every girl at work. *Really nice gesture though.* The rose that I received from Stephen also definitely does not count. In fact, he was the one who got me into seeing how consumerist Valentine's Day is, and so I didn't expect anything and I didn't give anything either. We were walking back to his flat, and on the floor near his door was a red rose. It was in good condition, but slightly dirty. He picked it up and gave it to me. I felt bad refusing it, so I humbly accepted it. *Can you believe that?* I placed the single flower in a tall glass, looked at it and saw myself. I realised in that moment I felt stuck, sad, lost and I needed to bloom again. After six months together, I broke up with him. It wasn't really about the rose, but the rose signified I wanted more and was settling.

Maybe I really do like Valentine's Day, and saying I don't celebrate it due to consumerism is my defence from having no one to share it with? In the same breath, I know Valentine's originates from the festival of Lupercalia, which involved sacrificing animals and whipping and beating women, before men selected one to couple up with in the hope of producing a baby. Doesn't sound like love to me. It's all about candlelit dinners and red roses now, so yeah, consumerism. I like romance—I like giving and receiving gifts but I'm not a fan of feeling pressured into it. I therefore conclude that Valentine's Day is a forced statement of love.

Zaara calling breaks up my mini internal rant.

"Hey, girl! How are ya?" she says, practically singing down the phone.

"I'm good babe, what's up?"

"Why do you sound like that, Syms? Have you been crying?"

"No, I've just been sneezing. Lilies make me sneeze," I say as discreetly as possible.

"You got flowers?!" she exclaims excitedly.

"No, my work colleague did," I whisper.

"Why don't you tell her?"

"I'm not here to rain on anyone's love parade. It's fine, no biggie," I say, shrugging it off.

"Are you up for speed dating tomorrow?"

Speed dating after *Valentine's Day? Interesting.* I agree because I've never been before and I'm intrigued.

"Yeah, why not?"

*

The next evening, I'm looking forward to attending Cupid Strikes. I don't know what to expect, so I have no expectations. I freshen up in the work toilets and re-apply my neutral lipstick, before changing to Hollywood Red. If I have three minutes to make an impression it may as well start with my striking lips that make my Colgate-white teeth pop.

"Syms!"

Zaara sees me and shouts to get my attention. Of course, she is standing by a busker outside Piccadilly station cheering him on. *This woman.* We greet, she looks great and we head inside. Although on time, we're the first ones there, looking like eager beavers, which I express to Zaara as we pay for our drinks.

"Nah babe, we get to see them coming. This is great. First in, first dibs," she says, sussing out the best place to sit before deciding the grey velvet looking couch facing the door is the spot. I agree and we take a seat. "To make this more exciting, let's give the guys our own names," Zaara tells me. Before I can ask for an explanation, a guy walks in. "OK, lets, see… he has a strong walk, good dress sense, nice height. Oh, he just waved… Hmm—welcome, Mr Confident!" We watch as the host greets him before a second man walks in. Zaara nudges me to indicate it's my turn.

"Hmm, not really getting a vibe, but his rucksack looks bigger than him. Who comes to a speed dating event with such a big bag? Damn."

Zaara laughs and we agree to name him Rucksack Man. It's 6:15pm, the men are coming through, and by 6:30 nine men have arrived. They are…

1. Mr Confident
2. Rucksack Man
3. Italian Stallion

4. Pinstripes

5. Slimy

6. Stretch

7. I Walked Into The Wrong Room (IWITWR)

8. South Park Cartman

9. Dry Man

We become deflated with each new arrival. Zaara and I are the only Black women here, amongst fourteen women in total. The nine men look like they walked into Willy Wonka's factory. I don't want to insinuate they're punching above their weight, but they are. It's cool. We both accept it and agree to remain open and have fun—which right now, may also mean getting drunk.

Handing Zaara her mojito, I announce, "Tonight, Matthew, I'm Carrie Bradshaw from Sex and the City," before pretending to walk through the doors of Stars in Their Eyes, without the smoke or make-up to embody the blonde-hair-me-me-me brat of a character. Zaara follows my lead. *This is why I love her!* Adisa would have kissed her teeth at the idea, and Chantel would have just sat back looking at me like a feisty Persian cat.

"Tonight, Matthew, I'm Samantha... Actually, I think she's too close to my character already. I'm... I'm... I mean Charlotte and Miranda are boring, so..."

"Zaara, this isn't real, just choose one."

"OK. Tonight, Matthew, I'm Samantha!" she says, spinning like she's Wonder Woman.

We kick back and continue to suss everyone out, whilst overhearing a conversation between Pinstripes and IWITWR. So many questions in such a short time—we soon realise it's two men sussing each other out — and therefore the competition. Ego and testosterone, the cause of many issues. The bell rings, we grab a seat at the long table and listen to the instructions.

First up is Mr Confident, who takes a seat at my table, introduces himself and says with an outstretched hand, "What's your name?" I swiftly reply, "Symona," failing at the first hurdle. I clearly cannot lie, so I abandon 'Carrie.' After three minutes, I can say he's interesting, but after thirty seconds I'd already found his over-confidence off-putting. Zaara and I had obviously judged him right from the start. The bell rings, signifying the switch, and Pinstripes takes a seat.

His oversized pinstripe suit is harsh to the eyes, it's also too big for him and very dated.

"I'm a psychotherapist!" is his opening greeting. He's looking at me, waiting… For what, I'm not sure.

"So, why you are single?" I genuinely ask.

"Do you know why *you're* single?" he throws back. Deflection, why? It's a simple question.

"I asked you first," I say, very aware that this is starting to sound childish, but I'm not giving in to this display of power dynamics either. *Bell just ring, I beg.*

"Hmm, your assertiveness is…"

"I didn't ask for your opinion on me. I asked about you."

The bell rings. *Yes!* As he gets up, he smirks, which I interpret as, *I know exactly why you are single.* I pay no mind, because I don't care and I haven't mastered telepathy.

Rucksack Man takes a seat. He is from Kansas City. "Oh the

same place as Dorothy from the Wizard of Oz?"

"No, that fictional character was from Kansas. I'm real, and I'm from Kansas City." *Jheeze*. He's intense. I have nothing more to say, and although I am intrigued as to what's in his rucksack, I daren't ask, and as a result the three minutes drag.

Italian Stallion is next—well-groomed, but with too many shirt buttons open, exposing chest hair no-one wants to see. He is, indeed, from Italy, he is a breath of fresh air, literally. His aftershave smells so good. The conversation flows, and we're still talking when the bell goes. Stretch is literally pushing him out of his seat to start our conversation. Six foot three, personal instructor, he comes across as genuine and just a nice guy.

The bell rings. Before Slimy sits down, I'm already laughing. Quick-witted, serious lyrics, but just a bit too smooth, which comes across as… slimy. *Our judgements so far seem to be spot on*. He also has a problem with space; he keeps invading mine. I never understand why people feel the need to lean in so far forward. *I can hear you!* If I lean back anymore, I will fall off this chair.

The annoying bell rings again, and I want this over and done with now. There is no one here for me and, well, this is a waste of time. I catch Zaara's eye, which she widens into a stare that says "kill me now." I have seen this look many times in meetings when we used to work together five years ago. This is dire, but I'm gonna see this through, if only for the sake of my mission not to be single by forty.

IWITWR sits down and I can't say a bad word about him, other than he does look like he has walked into wrong room, wrong country even. The Hawaiian shirt is the thing that throws it all off. This is February, in London. "Symona, nice to meet you. I'm James. How are you finding this?" he asks.

"Well, James, I've never done speed dating before, so I'm just putting this down to experience."

"Ah yes, well looks like we're all, you know, punching above our weight. I mean, look at all you gorgeous gals, and look at us. One big mismatch against such lovely surroundings." *Damn straight! Thank you, James, for acknowledging this.* That's probably what me-me-me Carrie would say aloud. I prefer to agree with him in my head. My smile is my response, whilst expressing his other qualities. "Charming, self-aware, and funny also counts for a lot," I say.

"Yes, yes, this is very true, but we live in a judgmental world, and had this not been a forced three minutes to get to know you, I wouldn't have had the pleasure, especially as I didn't even know this was happening. I just walked in." I burst out laughing. You cannot make this up! The bell rings. "Nice to meet you, James," I say, holding my hand up for him to high-five.

"No, the pleasure is all mine. Boom!" he replies, slapping my hand. *Not caring what people think is also an art.*

South Park Cartman had me in stitches, and if I were a comedy agent I would pimp him out to the circuit. Hilarious guy. Dry man is the last man to take a seat. He is dry. I can feel it even more so now that he's sitting opposite me. I'm trying to listen, but his slow, monotone voice is just making me feel so lethargic. Zaara is sitting one seat away from me. I lean back, in an attempt to catch her eye. Not sure how this is going to work discreetly, but I do it anyway. She turns, looks at me. Looks to see who I'm talking too, smirks, and then focuses her attention back to South Park Cartman.

A few minutes later, Zaara calls my name and tells me, "My date is looking at your date cos he's bi-sexual."

South Park Cartman looks distraught and says, "You weren't meant to tell anyone! I told you in confidence." Standing up, in a dramatic fashion, he leaves through the double doors, with Zaara running behind shouting, "I'm sorry, I'm so sorry."

The room's silent. Everyone is now looking at me, looking for answers that I can't give. *WTF Zaara!* The bell rings, for the last time. A few seconds later, Zaara walks back in smiling, followed by South Park Cartman. "He's forgiven me," she announces. I'm relieved—everyone is relieved. No one more so than the host, who wraps the night up swiftly. We say our goodbyes and walk out to the station.

"How was it?" Zaara asks.

"You were there; cupid clearly wasn't in the house. It was OK, but we put in a lot of energy to make it OK," I say, being frank.

"I meant our performance." She sees my confused face. "OMG! You thought that outburst was real?" I'm still not computing. "Babe, me and South Park Cartman planned that little scene to inject some drama into a dead night."

"Oh my God! I can't take you anywhere!"

"I saw your face, I knew what you were about to go through with Dry Man so, I thought we would just spice it up."

I laugh my head off, and then feel bad. "It's funny to us, but Dry Man didn't know where to look, hun."

"That's his business. A compliment is a compliment. I'm not bi, but if a girl fancied me, I would be flattered. It doesn't mean anything other than a compliment—plus it was just a joke, no harm intended."

"Unless it's a Black-focused event, I don't think I would do this again," I tell her.

"I agree. It was marketed well, so why no bite? Where do Black men go when they want to meet someone? Whenever I go out, I look around and I don't see them. Where do they go?" I shrug. "No idea. *Nothing for you will pass you*—does that still apply if we're never in the same room?"

"Great question. It still applies, because the world is one big room. We pass people all the time, but there is something that makes us pay attention, look up and notice."

"It's all timing. Universal timing," I express.

"I think so. Which kinda makes me think all of this is point-less." She gestures back towards the speed-dating venue as we walk.

"No, nothing is wasted. We are developing ourselves, taking action, opening up to new experiences, which is far better than waiting."

Zaara nods in agreement as we head into the station. *The magnetic pull is divine intervention, timing aligned. I think.*

*

I'm on a roll.

Yesterday, by chance, I saw a flyer for an event called

Conversations with the UK 'Hitch'. DeAndre Anderson is a successful UK Black professional matchmaker, who's married, so apparently he knows what he's talking about. I'm always wary of matchmakers who are single. Selling what you can't find for yourself doesn't work in this nature of business.

Adisa is the only one who is free tomorrow, but I'm sure I'll be taking notes, so everyone's going to benefit, hopefully.

When we arrive, the room is full of beautiful Black women who, as always, outnumber the men. *They really are missing a trick here, and the five men who are here know it.* Lights are on, there's no blaring music, and enough breaks throughout the day to approach us, if they wish. Surely this is the perfect environment. With over sixty people here, they may have *too much* choice. Regardless, they are here to learn and I respect that.

"I didn't come to tell you what to do. I came to share what *I* do."

Adisa and I look at each other. I know she is just as sold as I am, already. In fact, I was sold when he walked out onto the stage. I could feel his aura from all the way over here. I imagine people like Oprah, Michelle Obama and Beyoncé have that same aura thing going on. *Is that extreme confidence, the smell of money, a kind of superpower, or are you born with it?*

Apparently there is a four per cent chance that we have commonality with random people. By identifying our values, personality and level of attraction to the person, in conjunction with our personality typographies, which fall into various categories, our commonality can increase by fifty per cent.

"Stand up, everyone. I'm going to show you what I mean,"

he says. "I'm going to ask a series of questions, and if they're not important to you, please sit down."

By the ninth question, both Adisa and I are still standing, and I'm beginning to feel there's a prize waiting—*ideally the secret identical twin to DeAndre*—but it's not to be, as my butt hits the seat when he asks, *"Is Christianity important to you?"* I believe in God, but I'm spiritual and there's a difference.

Fourteen people are left standing, which means they share the same values and personality typographies, and as a result are invited to the stage. Adisa, who's still standing, looks at me in shock.

"Yes! Quick, apply some more lipstick, hurry up and go." I say, as I watch Adisa join twelve women and one man walk to the stage to a round of applause.

I'm so excited, the only thing I need now is popcorn, because this is getting intense. One man, thirteen women, and one question with a yes or no answer: "Are you attracted to Michael?" No maybes, no fluff, just a straight yes or no to keep it moving. I can see Adisa's face, she's nervous. I think she's gonna say no, because I don't think he's her type—she likes men with a more athletic build and she is pickier than me, so… Let's see.

The first woman struggles to say no, so the audience help her out. Her feelings are obvious and her reluctance to express herself is just making the whole thing feel unnecessarily uncomfortable. She leaves the stage embarrassed and sits back down. The second woman comes forward. Before DeAndre can ask the question, a firm, "Yes!" has already left her mouth. *Loving the self-assuredness.* I'm literally on the edge of my seat. *What will he say?*

"Are you attracted to Selina?" the host asks.

Michael's eyes have already given the answer away. Selina steps to the side and remains on stage. Adisa steps forward.

"Are you attracted to Michael?"

There's a pause. Her face gives nothing away. *This woman! Look at her, she is loving this right now.* This pause is nothing to do with being unsure—she knows exactly what she is doing, and that is holding her power in a playful, teasing way. *Gwarn Adisa.* "Yes," she says eventually. I'm pleasantly surprised.

"WOOOOO," I shout, completely forgetting that now it's his turn to answer. *Please let him say yes, please...*

"Michael, are you attracted to Adisa?"

The pause isn't as long, but he decides to return the favour and make her sweat for a bit, too. I jump to my feet and start whooping, *"YESSSSSS, you go girl!"* when he finally says yes.

Adisa takes her place next to Selina, and she is beaming. I'm so proud of her. Thirteen women later, four remain on the stage. All attractive and very different from each other. The ball's now in Michael's court, as he has to choose whom he would like to go on a date with. This man is loving his power. *Who told him to walk up and down the stage? KMT, just pick someone already!*

*

"Adisa, you did great. How are you feeling?" I ask as comfortingly as I can.

"I knew he was going to pick Selina, they suit. And I'm glad, cos I didn't fancy him."

I nod. "I knew it. I was shocked when you said yes, but glad you did."

"Yeah, I thought I would just be more open. The exercise was a great way to see that although commonality is important, attraction is still a priority. I have to fancy the person I have something in common with."

"I hear you, girl. Still proud of you."

Journal
18th February 2017

Although finding love was the sell of the matchmaking event, self-love came to the forefront. Somewhere down the line we've lost connection with ourselves to such an extent that we look to others to complete us, rather than compliment us. I'm thankful that I've always known this and took the time out to be by myself. It was such a good event, so many 'ah-ha' moments today.

Apparently men like compliments too. It makes sense, but there really is an unspoken feeling that if you do approach, you're too confident and be may be viewed as fast. Where did I learn that view? Is this just my generation? Is my view out-dated? I mean, I haven't put it to the test since 2006. That's a long time ago.

The confidence I gained from approaching Aaron in Barbados carried me until I was twenty-five years old, and then I stopped. Whilst raving with the girls at Ten Rooms one time after we came back from the holiday, I saw a guy I fancied. I was so nervous, but I psyched myself up and went over to speak to him. I said, "Hi, I know girls don't really approach, but I saw you from over there and had to come over and say I really like your style. You look nice." Whilst remaining seated, he slowly looked at me and scanned me from head to toe and back up again to my face. He then shifted his whole body away from me, giving me his back as his response.

For that kind of reaction, I had to be ugly, right? I wanted to press pause, rewind and make a different decision so I didn't have to feel so shit. Instead, I had no choice but to walk back to my friends, who were watching. I didn't deserve that. He was a dickhead, but at the time I made it mean something about me, and the story of not feeling good enough or desirable enough was further cemented.

Regardless of whether I have liked a man or not, I have always been courteous, because I could see how difficult it was for some men to approach, especially when we're in a group. To them, we must look like a murder of crows in the circle—aka fortress—we create on the dance floor. Almost no man dares attempt to penetrate it and if they do, it's at their own risk, hence the reason why the approach usually happens when the circle is broken. The strong six becomes an approachable two as we head to the bar or toilet. The time is limited, they know it, and so there is an added pressure to deliver this masterful elevator pitch, the end goal being a smile, an agreement for a drink to be bought, a dance to be had or a number to be given, before the fortress reforms.

Whilst I believe being kind takes less energy than being unkind, I've *realised that my politeness in letting a man down is also to appease their reaction. Some men don't react well to "no." I've seen it, and would rather not have to deal with the childish cussing that sometimes follows. Learning from past experiences is important, but if my thinking and behaviour is stuck within my twenty-five-year-old self, then I'm behaving in old ways, which is far from empowering at this age.*

Commonality, lust or attraction is what brings people together. I couldn't get enough of Jaden, for example, but in hindsight we had no commonality—so was it just purely attraction and lust? Is the magnetic pull, that unexplainable feeling that makes me feel like I have no choice—lust or something bigger?

Because there was Jaden… but there was also Ramiro.

Chapter Ten

Mr Guyana

One of my favourite sounds was the wheels of my suitcase rolling on the ground coupled with thoughts of doing nothing but relaxing on a beautiful beach drinking cocktails and looking at the picturesque postcard view.

"Welcome back, babe. It's different but the same right?" Asta asked.

"I can't believe I've been away three years."

Since our last trip, Asta had been visiting Tyron yearly, whilst I decided to give it a break, primarily because Jaden had a girl-friend. He'd been such a big part of my holiday experience that I just needed time to detach Barbados from being synonymous with Jaden.

As I looked towards the view ahead of me, I was so pleased to see Accra Beach was just the same, and I instantly felt the warm welcome of familiarity. There was a strong sense of calm-ness, which intensified as I watched the big palm leaves sway back and forth. *What is that?* I felt something, it wasn't the wind, but an energy coming from somewhere. Asta was on the phone, so I didn't bother her. I looked out in all directions, searching for what had caught my attention, and I felt the pull to the left of me. I looked. *There*. Two tall men were in the distance. I focused on one, but it wasn't from him. As I turned my attention to the other tall man with brown skin and long afro hair, I felt a surge of energy. *It's definitely coming from him.* He wasn't even looking at me. *What is going on?* I watched, hoping they would walk in this direction, towards me. Instead, they got in a car and drove off. *Universe, what was the point of showing me that? I've just landed and I see you are up to your old tricks again. Don't play with my emotions.* Too late. The sinking feeling that had just arrived already made me feel like I'd lost something I never had.

That man, *who I didn't even really see*, popped in and out of my mind every so often throughout the day, and I did my best to push the memory out. *I'm not here for that, I just want to relax.*

Later that evening, Asta and I went to the local karaoke bar, and we quickly learned that Barbadians take this seriously. The daggers might as well have been real, because we could feel them.

"I beg you, Asta, please don't make me laugh," I whispered, whilst trying not to laugh.

"Why are you blaming me? You're the problem. Why can't you laugh silently like normal people?" she said with her face screwed up, indicating she was internally laughing herself.

"Normal people make a sound when they laugh, are you OK?" I said, bursting out laughing again—unfortunately at the same time the Rasta man, who was singing *Vision of Love* by Maria Carey, *I kid you not*, was attempting to reach the high note. I felt the stares but I just could not contain myself. The big, dirty, laughter had been released. You couldn't miss it, which right now was a problem.

"Shhh, you're gonna get us kicked out!" Asta said, whilst still soundlessly laughing. Her shoulders moving up and down was the only real giveaway. I was jealous; it's a skill I never had. The amount of detentions I received back in the day at school because my laugh gave something away! *Nonsense.*

I was now at the donkey laugh stage, where I was still laughing but also struggling to breathe. It was a mess, I even almost fell off my bar stool.

Rasta man finished and everyone clapped. They were being serious. I really needed to get myself together. *I refuse to be known as the rude girl from the UK.* I vowed to accept the stripped-down entertainment version and respect every singer, good and bad in equal measures. I used my phone to distract myself from laughing, and it worked.

The same Rasta man walked over to me and put the book of songs in front of me. "Lets see what you got," he said, smiling, before walking back to his seat. *Oh shit!* I deserved it. I embraced the challenge. The crowd got *Killing Me Softly* by The Fugees. I killed their ears as I struggled to remain in tune—I knew I would—but I really took the piss at the bridge. "*Sing along with me, Wooooooooo ahhhhhh…*"

It was a car crash, one which they loved. The applause that I was getting, I didn't deserve, but I took it.

Asta followed straight after with *You Can Make Me Whole Again* by Atomic Kitten, it's her go-to song that Ibiza and Mallorca also know well. She could sing, so she balanced out my mess. She, of course, received a loud round of applause and we were redeemed. *YES!*

"Well done, ladies."

We both half-swiveled around on our bar stools and were greeted by a tall man with long, jet black hair that was tied back into a ponytail. His skin was golden brown, whilst his eyes were light brown and shaped like cat's eyes. *He's gorgeous.*

"Thank you," Asta said, smiling. I was glad she spoke, because I couldn't, my brain felt a bit scrambled. *His aura is really strong. I feel like I know him, even though I don't recognise him.*

"By any chance, were you two at Accra Beach today?" he asked. My mouth was trying to open, but at the same time, I was trying to close it. *Same hair, same height... Is it him?*

"Yes, we were, we love that beach," Asta said.

"Yo, Ramiro, you ready?" He turned around. Asta looked at me. He nodded to his friend in the doorway.

"Anyway, it was nice to meet you, ladies—"

"By the way, I'm Asta, and this is Symona," Asta interrupts.

"So sorry, I didn't even ask," he said, looking at her. "Enjoy your stay, ladies." He looked at me this time. Asta said goodbye—I managed a smile and wave, and just like that he was gone, *again.* But thoughts of him floated around my mind for the rest of the evening, which I didn't dare entertain.

*

"Asta, do you believe in coincidences?" I asked as we got into our red rented car the next day. I'd been pondering over the question all night, and just didn't have the answers.

"Erm, no, I think everything happens for a reason. Why?"

she asked as she put her seatbelt on before pulling out of the driveway.

"I know Barbados is small, but what are the chances of seeing someone on a beach in the day and meeting them in a karaoke joint at night?"

"Had you seen that guy at the beach?" she asked.

"They were far away but, I saw a guy with the same frame and hair, so it must have been him."

She raised her eyebrows. "Erm, I don't believe it was a coincidence. Perhaps it was synchronicity—we were there at the same time, but there's no connection."

"Doesn't that go against your there are no-coincidences theory?" I ask.

"Damn, Yeah, it does," she said, laughing.

"OK, what beach do you fancy, today? Accra again, or Miami? They're not far from each other?"

"Let's try something new." I regretted it as soon as the words left my mouth.

"Miami it is, then," Asta said, turning the volume up and winding the windows down.

The breeze glided over my skin in gentle waves, taking away my work stress and tiredness. The beaming sun kicked to the curb any additional stress trying to arrive. I tied up my box braids and forced my mind to stay in each moment.

The uninterrupted panoramic views were just breath-taking at the beach. *Paradise is all around.* Asta ordered a roti, whilst I went for the Ital wrap. It was never too early for that, and we took a seat under an umbrella. "What's your favourite beach?" I asked her with a mouth full of food.

"Erm..."

"Hey ladies, do you mind if I take a seat?" I nodded and remained looking at Asta for her answer, because I was frozen. I recognised the energy, but I could not bring myself to turn around. *This is not happening.* Asta's eyes told me it was.

"Ram... Sorry, I can't remember your name?" she said.

"Nearly, it's Ramiro" he replied.

I turned around and went straight into questioning mode, because as much as I loved random moments, that right there was nuts.

"Hey..." I said as breezily as possible. "What are you doing here?" It could have come out better, I know.

He laughed, and answered without defense, "I'm a conservationist. Accra, Dover and Miami are the beaches under my remit." He knew where I was heading and saved me from asking another question.

"Oh I see," I said, as I discreetly checked what he was wearing and decided his green overalls showed he was telling the truth. Even though I had no idea what conservationists wore. I was relieved. *He's not a stalker, phew!*

"What do you both do back home? You're from London right?"

"Yeah, I work in a bank, but I'm currently upskilling as I specifically want to work in investment," Asta said.

I don't know what's in the food here, but these men don't look like anything I've ever seen back home.

"Ah nice, and Symona, what do you do?"

"I work in PR," I said, just about looking at him, because his energy was so strong.

"Ok, office ladies! I can't survive that environment at all."

We chatted as we ate, and his calm confidence was really intriguing. *Why is Asta tapping my arm?* I ignored her, until I was too irritated to continue.

"What's up hun?" I asked, turning to her.

"I think you need to stop touching him up, love," she said, raising her eyebrow and pointing. I looked, and to my horror my hand was running itself up and down Ramiro's bicep.

"Oh my God, I'm so sorry, I didn't even realise," I said, removing my hand in embarrassment and horror at my complete lack of control and awareness.

"It's all good," he said, smiling.

As I was on holiday, I had no concept of time, so I was surprised when he informed me he'd had a two-hour lunch break and needed to head back to work. Asta had checked out of the conversation ages ago to give me space and to stop herself from vomiting, because my arm touching didn't stop. *I couldn't stop*, which sounded so bad. We exchanged numbers and he drove to his next location. I walked back over to Asta and immediately apologised.

"I'm so sorry, I didn't realise I was there for so long."

"You are smitten. How you gonna touch a man like that!" she said, laughing her head off.

I could only manage a shrug and a laugh because I didn't have the answers.

"The attraction you have for each other is off the Richter scale. He is fine. A vegetarian like you and clearly into the spiritual stuff, like you."

"I know, right? Like me, he's also intelligent, wise, calm and graceful."

"You are so reaching," she said, laughing.

"OK, so now what do you call this... this encounter? Coincidence, synchronicity or fate? Because I'm truly baffled now."

"I think it's fate, hun. Destined, designed and already written."

I lie back and pondered over this idea. Asta was Christian, so she believed God planned this. I was spiritual, so I believed our spirits agreed we would meet ahead of us coming to Earth, which explained why I felt Ramiro's energy first. I recognised him and he recognised me.

*

"Where are you taking me?" I asked.

"Just relax, we'll be there soon," he said gently as he led me down a slight hill. I was blindfolded, and giving a lot of trust into this man that I'd properly met only two days ago. *This could be the start of a murder scene...* My anxiety was about to run wild, but the smell of incense and sea air triggered the voice of reason in me. *Anxiety, when was the last time you watched a movie where the murderer prepped the crime scene first by burning incense? Exactly. Just breathe. Plus, you're not reckless, you've gained a sense of him over the last couple of days. If something was off, you would have sensed it.*

"We're here," he announced. "But I need you to keep your blindfold on for a little longer, OK?"

I nodded. "*Oh!*" He was by my feet suddenly. He unbuckled my sandals and removed them from my feet. The leather material under my soles was replaced by sand. As he asked me to step forward, and sand was replaced by a silky fabric, which surprised me.

"Symona, I now want you to sit down, crossed-legged, whilst keeping your eyes shut. I will help you." He assisted me to the ground and I crossed my legs. He placed my hands on my legs and turned my palms up, as if I was about to meditate. I breathed deeply because the excitement was making me sweat. I just wanted to see where I was. He moved my hands closer together, and something round was placed into them. He removed the blindfold and told me to open my eyes.

My first instinct was to look around at my surroundings.

"Oh my God, this is beautiful, hun. You have gone to so much trouble. I feel special."

"A special lady deserves special treatment," he said, beaming.

I was greeted by the rhythm of the sea, the light from the full moon and a sky full of stars, whilst sat on a pink silk sheet inside an alcove cave. Four encased candles were burning at each corner of the sheet, and two incense sticks were dancing in the gentle breeze. If that wasn't enough, he had made dinner. I was holding a plate of chickpea curry, rice, and of course, a side of macaroni pie. *I cannot wait to tell Asta.*

"This is the most well-thought-out and original date I've ever been on," I gushed. "Bloody hell, you can cook too," I gushed again. He smiled and it became apparent in that moment that what I liked about him the most was—he was devoid of ego. Humble whilst knowing exactly who he was and the power he had. It was so attractive.

I lay back when I finished my food because I was stuffed. He poured me a grape juice and joined me. We kissed and caressed each other. My top came off, he took off his T-shirt, my skirt, his shorts, my bra, his boxers, and lastly my knickers. Butt naked under the stars and in his arms. I felt so comfortable, which felt so good. *But what if he wants sex? I don't want to do anything, but what if he gets the wrong idea?*

"Just so you know, this isn't about sex," he said. "This is about being at one with nature and us getting to know each other before spiritual intimacy." *Did he just hear my thoughts?* Somewhat relieved, I sighed more deeply and loudly than I expected.

"We're just getting to know each other, hun," he said, kissing my forehead. *Shit I think he's got the wrong end of the stick.*

"Oh, no, I sighed because I was relieved. This is already such a beautiful evening and I although this is so nice, I hoped you also didn't want sex, even though I feel like I know you already. Does that sound weird?" I asked, looking up at the blanket of twinkling stars in the sky.

"Not at all. I feel exactly the same. I read somewhere that an instant connection is established lifetimes ago. We have met before, no doubt about it."

"It was only when I saw you at the karaoke bar, that I realised you had seen me on the beach. You were so far away, so how did you recognise me?"

He smiled. "I felt your energy. I really wanted to come and say hi, but I had to drive my work mate to Crane Beach."

"Wow, it was exactly the same for me. I was upset when I saw you drive off."

"I had a feeling I would see you again, so I didn't worry."

"Coincidence, fate or synchronicity? What do you believe this is?" I asked, intrigued to hear his perspective.

"This is destiny for sure. Our encounter was pre-determined. We, our spirits, agreed this a long time ago. The energy we both felt was irresistible. Agree?" I nodded and he continued, "Which was to ensure we wouldn't miss this moment."

He is a breath of fresh air. "I fully agree, one hundred per cent. Third time lucky. What you do believe this is? I mean, why do you think, feel we've met?"

"Let's discuss this at the end of the week, before you go home."

This man was different. I loved it. I lay in his arms feeling content, at ease, happy, understood and connected. *The universe is gifting me.*

"Are you sure it's the universe?"

I heard the question inside me, but didn't have an answer.

*

This is what I learnt from meeting Ramiro. Trust your intuition in regards to people and their energy, and pay attention to the sign-posts. The magnetic pull is one of the sign-posts, linked to destiny. Be selective with who you sleep with, because their energy stays on you. Believe in your knowledge about how the universe works, even though you won't always have proof. In the moments that click, believe it.

Do all relationships stem from a place of destiny? If the magnetic pull is the sign-post, and I have only ever experienced it twice, then the answer has to be no. It's based on a decision, whether that is from commonality, lust or attraction. Beliefs also play a part—tradition and mindset—and compromises or patterns in behaviour also need to be considered in understanding why people make the decisions they make. If this is the only time I'll be Symona Brown in this lifetime, I would love the match to be destined. That has nothing to do with my timelines, because that's not how it works. *Wait, what am I saying? My biological clock is ticking…!* What I mean is, I would love to be with The One, the one for me in this lifetime. That's it.

Jaden and Ramiro were sign-posts, showing me that the type of man I'm looking for does exist.

It's time to get clear, be specific and *learn from the learning.* I need to update my requirements.

Chapter Eleven

My Future Partner

Future ~~Husband~~ Partner Requirements

My future partner is in touch with his feelings and can express himself. So many men struggle with this because they have been taught that showing emotion is a sign of weakness. Emotional intelligence and the ability to process thoughts and feelings is a strength—and therefore my future partner also knows how to communicate without shouting.

My future partner has done the inner work. He knows who he is, in spite of any labels and stereotypes placed on him. He is ambitious, head-strong and knows what he wants. He understands that I am my own person in my own right, and we are equal in power within our union.

My future partner is honest, intelligent, and humorous. He makes me laugh and smile but he also knows it is not his job to make me happy, as it is not my job to make him happy.

My future partner believes in commitment, the act of being with and remaining faithful to one person. *(I'm not sharing by consent, polygamous living, or non-consent because I didn't know he was a cheater. Imagine being with a man thinking you are the main meal and the dessert and this man and his greedy gut goes out for sides and extra helpings, only to return to you like butter wouldn't melt? I'm not here for it. Honesty counts for something. If that is what you want, just tell me, because at this big old age I don't have time to waste. Don't even get me started on the emotional impact. Hmm, I may as well add self-restraint…).*

My future partner appreciates what he has at home and values it and whilst he acknowledges other beautiful women, he isn't about to lose his whole damn mind and disrespect me and what we have.

I'm a sapiosexual because an intelligent man turns me on. But don't get it twisted, my future partner also has beauty to accompany the brains, along with a slice of charm, a winning smile and kissable lips. He is taller than me, even with my heels on, so let's say he is five feet eleven inches minimum. He has an athletic build naturally, but he also loves exercising. Contact sports is his thing. He is agile and can touch his toes. *(What? It's important).* He is also a fan of couples working out together. *(Apparently they are more likely to stay together).*

He has firm biceps that, when wrapped around me, make me feel safe and protected as I nuzzle into his chest. His washboard stomach is accompanied by a cute belly button *(may as well be specific)*. His hands are big, well looked after and he knows how to give a good massage. He has footballer thighs and skin that is a rich shade of brown from head to toe with no interruptions from tattoos.

My future partner, like me, doesn't eat meat. He is a vegetarian or pescatarian, and conscentious of what he puts in his body. Spiritual over religious, and well-read. He understands the world we live in and has a willingness to effectively navigate it, writing and re-defining his own story.

My future partner LOVES Black women and holds them—and therefore me—in high regard.

My future partner is a friend, supporter and cheerleader who will hold me accountable when required. He has a smooth, deep voice and a way with words that land to my ears in the mindful way he intended. He is kind, considerate, sensual and loving, both in and out of the bedroom.

My future partner has a close group of male like-minded friends whom he can confide in, chill and have fun with.

My future partner has warm brown eyes that exude his kindness and love for me, whilst being transparent enough for me to read his emotions and soul.

My future partner, is a modern man, my kindred spirit, my

destined soul mate. The One.

I'm not looking for perfection, because I'm not perfect—no-one is. Everyone has issues, including me. Heartbreak has caused me to reduce the flow of love I give, and build a protective wall around my heart. Trust has to be earned. My career has taken over the space a relationship should be in. I'm married to my job… instead of a man. I filled the space to create my lifestyle, and now I need to create some balance.

My future partner is as well-rounded as can be, so that we can come together and be enriched by each other.

And so it is.

Chapter Twelve

Mr Bus Driver

I jump on the number 23 bus to Oxford Street from Charing Cross station. I usually walk, but I don't have the energy this morning. I tap my Oyster and acknowledge the bus driver, who is just staring at me. His striking green eyes and caramel skin make him hard to miss. Of course my mind flashes back to Jaden, who I haven't thought about in years. I give a slight smile before sitting in the middle seat at the back of the bus. It's cold outside and this additional heating is what I need right now.

The bus moves off and I look out the window, prepping my to-do list in my head. I glance forward again and briefly catch the driver's eyes. It was so quick that I doubt he was even looking at me. I turn my head away and look back out the window. It's hard to act natural when you think—or know—someone is watching you, but I give it my best shot whilst knowing I'm failing. *I can't help it.* Event photographers hate me, because I can't act natural. As soon as I know a camera is aimed at me, I instinctively pose.

I glance back when the bus stops at a red light and I'm right. He's looking at me. *What are you gonna do about it?* Now I know he's looking, I'm finding it hard to look back. I mean, I'm intrigued but anxiety has arrived, attempting to kill the party. *Girl, you don't need to act on everything you see.* It's true. Perhaps this isn't even anxiety but sense talking? Remembering my promise to challenge myself, I decide to just seize the day, but time is running out as my stop is approaching. I search my bag and find a pen, open my purse and find an old receipt. I write my name, number and 'Call me' with a smiley face. I ring the bell, fold the receipt in half and walk to the front of the bus. My heart is beating loudly. The bus pulls in to my stop, I move towards the driver and slip my details under the screen beside him, into the change reservoir. He looks at me and takes the paper. I watch him open it whilst questioning why I'm still standing here. *Get off the bus, you don't need to see his reaction!* But I do. Although it's unnerving, I don't want to run away based on past embarrassment. I'm older now and more confident. He smiles as he reads my message, and that's enough for me. I step off the bus via the front doors without looking back.

I have no idea what just happened, but I feel good, like a boss woman taking charge. I bop to work with a Beyoncé beat in my head. *What if he doesn't call?* The excitement is short-lived. *What if he does?* The beat come back. *Him not calling me doesn't mean anything. It would be nice if he did, but I lose nothing from trying.* I feel pumped for the day. I can do anything. My team are not gonna know what's hit them. *Lets go!*

*

Private number? I never answer hidden numbers, but I answer because I hope it's the bus driver. It's been three days since I gave him my details. I thought only women did the "Let me not look eager wait game," but this is 2017 and with all these dating apps, things tend to move a lot faster now. *So what took him so long? It's him.*

His name is Ryan, he seems nice but I'm not really feeling much punch from him. All I know about him so far is that he is thirty years old. *I'm surprised—he looked older.* He has a degree in International Business and has worked as a bus driver for three years, though he doesn't really enjoy it. He has one older brother, no kids, lives on his own in North London and has been single for six months. We've decided to meet on Saturday, so I'm sure I'll find out more. He asked me where I want to go. *I'm not impressed, like I approached you, can you now take some initiative?* Of course, I didn't say that. I just suggested we both have a think and send suggestions by Friday.

*

I walk into the nice French restaurant in Islington that he chose, feeling good and looking good. I've made an effort, but I haven't gone all out. I'm wearing a grey oversized coat over a simple black V-neck, figure-hugging dress and black biker boots—my heat tech socks can't fit into my high-heeled boots, and in this weather it's not about looking sexy but feeling cold. My hair is in a bun and I'm wearing deep red lipstick and gold hoops. Simple.

The booking is in his name and I'm shown to our table, which is a nice two-seater by the candlelit window. He hasn't arrived yet. *He lives in North London, this restaurant is in North*

London; I live in South. If anyone was to be late, it should have been me and my no-local-Underground self. I order a glass of wine and acknowledge that although I haven't been on a date in a while, I'm not nervous. As I made the approach, I feel more... *in control?* Perhaps that's the reason, not sure.

A guy walks in ten minutes later. I look up, and then look back down to my phone.

"Hey, Symona!" he says.

I look back up and it *is* him. *OMG, erm...!* "Oh, hi Ryan! I didn't recognise you, you look different. How are you?" I say as I stand to greet him. *He is short. Like, really short. Like five foot. Too-short-for-me short.* I bend slightly to hug him, feeling awkward and disappointed, but I refuse to let it affect the evening.

"Sorry I'm late. As I live so close, I just took the time for granted."

I don't respond because I'm not impressed, but I choose to let it go, so I throw a smile at him as I suggest we look at the menu. He tells the waiter his order, and I notice three gold teeth. Nothing wrong with gold teeth, I just don't like them, especially if they cover perfect white, straight teeth, which is exactly what he has. I try and push the judgement out my head.

"You're just so beautiful and I'm so glad you dropped me your number like that. It made my day," he says, smiling, before continuing, "So, how many times have you done that then?"

I genuinely don't know what to say, but disappointment is coming faster than my food will arrive.

"I haven't done that before actually, so you should feel privileged." As soon as the words leave my mouth I feel bad, because

I know he didn't mean it as an insult. He was genuinely asking. Lack of tact was the only thing he served. "Why do you ask?" I'm intrigued to hear what he has to say, and I'm already telling my brain not to react.

"I just want to get a sense of how confident you are."

"Why? Does a confident woman unnerve you?"

"A confident woman who is forward can get any man!"

My whole body just screams *WHAT!* I have even more questions, but I decide to just sip my wine, because from what I have already seen, I know he will dig himself a deeper hole.

After a moment of silence, he asks, "So you wear Tampax?" He laughs, seeing the confusion on my face, and elaborates. "The receipt? The one you put your details on showed that you bought Tampax from Boots."

A red cross flashes. My soul has spoken, and we are in sync. I'm done with this man. If I was younger, I would have wanted the ground to swallow me up, but I have nothing to be ashamed off. I wear Tampax. So? The food arrives. I could leave, but I decide to stay, enjoy the food and use this time to learn to sit in my power. He is no threat to me, and I learn nothing more about this experience by walking away.

I think nerves got the better of him at the start, because he relaxes after the starters arrive. We speak about different things and it's OK, there just isn't much depth. He tends to just agree with everything I say. By the time the main course comes, it becomes apparent that my questions, answers, in fact my whole being makes him uncomfortable. *The seven year age difference isn't the problem—his lack of confidence, tact and ability to effectively communicate is.* He asks me about my job and then says, "You clearly don't have time for a man." I nearly spit chocolate cake out of my mouth. *Is he OK?* I tried, but I'm done. This now just feels like torture. I ask the waiter for the bill, which we split, and we walk out together.

"I really enjoyed this date. I would love to see you again," he says when we get outside, doing that stare thing he does with his eyes, trying to seduce me, which I now realise is all he has.

"I think you're a good guy, but there's just no spark for me," I say honestly.

He nods, I think he gets it, and then says he will call me tomorrow. I cannot be bothered to explain myself again, so I wave goodbye, and as soon as I enter the station I block him on my phone. *Harsh?* Perhaps, but what do you do if you feel you're not getting through?

When I get home, I take a quick shower as soon as I get in, and instantly feel my frustrations and expensive perfume wash away. I'm back earlier than I thought I would be, but it's all good, because I feel proud of myself. Once I'm dry and wrapped in my warm dressing gown, I grab a hot chocolate with Baileys and begin to journal.

Journal
21st January 2017

My first date in five years was disappointing. Looks alone cannot keep me. He lacked in so many departments: communication, assertiveness, character, confidence, tact, height and drive! No pun intended

(Ryan is a bus driver). Equal to or greater than, the match has to make sense. I'm a modern woman, looking for a modern man. Do they exist? We have levelled up from being pretty things on men's arms, great at keeping a home and raising children. Beautiful, confident, smart, qualifications, a good job and an entrepreneurial mind-set. Well read, good communication skills, humour, emotionally intelligent, the willingness to constantly learn and improve, whilst still striving to have a family. This is who I am—the definition of a modern woman. Do all men want this? I'm not sure, and that is why I'm looking for a modern man. I'm not compromising. Picky? Yeah, I'm real picky.

Anyway, approaching Ryan was a big deal, and I'm glad I have overcome it, because I think it's a skill needed in this day and age. We have to also be willing to approach, and to strengthen that rejection muscle. We do it in business, dating is no different. I also need to add flirting to my tool box, because I have only just found out that flirting is more than just smiling. I know... nuts!

*

Hey Ladies, how are you doing? So, I have just got back from my first official date and it's not really worth talking about. Too short, gold teeth and no stimulating chat. #Theend. If you're in, up and free, fancy a chat about flirting? I was today years old when I realised that I realised it's a bloody skill. Sending the video link to join a group vid chat now.

"Hey girl, I wanna hear more about this date!" Adisa squeals when she appears on the screen.

"Hey, hun. There is literally nothing to say. It was dead. The food was nice, though."

"Yeah? I've been swiping left more than right. It's addictive. Sometimes I swipe so fast that I miss good-looking men, but it's cool as they seem to come back around… eventually. It eats into time though," she adds, raising her eyebrow.

"Hey girl! How short we talking? I don't mind gold teeth…" Zaara says, joining the video chat.

"Hey Zaara, you would be so bored with him. I wouldn't do that to you, or any person I call a friend. On top of that, how can he be so unaware that he doesn't even realise he's insulting someone?" I say, shaking my head. "How come you're in?"

"I'm doing the challenge, remember? Quality over quantity. I'm cutting back on dating for dating's sake."

"Oh yes! Proud of you!"

"I'm bored. It's been a while since I've been home on a Saturday night."

"Welcome to our world," Adisa says, laughing.

I get straight to it. "Flirting is an art, ladies. It's more than smiling or flicking your hair, there is a whole bloody strategy, let me tell you. So… I went to Shoreditch BoxPark on Friday night with a work friend for a few drinks. She was sitting opposite me, and the seat next to me was free. As it got later into the evening, the music became louder and the place became more crowded. The seat next to me was taken by an attractive-looking white woman who was waiting for her friend. She had short-cropped black hair, with piercing blue eyes—think Madonna circa 1993, when she released *Rain*—"

"Yes! I loved that video, she looked so striking," Zaara interrupts.

"I don't remember it. Hold on, let me Google," Adisa says. "Yes, Syms, I know you hate this shit, just chill…" *She knows me well.* "*Ah yes,* I remember."

"Anyway," I continue, "I forgot the woman's name, so for the purpose of this, I'm gonna call her MUA, because she looked like a make-up artist. I can see you both rolling your eyes. Anyway, as the drinks were flowing, we got talking and our twosome became a threesome… not like that." It was my turn to roll my eyes. "We all just got on, and MUA was also single, which I couldn't understand. There were more men than women there that night, which is so rare, and that's when I found out there's a whole strategy. In order to get what you want, you have to show you are interested—and you do that through the eyes. You would have thought I already knew this, right?"

"Yeah, especially as you seem to have an obsession with them," Adisa chips in.

"I know, but that's because I need to be able to read a man. It's not about the colour."

Zaara coughs. "Out of interest, what colour eyes did the date-dude have? What's his name?"

"His name's Ryan and his eyes were green." *Here we go.*

"Like that Barbadian guy you told me about?" asks Zaara.

"I rest my case," states Adisa.

"I get it, it looks that way, but I promise it's not. Yes, the rare eye colour on Black skin is striking, yes I'm attracted to it, but that's not what I'm intentionally looking for. So—"

"Yes it is. You want a pretty man with pretty eyes… Who doesn't?"

They both laugh and I join in, giving up on protesting. "*Anyway*, our new friend said flirting begins in the eyes, and to prove her point, she pointed out a guy to us who she noticed had been watching her. She didn't literally point, she referenced the time and clothes he was wearing, like 'four o'clock, dude in all denim, look now, don't be obvious.' We both discreetly looked over and yes, he was nice and he knew it."

"How did he know it?" asks Adisa.

I pause before answering, because I realise I've made a general statement based on my own stuff and I need a little longer to think about what I've said. I give up and just own it. "He was light-skinned or mixed heritage, good looking and had a confidence about him. Nothing wrong with that at all, but you could just see it and feel it." However, underneath what I said is my belief that a man who looks like that wouldn't want me as I'm too dark in comparison to them. I've always felt overlooked by men of his complexion and so rule myself out of them liking me before I know whether they do or not. Whilst I'm self-sabotaging myself, there's also enough evidence that proves my feeling. "As he looked over again, she glanced at him and looked away, turning back to us she said, 'See, I told you! Now the play begins. I need to show him that I'm interested. You start subtly at first and then you build up in stages. When he looks over next, I am going to catch his eye, look away, and this time, smile.' When

Michelle, my work colleague, questioned why you look away and then smile, MUA said very matter-of-factly, 'I'm reeling him in slowly. You don't give everything in one hit.' Who knew! Where did she learn this? Did you guys know?"

"You know I had no clue," says Adisa, retying her headscarf.

"I see… so that's where I'm going wrong. I'm going straight for the kill. No wonder some men view me as over-confident or too forward. This is just a subtler way of doing it. OK, I'm learning," Zaara says.

I continue my story. "Then she ignores him for a bit, although she was always aware of where he was, and then she started the whole process again—but this time, she held his gaze for longer before breaking away. She then said, 'you keep doing this until he comes over.' *He* comes over! Did you hear that? She was not going to approach, even though I damn well knew she had the confidence to. Why do I approach men, again? What am I giving up when I do this? Why do I feel I need to do this when she doesn't? HELLO! I need answers!" I finish passionately, with a slice of frustration.

"Entitlement," Adisa announces.

"Do you think it's really just that?" I ask.

"Whilst you're there doubting your level of attractiveness, my girl knows the level of hers, and the level of skill in her toolbox. There is no doubt about it."

"Perhaps she was just his type?" offers Zaara.

"White girls are every man's type," quips Adisa.

"That's a massive generalisation," I say.

"No different to the generalisation you think light-skinned

or mixed heritage men have towards you," she retorts back.

"I said what I said, and I owned it—you are the one with sweeping generalisations."

"I also said what I said. MUA didn't need to move because her experience has told her of course she is desired. Even if she's not, she will think she is because as much as this is a white man's world, white women aren't too far behind them. She knows she doesn't need to move," Adisa says very matter-of-factly.

I watch Zaara on the screen, and she is where I'm at—nodding, frowning, kind of agreeing but not sure, all at the same time. "An interesting take," I say. "I hear you."

Zaara speaks up. "Black is always in. I mean Black culture is always in. Black girls? A whole different story."

"We are ridiculed but mimicked, whilst the mimic is being celebrated," I respond. "Now the mimicked is mimicking the mimicker. You can't make this shit up. Trends affect confidence and dating more than we think. Is your look in or out?" I ask, before continuing. "She knew he would come over; she was sure of it. She said it was 'a tried and tested method that worked every time.' Not gonna lie, I found her level of confidence sexy and empowering, regardless and I have work to do. We continued our discussions about life and work, and throughout I was sporadically distracted by the game that was happening as MUA's head kept turning to make eye contact with him. Whilst it was interesting to watch, it was also a bit depressing. A room full of men, and Michelle and I both felt overlooked. I went to the toilet, not because I needed to go, but because I needed a break. I had to mentally slow clap on my return back to the table when I saw the dude in my seat. I mean, take a flipping bow, love. As I arrived, he finished putting his number into her phone, handed it back and said he'd call her tomorrow. Job done. No sooner did he leave, her friend arrived and that was that. Lesson done." I sighed. "So what flirting tools do you girls have in your tool box? Cos I don't even *have* a toolbox. I didn't even know I needed one. On a different level, MUA had a kind of liberation and freedom that I didn't recognise in myself anymore."

"Of course you are missing out on freedom and liberation— you're not having sex," Zaara says. I can't even argue with her. She's right. *But I know I'm also talking about self-power. My ability to tap into myself.*

"Well, I don't have enough skills to require a whole tool box," laughs Adisa.

"In all seriousness, we are learning and figuring things out as we go, but why don't we know this?" I ask.

"We never practiced. We spent too many years expecting men to approach and judging their approach, as opposed to learning to 'reel them in'," offers Adisa.

"I agree—the one thing I can say about Becky and her crew… you know what, let me not even say that, because I wouldn't want to be referred to by a stereotypical Black sounding name, that lumps us all in the same way of behaving. The one thing I can say about white girls that I've noticed, is that they have a level of openness that we—let me talk for myself, my crew back in the day—weren't always willing to entertain. There's an art to having fun, and looking back I think we sometimes saw the approach as an interruption to our fun," Zaara says candidly.

"There is also an art to an approach," Adisa says, to which I also agree.

"There isn't just one answer, but I hear all your points. Regarding flirting, I'm going to do some research," I announce.

"Research? Hahah, well Chan did say it was like a job. I guess we're up-skilling," says Zaara.

"Lord help me!" Adisa exclaims. "I'm going to my bed, ladies."

"Confidence to flirt! I'll let you know if I find an event to try it out. Night, ya'll," I tell them, smiling, waving and ending the call.

Chapter Thirteen

Mr Irish

"Excuse me, Excuse me."

I'm not sure if the call out is for me, but I turn around anyway.

"You dropped this." I look at the outstretched hand, and he is holding an Oyster card holder that says 'Keep Calm and Go for Gold'. It's definitely mine.

"Thank you so much," I say to this young Black man, who looks like he's on his way to football training. I'm really grateful as I have just done a monthly top up.

"No problem, have a nice day," he says, smiling.

I hear someone say, "Hey!" but I keep walking, as I really don't think that one is for me. It's only when I feel a tap on my arm that I turnaround. I'm greeted by a tall white man, good looking, around forty years old. He looks like he has just left a fashion shoot, and I'm interested to hear what he has to say.

"Hey. I just saw you and decided to say hey."

"OK. Hey right back to you," I say, not really sure where this is going.

Sounding nervous, he says, "Well that's all I wanted to say."

Huh? "Really? That is all you wanted to say?"

"No but…" I can see he is struggling and I decide to save him.

"Are you in a rush?" I ask, and he shakes his head.

"I'm grabbing a coffee, feel free to escort me if you want." *Escort?* Don't ask me where my brightness came from. I was intrigued as to what he actually wanted to say, and thought this was a great way to give him some time to say it. I knew he liked me, I could see it in his eyes and I was prepared to play with this power that I felt I had, in the form of subtle flirting. *I'm learning.*

We line up in the queue in the coffee shop, side by side. He's not talking and I'm not going to save him. He's looking at me, and I can feel his eyes travelling the profile of my body. He can look, I don't mind, I just want to hear what he says after this information he is silently gathering. I order, he pays, *didn't expect that.* We wait in silence. It feels awkward but I don't care.

"Symona and Conor!"

Our coffees are ready. As we go to collect them, he says, "Jesus, I didn't even properly introduce myself. Symona, I'm Conor, nice to meet you."

I shake his hand and we walk out together, in the same direction. Conor is Irish, thirty-eight, works for an advertising company, roughly six feet tall, dark hair, chiselled model looks and quite charming, with a slight Irish accent. As we walk down Argyll Street, I ask, "What made you come over?"

"Honestly, I think you're stunning. I like Black girls." *Hmm, not sure why he felt the need to say that.* When this kind of information is offered up so readily, it makes me feel like they might have a fetish. It may be a reach but it kind of throws me off, *even though I guess it's good to know?* We parted ways when I came to my work building. I thank him for paying for my coffee and for the chat. He leans in and gives me a kiss on both cheeks. *He smells good.* Random, but something different for a Thursday morning…

*

How is it lunchtime already? I have two deadlines to meet today and right now, I'm not sure if I can meet them, but I'm gonna try—hence why I'm sitting at my desk eating this lame three-bean wrap. The phone only ever seems to ring non-stop when I'm on deadlines, why? *Just go away!!!*

"Hello!" I answer with urgency.

"Is this Symona?"

"Yes, who's calling?"

"It's Conor." My brain takes a while to compute, which explains why he helps me. "Oh, erm, I met you this morning. We grabbed coffee?"

"Oh! Hello, how are you?" *How did you get my number?* is what I really wanted to say, but it's obvious. He practically walked me to work, so knows the building I work in. You need a last name to be patched through, but knowing him and his bright self he just sweet-talked the receptionist. I'm the only person called Symona here, so not hard at all.

"I'm calling to see if you would like to meet for a drink after work this evening? I can pick you up at say six fifteen?"

"Erm… sure. I have a deadline, but should be done by then. So fine, meet me outside my work then?"

"OK, see you then. I look forward to it."

What am I doing? I love Black men like I love apple crumble and custard, bun and cheese, amaretto and lemonade—perfect combinations which understand and compliment each other with no explanation needed. Whilst I appreciate other races, Black is my preference. Do I need to cast my net wider? The internal conflict regarding this is real. Black men—SOME Black men—have no problem dating outside of their race, yet I find many of my Black female friends are reluctant, like me. Is it time for my ideals to be re-evaluated? Or am I compromising by looking outside of what I want? *Hmm.* Is loving someone outside of your race based on love, commonality, lust, attractiveness, beliefs or destiny? I'm not in that position, so I can't answer that. In the past I've heard ignorant comments like 'Black women are too difficult and white women are easier to be with.' That's a double insult from where I'm sitting. *KMT.* Let me just focus on completing these deadlines.

*

The time has flown by, and I feel more anxious than excited right now. *It is what it is.* I freshen up and leave my four-inch heels on. I'm going to firm it as long as possible—my flats are in my bag if I'm struggling.

Look at this dude, just casually leaning on the pillar. GQ magazine shot right there. I walk through the double doors and greet him.

"Did you complete the deadline?" Conor asks. I nod, and he animatedly punches the air. I laugh; it's not what I expected, but it's cute. We head to a bar he knows around the corner and he gets the drinks in.

Four drinks and two hours later, I ask, "So, what is it about Black girls that you like? It's been playing on my mind... I mean, if I approached a man, I wouldn't say 'I like white guys', even if I did."

He kisses me in response. Who does he think— *He's a good kisser.* His hand cups the nape of my neck and slowly moves down to my breast. Red flags flash. I pull back and break away. We're in public, I feel self-conscious, and he's way too forward. I compose myself and ask the question again. "So what is it about Black girls that you like?" I want to hear the answer more so now because that kiss, *whilst nice,* doesn't mean he gets away from answering.

"I'm attracted to Black girls, always have been. Specifically regarding you, I find you very attractive, I love your twist out..." He sees my expression that reveals I'm surprised he knows what a twist out is, let alone that he's able to correctly identify it. He smiles. "You have a classy way about you which is intriguing and well, I want to get to know you."

I'm somewhat satisfied by the answer. No hints of fetishism, just forwardness. I can deal with that, *I think.*

We walk together back to Oxford Circus station, and he suddenly stops me.

"This is the spot where we met fourteen hours ago, so erm..."

Hey! Again," Conor says.

A romantic. I see. "Hey you."

He comes closer. *Is this dude gonna kiss me again? OMG, he is.* I step back, move to the side and continue walking. The sound of his jangling keys tell me he's doing a little jog to catch up. "Come home with me," he says playfully.

I shake my head and inform him that he's going to have to work a lot harder than that. I sound like I'm teasing him, but I'm not. This is all new to me—not the pace, but the pace with a white man. *This is gonna need to slow right the way down.* The look he gives back tells me he will happily take the challenge.

We say our goodbyes, and just as we split to head to our respective platforms (he needs the Victoria line and I the Bakerloo line), I ask him to meet me outside my work again tomorrow at six thirty. I leave before he answers, because I want to see what he'll do. Tomorrow is Friday, he may have other plans, we'll see. Unfortunately, dating is not as clear the TFL Underground map. I wish it were.

Conor intrigues me. I like his confidence, if not so much his forwardness. I'm comfortable, whilst at times I feel self-conscious. I know you aren't meant to entertain everything that comes into your path, but I will only know if I need to cast my net wider if I come out of my comfort zone to find out.

*

I don't mean to stare, but it's the first time I've really seen the difference. My deep brown skin next to such pale skin. I mean, it's not exactly white, as I can see the hint of yellow, red, brown and blue blended together to makes up this colour referred to as 'white'.

My second one-night stand in my life is with a white man. *I never would have guessed that in a million years.* And all it took was a self-imposed challenge. *What am I doing?*

Conor is barely breathing now, but he literally snored his head off last night, and I haven't slept as well as I wanted to. I need to pee but I don't want to wake him. I remove the cover from my body and gently slide out of the bed, tip-toeing to the bedroom door across the heated floor boards, collecting my discarded clothes along the way. I open the door slowly and I'm greeted by a loud creaking sound.

Of course he has a squeaky door, of course he does

"Hey darling, you OK?" he asks, rolling over to look at me.

"Yeah, I'm just going to the bathroom," I say effortlessly.

"Hmm well hurry up and come back."

I can feel the tears as soon as I shut the door. I sit on the toilet seat, face in hands, and shake my head in disbelief. I just cannot believe last night happened…

I was surprised to see him outside my work place, it being a Friday night and short notice. I assumed he already had plans. The aim was to go to a bar in Shoreditch, but after rain fell from nowhere and I was clearly losing the battle with my broken umbrella, he suggested we go to his. My hair and scalp was under attack from the cold wet drops, and the last thing I wanted was to be in a bar with other damp people in a confined space, looking like a drowned Troll doll with streaks of gel and foundation running down my face. I said yes, I mean, I could have just gone home, but I was intrigued. Intrigued to see Conor's space and how I navigated in it away from prying eyes. We may be in 2017, but I see the judgement and it does make me feel uneasy. I'm not used to this enough to not care.

From Shoreditch High Street Station we zig-zag through the back streets, and roughly ten minutes later, arrive at a black door with graffiti on it. I was unimpressed when I saw it—*derelict drug den* was the first thought—but I was pleasantly surprised when I walked inside. A converted warehouse, *my dream home*, cleverly adapted into flats. He was on the fourth floor, Flat 10—surprisingly minimalist and neat. Everything had a place, making the space even larger and more tranquil. Only one year older than me, his earning capacity was nowhere near mine. I was in awe, whilst wrapped in jealousy.

He would have taken my clothes off on the train if he could have, but he waited until his flat tour reached the bedroom. I liked how he kissed me, I liked how he held the nape of my neck with his big hands that eventually travelled to my back and over to my breasts. I let go of my thoughts and went with the flow… both naked, I ran my eyes down his body. Stopping at his package, I could see why he was so confident. Aware of the jokes and rumours within my community about the size of white men's penises, I was pleasantly surprised. Not only had I never slept with a white man before, I'd never watched porn with white men in it. I had to consciously choose to experience him as he was, not what I'm used to. Really attentive and considerate. It was nice, I enjoyed it and I allowed myself to enjoy him—

and yet I'm sitting on the toilet seat, crying. *When will this stop?*

Of course the headscarf I'd had in my bag has come off. Can someone just make a non-slip silk one please? This time I don't care, because I predicted Conor would ask me back at some point in the evening—the man is so forward it wasn't hard to guess. I'd packed the mini-essentials: headscarf, gel, coconut oil, change of knickers and a fresh top. "Sometimes no plan is the best plan, but you need one when you are staying at a white man's house, cos he ain't gonna have any of the shit you need," was the advice Zaara gave me when I told her how Conor and I met.

Re-twisting my hair on his dark brown leather couch made me feel defiant. I'm a Black girl making no apologies about that fact. *This is my hair, this is my process, this is how you get the twist out term that you know.* He wasn't fazed at all by it when he came out of the shower, so I'm not really sure who the defiance stance was for. *Hah.* Chinese takeaway, wine, a film, talking and kissing in between. It was a lovely evening; his tongue is amazing. I was loud and didn't care.

"You alright petal?" Conor calls out from the bedroom now. *Damn, I've been here a long time.*

"Yeah, all good. I will be there in sec," I shout back as I flush the toilet and wash my face.

Journal
8th April 2017

It's been a month since I've seen Conor, because I'm avoiding him. I guess that classifies as ghosting. He's done nothing wrong, we get on, I feel comfortable with him—in fact, I like being with him, and that kind of scares me. I don't want to get to a stage where I catch feelings and actually think about having a future with him. Yes, I may be jumping ahead, but these are things to think about now, because casual sex isn't the path I'm trying to be on, even though it was so good. I cannot afford to be distracted. Love is blind for some, but all I see is that I'm not with my preference, and that upsets me. Mum and sis will say they don't care who I'm with as long as they love me and treat me right, which is great, but I cannot see it for myself. And here lies the problem. I don't like being ghosted and here I am doing what I don't like.

*

My palms and armpits are sweating. *Shit, it's ringing. Please don't pick up, please don't pick up.*

"Hey, you're alive then?"

Conor's tone is light and breezy, but I hear the dig. I really wanted to just send a text message after a missed call, but that would have been too easy.

"I'm sorry I've left it til now to get in touch. Can I come and see you to explain?" I ask, even though that was not the plan. *Night turns into day, tumbleweed rolls across the ground, day turns into night before the cockerel crows symbolising morning had indeed come again.* Conor makes me wait and the silence is unbearable, but I firm it.

"I'm here," he says eventually breaking the silence and disconnecting the call. *Who the hell does he think he is?* I would have phoned back and cussed him if I wasn't in the wrong. Out of respect I told him via WhatsApp that I would be there in an hour.

I arrive looking effortlessly casual, which took some effort. He opens the door and I fix my face to an open but solemn state. Tight vest, grey tracksuit bottoms, he looks casual. I walk past him and into the lift at his invitation, and the whiff of cologne tells me he also went for the effortless effort look. I catch myself smiling and stop, as I also don't want him to get the wrong impression.

I take a seat on the brown leather couch while he's in the kitchen making me a cup of tea. I'm praying my rehearsed words leave my mouth in the best way possible.

"Babe, I'm so sorry I didn't return your calls. I just needed time to think. I really, really like being with you, but I have an issue that I feel so embarrassed about," I say as he hands me the hot mug.

"What, you have an STD or something?" he asks, scrunching his face up.

"No," I say mirroring his expression. "I really like you, and I'm comfortable with you when it's just us, but not when we are out and about. I just feel so self-conscious. I feel rubbish for saying it, but it's true."

"Are you ashamed of me?"

"No. I'm just not used to being with a white guy."

"Why do you care so much?" It's a good question, and one that a shrug doesn't answer, but that's all I've got.

"So you just avoided me?"

"I needed the time to work out what it was, what I was feeling.

I should have said something, I know, and I'm sorry, but—"

"Conor, can you make me a cuppa please?" *Who said that?* I look at him.

"Sure hun, give me a minute," he calls back. I look at him still, with confusion on my face.

"What?" he says. "Did you just expect me to wait in the hope that you would call and give me an explanation?"

I'm shocked. "No, not at all, but I could have just explained all this on the phone in that case. I didn't need to be here."

"You asked to come round."

"And you COULD HAVE JUST SAID NO, as you are clearly busy!" I shout back. *Who does that?*

"WHAT'S GOING ON!?" shouts a woman's voice from down the hallway, before appearing in front of us. Fantastic body, impressive lingerie that pops against her brown skin and 3a tumbling curls.

I move off the couch as elegantly as possible. "I've said what I wanted to say, I'll let myself out," I say to Conor, as I grab my bag and walk to the lift. "And you can have my cuppa love, I haven't touched it," I shout as the doors close. Yeah, I know that was unnecessary, but whatever.

I head back to the station. I'm pissed off but not pissed off, even though I'm walking fast like I am. He's moved on, I'm happy for him. I'm pissed because I didn't need to go round there. *Anyway, anyway, anyway,* it's done. I now know for sure. My net can be cast wider, but I'm still looking for Bluefin tuna.

Chapter Fourteen

Boxed In

"Happy birthday to you... Happy Birthday to you..."

Surely I look too old for strangers to want to sing happy birthday to me. But no, my big ole thirty-eight-year-old self isn't, it seems. I was considering holidaying alone, but decided I didn't want to be alone and so here I am, having a low-key dinner with the fam instead. It's all good. I'm OK, just feeling a bit *meh*, but I'm sure I'll snap out of it.

"...Happy Birthday to youuuuuuuu."

I quickly glance at the people sitting nearest to me, in what has to be the hidden gem of Blackheath, to acknowledge their kind wishes before making a wish, *never too old for that*, and blowing out my candles. Mum claps in delight, and I feel eight years old all over again.

Cutting into the rich chocolate cake, I know it's coming, because nothing was said over starters, or mains. I can feel it...

"Syms, when are you going to settle down?" mum asks. *Knew it.* "I'm just here waiting for my grandchildren now, and I want to see them whilst I'm still agile, fit and can help out."

"Mum, you ask this all the time. Settling down means I have someone to settle down with. As the man is not here... yet... I can't actually answer your question." I quickly change the subject. "Chan, how is Seyi?" I ask, whilst putting a slab of indulgence on mum's dessert plate.

"I haven't finished with you yet," she says, cutting into the cake with her fork.

"Mum, I don't have the answers. When are *you* gonna find a man?" I ask as a further attempt at deflection, knowing full well I'm teetering on the line of over-familiarity.

"Meh! KMT, don't worry about me ya nuh, me and you are not size," my Mum says. "I did my time, had my child, it's you I'm looking at now."

Mum gave up on finding another man the day she kicked Dad out fifteen years ago. She keeps saying she's 'past it,' *which isn't true,* and that 'men her age want younger versions,' which I think is partly true, based on the big men that have tried to chirps me. *Just so wrong.* Heartbreak is the truth of the matter, though; she doesn't want to feel hurt or disappointment again. "Too old for that," she says. I understand the fear. I thought things were meant to get easier as you got older, which would only apply if you discard the emotional baggage on the way. I respect where she's coming from, but she deserves to be with someone and feel loved, regardless of her age.

"So are you at least seeing anyone?" she asks.

"No, but Chan is. Chan how's it going?" I say again with wide eyes, hoping she takes the obvious bait.

"It's going OK. I've been seeing him for four months now." *That has to be a record.* I'm dying to ask if she's deleted all her apps, but that isn't a question for now.

"Remind me what he does again?" says mum.

"He works in the same industry as me, tech, as a Business Insights Analyst. He's kind, clever and considerate. He has a younger brother and he's close to his mum and dad, who are still married. They spend the winter months in Nigeria—they own properties which they rent out. He wants children, and he believes in marriage," Chan says, satisfied she has covered all of Mum's questions.

"So do you like him?" Mum asks.

"Yes, but I'm taking my time. Don't worry, you will meet him when I'm sure-sure. No one gets to meet the Mumzy otherwise." She's given just enough information with a little sweetener on top to make her happy—she knows no other questions are coming her way. Me on the other hand…

"So Syms, why do you think you're still single?"

A shrug is all she gets. I feel rude, but I can't, I just can't, not now. "Shall we get the bill?" I ask, whilst catching the waitresses eye and signalling for the bill. *No one signs by pen anymore, so I have no idea why we still do that squiggle thing in the air.*

I place the leftover cake in the box provided and note that I, too, feel boxed in. Boxed into timelines I cannot meet. Boxed into pressure. Boxed into the belief that I don't feel good enough or desirable enough to get and keep a committed man, and when I do, I worry that my intimacy issues will just destroy what I have. I'm OK, I just don't know how to unbox myself.

Chapter Fifteen

Blind Spot

I'm loving these hot summers that London seems to be experiencing these past few years. I know it's down to global warming, but it just feels so good. I take Vitamin D supplements all year round regardless, but it's nice to get it direct to the skin. I'm not sure if it's in the air or some hidden clock that sounds an alarm that only men hear, but summer really begins when I get chirpsed several times in close succession. I step out my house: *"Yes sweetness, ya alright?"* I nod, smile and keep it moving. Turn onto the main road: *"Hello darling, can I have your number?"* I glance to acknowledge and keep it moving. *"Hello miss, you are looking good!"* I say thank you and keep it moving. It's harmless appreciation, which I gladly take—more so when my hair is in a twist out. My hair isn't down to my back, I don't wear weaves any more, I don't look like the girls in the videos, so I really do feel seen and appreciated in my natural state—and I feel appreciated today.

*

May is birthday season—just so many! Why? I would try and

attend them all back in the day, but now that I'm older it's all about value. Do we both make an effort to see and speak to each other outside of 'occasions'? I'll do my best to attend if the answer is yes. It's Angela's birthday today, she's a work friend who has become a friend. As the only other Black woman on my floor at work, she is a breath of fresh air. Just seeing her across the table from me in meetings and catching her glance is enough to tell me she also heard the off-key comment laced in passive aggression that no one else seems to have noticed. We have had so many meetings of our own after the main meetings to literally call out and process what just occurred, which has saved my mental health, because it proves I'm not mad. Every red flag, every feeling in the pit of my stomach meant something, and I was right to pay attention. "Some battles aren't worth fighting," Angela would tell me, "and some are. Your job is to identify the ones that are. Remember, this is not your dad's company—you are replaceable. Do your best and leave your work in your workplace when you leave at six pm. That is the only navigating to do. Save your energy." Those words changed my whole working outlook. Angela is a boss lady, my mentor and friend.

"Happy Birthday, hun! You look great!" I squeal, upon entering into the plush restaurant in Chelsea. She looks fabulous in a tight coral pink bandeau dress and gold heels. *This is forty, wow!* We embrace.

"Thanks for coming, hun. So good to see you. Let me introduce you to peeps."

She introduces me to four people I've not met before. I say 'hi' as I take my seat and pray I don't have a person either side of me who thinks this is a networking party. Thankfully, everyone is lovely and the conversation flows just as fast as my glass keeps magically filling up.

Just as I finish my seared tuna starter, Angela introduces us to Troy and Sienna, who have just walked in. Troy is handsome and Sienna is stunning. *They make a really good couple.*

Throughout the dinner I try to engage in the wider conversations across the round table, but it's difficult and my neck begins to hurt a bit, so I chose to just talk to people in close proximity. Troy and a few others head outside for a quick smoke before dessert arrives. There are vacant chairs around the table, and Sienna decides to move closer to me.

"Hey, I thought I'd come closer instead of shouting. I'm, Sienna. I didn't catch your name?"

"Thanks! I'm Symona. Nice to meet you. So how do you know Angela?" I ask, even though that isn't the first question in my head.

"I run an events company and I enlisted Angela to help with my PR on launch day. This was over seven years ago. She's my go-to person." The smokers begin to head back in and take their seats, in what must have been the quickest smoker's break ever. I swear the people in my workplace go for twenty minutes at a time.

"She's fabulous, isn't she? We work together," I tell Sienna, pre-empting her next question, which she doesn't get to ask.

"I'll speak to you later," she says getting up and allowing the original occupant to re-take their space. Whilst she goes back to her seat, I excuse myself and head to the bathroom. With each step I take, I receive further confirmation that I need to slow down on the drinks. By the time I flush the toilet and wash my hands, Conor pops in my head. I push him out with ease, only to be replaced with the beginnings of a pity party. *Why are you still single? You are thirty-eight, you should be here with a man as your plus one, but no.* I shake my head in a physical attempt to shake the thoughts out. *I'm really drunk.* I focus on attempting to re-touch my lipstick within my lip line.

The bathroom door opens. It's Sienna, who I can see behind me through this long rectangular mirror. She pauses before entering a cubicle.

"I really like that lip colour, where's it from?" she asks from behind the closed door. "Ahh thanks. The colour is called Supreme, from MDMFlow," I shout back.

"Ah Flo's brand. She's such an inspiration, and so cool. If I knew studying Cosmetic Science would have meant I could make my own lipsticks, I would have paid more attention in science class," Sienna says, flushing the toilet, emerging from the cubicle and walking to the sink. I smile and agree with her, even though I wasn't good at science.

"I love the gold packaging, and the shape reminds me of my bullet."

"Oh, do you have one of her lipsticks, too?" I ask.

"No, I mean my bullet," she says, pulling out and holding up her gold bullet vibrator, before placing it back into her make-up bag like it's nothing.

I mean, it *is* nothing—but how often does a stranger randomly show you what they use to get off? I smile. *What's going on?* But before I know it, she *kisses* me. She is kissing me and I'm not doing anything about it. It fells different… *nice different.* I'm not stopping her. I'm dancing with her in this world I've never explored. *I don't understand it, what am I doing?* I pull away eventually, not sure of where to look. I glance down and fiddle with my ring. I'm not embarrassed, I just don't understand. I liked it. I'm not a lesbian, bi, or bi-curious, so…

"You OK?" Sienna asks, lifting my chin up and forcing me to look at her.

"Yeah, erm… You and Troy make a great couple," I say as an off-key attempt to remind her she has a man.

"Troy's not my man, we're just good friends. I'm sorry, I shouldn't have done that, I just… I'm really sorry."

I'd spent all night trying not to look at her gorgeous man, who isn't her man, only to find out that she was looking at me. "No, erm, it's fine, really. I mean, I was taken by surprise, but you're a good kisser and I'm… I guess flattered." I'm not lying.

Her lovely rich brown skin and her long, jet-black braids, along with the silver nose ring, gave her a Lisa Bonet vibe, whilst her deep brown eyes, accentuated with eyeliner and mascara, exude a power and presence that I hadn't noticed from across the table. *I kissed her back.* Yeah, I'm shocked. We both fix our lipsticks and head back to the table. I'm finding it hard not to look in her direction, but I'm also trying to act normal. After dessert, the smokers head out again for that good ole nicotine-laced air— and once again, Sienna comes over.

"I'm just checking you're OK?"

"I am, thank you. I'm just shocked and a little intrigued. I haven't done anything like that before, so it's kind of a big deal… Well, a big deal for me, anyway."

"What are you intrigued about?"

I would have picked up on that word too if this was the other way round. *How do I say this?* "Erm… I appreciate women," I tell her with openness, "but I've never been attracted to them like that. I'm intrigued as to why you may be different for me."

"What are you doing after this?" she asks. I shake my head and shrug, my way of saying nothing.

"OK. Let's hang. If you want to, that is?"

"Sure," I reply, far to breezily for my liking.

We split the bill and everyone begins to say their goodbyes and go their separate ways.

"Angela, this was such a lovely, dinner," I tell her. "Happy Birthday again, and I'll see you when you get back from your hols."

"Sure thing. Thanks for coming, I've had such a great time."

Sienna says her goodbyes too—first to Angela, and then Troy, who she playfully embraces. *I see the brotherly love now…* We step out and head towards Soho, but we end up in Stockwell—here, at her place. I'm not gonna use alcohol as an excuse because I'm not drunk now. I'm just lean, you know, nice—and aware of what I'm doing. She's so easy to talk to. I feel comfortable, and I'm attracted to her vibe. Her groundedness, her well-balanced alpha-and-sensual feminine energy. It's attractive.

If eyes are the windows to the soul, a person's book collection is a commentary on their character, interests and sense of self. As I scan her shelves, I have never seen so many eclectic books, from poetry, ancient Egyptology, self-help to tantric sex, herbal remedies and an array of Black history books, written by Black historians. A lover of crystals, art and plants, Sienna's flat is small but beautiful.

"So, are you gay, bi or...?" I ask eventually. A bit late, especially as I'm in her bed. *I feel stupid.*

"I'm bi, I'm attracted to men and woman. My last relationship was with a man, but I've dated women, too."

"When did you know?"

"Hmm, around eighteen, nineteen-ish, but I didn't really explore it until my early twenties."

We chat for ages on just every single topic. Girls share beds all the time, and I didn't feel awkward at all, not even when she kissed me... my breasts, navel, clit. Not even when I gasped for air as I came. Came. Came. I came. Released. Cried. I cried tears of joy, she understood, she knew, she understood.

*

I usually set the scene in my head and then slowly tease myself, adjusting the speed to mimic the pulses, eventually going faster and faster. Then, as I hear my moans getting louder, I open my eyes, catch myself in the mirror and cue the internal voice: *What are you doing? Are things so bad that you have to get your sexy on with a bright pink dick?* The romantic scene in my head is over. Dildo flung on the floor. Needs suppressed.

This is how it used to be. Since I met Sienna two days ago, I have made myself cum four times. I feel empowered and sexy

Lisa Bent

in a different way to how I feel when I'm with a man. *A woman knows what a woman wants.* I've always heard this saying, but it's true. She tapped into the next level of my organismic experience. I feel I should have known for myself, but I'm not going to beat myself up about it. Her touch, her *everything*, was so soft and sensual, in ways I don't think men can re-create. It's so much more than saying, "less of the deep dive tongue stabbing." It's so much more than that. She awakened something buried so deep. Trauma. Trauma so deep. My blind spot. Her unspoken words allowed me to enjoy without judgement. Liberation is the word, but so is healing. Sexual healing. *Who knew?*

I have thought about Sienna a lot, and part of me really wants to get in contact again, but I'm not trying to open up Pandora's box any wider. I don't have anything to avoid, I just fully believe that experience was meant to happen, and that's it. I know what I have gained as a result of it.

We'll remain friends though, and I'll keep searching.

179

Chapter Sixteen

To Submit or Not to Submit

"Hey guys, so sorry, I took so long," Chantel says, flopping into the empty chair whilst shoving her big yellow bags under the table. "I couldn't decide which outfit to buy, so I bought both to try at home. Things always look different in my mirror anyway. Have you noticed that?" she asks, sipping the spare water in front of her. Adisa, Zaara, Tasha and I look at her in silence, as we need to catch a moment from this whirlwind of a woman.

"How do two outfits equate to four big bags?" I ask.

"Well, I also saw a few outfits that I could wear for my birthday, so just got them to try on, too."

"Your birthday is a whole four months away, are you OK?" I ask with genuine confusion.

"I'm a Scorpio, you should know this—go hard or go home. It's my thirtieth, I'm gonna need lots of options. I'm famished, have you lot ordered already?" We all nod.

"So, are you looking forward to meeting Seyi's parents?" Zaara asks.

"Yeah, but I'm nervous," Chantel says honestly, calling the waitress over.

"Ah, you're a fine girl, no pimples. You'll be fine. Just be yourself," offers Adisa.

"Hold on… Can I have an almond milk mocha and a cheese and tuna panini, please…?"

Almond milk, since when? And a meal without meat? Who is she?

"…Yeah. Seven months in, the most committed I've ever been, and it's been kinda nice. Scary, but nice. I de-activated my dating apps, can you believe that? I mean, I don't even know who I am," she says laughing.

Exactly, nor me. I'm so proud of her. Since our little moment at the summit a few months ago she's been a different person. Just more grounded, open and not so reactive. Seyi seems to be a positive influence, I still need to check him out with my own two eyes, but I will when Chan is ready.

"Ah we're proud of you," Adisa says, for us all. "How are you all getting on? I know there's been snippets in the group, but any updates? I've been so busy with work, I haven't really given the dating stuff the time it requires,"

She pauses after answering her own question.

"I just swipe after work, on my way home. I haven't really had any luck though, but the church strategy is still on-going. There's a lot of churches to get through!" She laughs. "I'm being serious, though. You can't just go and move on to another one the following Sunday, nooo. We go at least three to four times first, in case someone was away the previous weeks."

"Wow, you are not ramping," I say, surprised at the level of dedication.

"No, I'm not. I have time for God, and I want my husband

to be a Christian so I'm doing the work in God's house, preparing so, you know, I'm ready for when commonality and values meet opportunity."

"Amen!" Chantel says in support.

"To be honest, I think your strategy is such a good idea, and geared for success," Zaara says.

"Ah, why do you say that?" asks Adisa.

"Look around—where are the Black men?" We look around our environment. She's right, not a Black man in sight. "It's not just here, it's whenever we go out," I say. "Where are they? Where do they go to dine, hang out? It's such a mystery to me."

"We only make up three per cent of the whole of UK, perhaps that's why?" Zaara suggests.

"Yes, but we're *thirteen* point three per cent in London. Look, I've just checked," I say, pointing at my phone screen.

"I think it's bigger than that, though," Tasha says. "Chinese people make up a smaller percentage in the UK and they know where to find each other, like Asians. We don't have that… that… bond. *Unity*, for want of a better word. A lot of places aren't designed with us in mind. Brixton had that vibe thanks to our culture, but gentrification has turned it into something else which feels less authentic and welcoming. Other factors—less surplus money to play with due to inequality of pay, and maybe already being parents, potential higher rent rates and event bias due to discrimination, make it difficult for Black business owners to thrive."

"And maybe intention also has a part to play that informs Black men's decisions," I add. "If they want to meet girls, they go to the places that ensure they'll see some. Perhaps it's that simple? But I go raving to have fun, I don't intentionally look for someone whilst there—"

"There's more Black-led events now though," interrupts Chantel.

"When was the last time you went to a Black event and the room was filled with Black men?" I ask.

Chan doesn't find an answer. "And this is why actively looking in Churches makes sense," Adisa says, laughing.

"Tash, can you ask Tevin what his single boys do? In fact, what is their strategy? Do they have one? So many factors, it's actually quite deep when you think about it," I say.

Tasha agrees, and the attention turns on me. "And this is why dating apps are important," Chantel says. "Syms, how are you getting on?"

"No change. It's all good though. Chatting to a few people on dating apps, even spoken to one on the phone but, nah, no one that I really want to meet in person." I haven't shared the girl-on-girl experience with anyone. These ladies who are my close friends are cool, and even though I don't think there would be any judgement, I don't want to chance it. I've never heard anyone in my circle talk openly about attraction or a sexual encounter with someone of the same sex before, and I don't want to be the person to give that insight. I don't want to be questioned. We look to Zaara to hear her update.

"I've been on one date. It was OK, nothing much to report. I'm getting used to being at home on Saturdays, and I didn't realise how many dresses I own. I need to learn to recycle good quality clothes and stop buying one-wear-and-throw-away cheap ones. Oh... See that? My new stance on looking for quality men has also transcended to my clothes!" Zaara says, dancing in her chair.

Just as I'm about to complain that our food is taking too long, the waitress arrives. She sees my face and apologises. I smile, grateful for the acknowledgement, and begin to tuck in. *Shopping on an empty stomach, I should know better by now.*

"I'm attending a modern church at the moment, and last week's sermon had me fuming and in stiches in the same breath—"

"Wait, Adisa, what do you mean by modern?" asks Chan.

"I say modern, because unlike most traditional churches I've been to, this pastor uses everyday situations to further explain teachings. He mentioned he was conducting a wedding in the afternoon and used that as catalyst to discuss the union of marriage. He was doing well until his opinion came into it. Can you believe— You know what, I actually wrote it down. Let me tell you word for word." Adisa pulls out her phone and begins to read aloud.

"In order to keep a woman happy, men, you must give her compliments, listen to her when she's speaking and buy her gifts, often. Women, to keep a man happy you must look good. He wants to see the same woman he married in years to come. And we all know the way to a man's heart is through his stomach. A man will never stray when these two things are in order. Don't nag him, leave him be—he works hard to provide. It goes without saying, but you must also have the energy to satisfy him."

"What? You call this a modern church?" I say with surprise.

"Misogynist," states Tasha.

"The joke is, this church films their services, so people who weren't there still get to see rolling eyes and hear the sounds of kissing teeth. I literally couldn't believe it. Imagine having him as your marriage counsellor? That's a rocky foundation to build a stable and successful marriage on."

In a chorus of *hmms*, we all agree with Adisa.

"What do you think about the word 'submit'? Like, would you 'submit' to your partner?" I ask.

"I think we all do it unconsciously anyway; this is a patriarchal society remember," says Adisa.

"I hear you, but I'm specifically asking, if a man asks you to submit to him, would you?"

"No one really talks like that these days. When was the last time you heard a man say, 'And you shall submit to me?'" she says in a low booming voice that sends me into fits of laughter even though she is pissing me off.

"OMG, can you just answer the question?" I stress.

"If a man wants you to always compromise because he feels his opinion and authority matters over yours, what would you do?" Zaara offers instead.

"I would tell him to get the fuck outta here," Adisa answers, laughing.

"So you wouldn't compromise, but you would submit?"

Adisa shrugs and I'm baffled. "That makes no sense. To submit is to yield or give way to a more 'superior' force. Compromise is all about coming to an agreement, that's my understanding," I say.

"So, if a woman is expected to compromise because a man

feels his opinion matters more and you give in, this is still submitting from where I'm sitting," Adisa responds.

Chantel shrugs, sips her coffee and says, "we already submit unconsciously anyway. Men influence how we behave."

"I agree, but let's purely focus on relationships," I suggest. "This conversation is already difficult because we're all working from different reference points. 'To honour and obey,' honour your husband by respecting him, and obey by listening to him. Submission is giving up *your* wants in order to comply. That's just my opinion. So, to put it a different way, will you allow your man to dim your light? Suppress your voice and contributions to decisions?"

Adisa considers this for a moment. "I've heard other pastors talk about submission from a place of humility in order for a union to work. I also see it as trust in a man's authority as the head of the household." We all exchange looks. "I can see how the word can be viewed as negative, however, my mum and dad have a successful marriage. Their roles are clear, they talk about everything, but the ultimate decision lies with him," she says, before continuing, "I can see the positives of having that understanding."

"OK, would you like to, or can you see yourself adopting what has worked for your parents?" *I feel like I'm working really hard today. Adisa is usually more to the point.*

"Honestly… yes. I want my husband to be a man, make decisions and be in charge, whilst still having a say. I respect him and he respects me. I want him to feel like he is the king of the castle, I want to give him the biggest piece of chicken. I don't lose any power from this stance."

I can only guess the silence we are sitting in, is due to not knowing how to communicate the plethora of words that are edged onto our faces. I look confused, like everyone else, and I'm not trying to hide it. I sip my peppermint tea, pondering if I should express myself more on the topic, or leave it. I really don't want to come across as cantankerous. Zaara asks for my view.

I draw in a breath. "I just want to be with someone who understands we have differences, and my opinions shouldn't make him feel less of a person, man, king. My vagina is a portal to another world that brings life—that is powerful on a mind bending level. We literally birth out miracles. I think our power makes men feel inferior and that is why we are asked to submit. No one should need anyone to be less-than to feel good about themselves or in control. My husband should already know he's a king, because I already know I'm a queen. Respect is what he should feel. I want to be with someone who respects and understands that we bring different things to the table, and that makes it equal. I don't have energy for unnecessary power struggles."

"If you submitted, you wouldn't have loss of energy because there would be no arguments," offers Chantel.

"I would. A lack of voice, sense of self, is a loss of energy," I inform her. "I'm not saying I'm right, I'm just saying this is my opinion."

"Maybe you struggle with masculine energy...?" offers Adisa. I have no idea how we got to this next level of explaining. *I know this is already an issue.* I'm boiling like a volcano inside, whilst my face, *I think*, is as cool as a cucumber.

"You do have problems with male fitness instructors," Zaara agrees. "You cannot stand them telling you what to do—and do I need to remind you what happened when we all did salsa lessons?"

"Syms, I get everything you've said, but Zaara is right. It's specifically authoritative masculine energy that pisses you off," Chan says. "In salsa, the man leads, that is the rule, but you struggled with it—and dare I say, resisted it?"

"What? That old white man was in his element. He was rough and forceful, I felt like a wild horse he wanted to break in. Regardless of the dance rule, surely it shouldn't feel like that. I refused to dance with him because he was a dickhead. And yeah, the situation at salsa is a visual representation of what submission looks like to me. Just going along with whatever the man wants and says."

"But sis, maybe it felt like that because you were resisting? I didn't think it was that bad. I guess he was forceful, but he was pushing me into the next move. He led, and knew what he was doing," Chantel says calmly.

"Hmm, I partly agree, but I think Symona's right. There was something about him and the way he was that I didn't like either," Tasha says. Adisa nods in agreement which I'm grateful for. I'm always ready to stand by my opinions even if it means I'm by myself, but it's nice to have some support.

"He got off on it. I know what I saw and felt," I say, trying not to sound defensive, *because I knew they were hitting a nerve about how I feel around men like that?* "Anyway… What do you guys think of the word submit? JOKE. Are you guys ready to go?"

Chapter Seventeen

Mr Coffee Cup

The girls want to continue shopping, but I'm all shopped out, so I leave them and make my way to Bond Street station, before changing my mind and walking to the bus stop. The thought of being on the Central line just fills me with dread. The idea of this intense heat for just one stop to Oxford Circus before changing to get to the overground at Charing Cross is too much for a hot, busy Saturday afternoon. There is a lot of traffic, but air, real air, just seems more appealing right now. The 159 greets me at the bus stop, and I have a choice of seats upstairs.

Mindlessly gazing out at the sea of people below, I'm in my own world, until a man decides to sit in front of me. *There are so many seats on the top deck, why this one?*

And drinking coffee, in this heat? Anyway, I turn my attention back to gazing out of the window, allowing my mind to wander. It heads straight back to the last conversation with the girls and my struggle with 'masculine energy.' *Hmm.* I don't see it as a struggle. I see me not giving up my power just because the person I'm talking to is a man. *Perhaps my issue is not my issue but men's, based on their expectations of me as a woman?* My train of thought is momentarily distracted by the guy in front of me, who keeps turning around, in the way tourists do when sightseeing. *But this is Regent's Street, there aren't really any landmark sights here…*

I choose to ignore him as I settle back into my thoughts. I realise outside of my Dad, I've never had a Black male teacher, lecturer, boss or CEO heading up a company.

They exist, of course they do, but I haven't experienced it. The only authoritative man in a position of power whom I know is my Dad, and I stopped taking orders from him when I was eighteen because he allowed me to make my own decisions. Then I stopped talking to him all together at twenty-three, because of his actions. So the question is, how well-versed am I in communicating with Black men? And how open am I in taking direction from Black men? Especially, if I have latent anger that causes me to be hypersensitive. Black fragility exists. The destruction of the Black family on a systematic level is well known, to me. How it impacts and shows up in our relationships and how we communicate isn't. So what is the cost to love?

My *a-ha* moment is broken by my phone vibrating.

Hey sis, I forgot to say, I loved the book you recommended. In fact, it's really helped me to process my patterns and emotions. Thank you. Love ya x

I type out a reply.

Hey Chan, I'm so glad you got something from it. Love you too x

I press send, and when I look up, dude in front is taking selfies. *He's definitely a tourist.* I press the bell, which is on a pole near the back of his head. He gets up too, and indicates I should pass him. *Strange.* He follows behind me as the bus slows down and stops at a traffic light. Standing on the other side of the pole we're both holding on to, he says, "Hi."

Suddenly the bus starts up again as the light turns green, and we both stumble. I grab the pole again, but he misses it, lurching forward and spilling his drink all over the floor. *It's not coffee—it's alcohol.* "Oh man, it's your fault that I stumbled, you're just too beautiful."

Nice ice-breaker. I smile cautiously and hand him a tissue. "Thank you," he says as he wipes the liquid from his ankles. *Hmm, around my age, tall and handsome.* He's in a crisp white shirt, beige trousers, nice watch, brown loafers, no socks. Sunglasses on his head—he's definitely not a Londoner.

"Hey, I have alcohol because it's a sunny day," he says as we both step off the bus. I didn't care to ask because it's none of my business and I didn't want to engage. *I'm just not in the mood.* However, his explanation still doesn't make sense. 'Why is it in a coffee cup?' is the real question.

"I'm from Zambia," he continues, regardless. "I have been here for three months and it's interesting so far." I decide to humour him, because if I was in a new country, I would also like to be shown kindness.

"What's been interesting so far?" I ask.

"I'm in Sevenoaks. It's a nice place, but I haven't really seen any Black people there, which is so strange to me… Sorry, I need to find a bathroom ASAP. Please stay whilst I run to that pub? Please?" He shoves the coffee cup into my hand and darts across the road. *Why me? Can I just have an easy life? I should just dash this cup and leave.* He reaches the other side without getting killed, looks back and throws me a boyish-yet-charming smile. *Cute*, I think, though I feel like an idiot!

No sooner than he walks into the pub, he walks out, and I'm thankful whilst still feeling like an idiot.

"I'm sorry," he says out of breath by the light jog back. "I just really needed to go. I'm Luckson." He stretches out his hand.

"Did you wash that?" I ask seriously, because not all men do. *Facts!*

"Erm, actually… yes, I did," he says, bursting into laughter. *I like his playfulness.*

"Look, I don't want to keep you, but I would like to call you, get to know you." He didn't actually ask for my number, but his non-ask was clear in its intention. *Hmm.* Alcohol in the coffee cup was weird, but he seems fun, and I don't know much about Zambia—or Zambian men. He looks just as surprised as I do. I give him my number.

"Oh wow, thank you. I'm going to call you later, is that OK?"

I nod, and begin to say goodbye, because his level of his merriness is increasing and becoming annoying.

"Bye, Symona. Bye, Symonnnnnnnnnnna!"

I keep walking. *What have I done?*

Five minutes later, my phone rings, "Hello?"

"Hello Symona, it's Luckson. I couldn't wait until tomorrow.

Let's seize the day! Fancy a drink now?"

"Err... no sorry. I'm on my way home. Plus, don't you think you've had enough to drink already?" I ask.

"No, I'm doing... how you guys say... hair of the dog, liquid lunch." I remain silent. "Come onnnn, don't be a bore."

"Nope, sorry, I've just got on my train. Take it easy, stop drinking, bye."

I'm not entertaining any of that nonsense. Drinking at 3pm on a weekend is acceptable, but alcohol in a coffee cup, whilst riding a bus with no real place to go is weird. *Or is it?* London isn't always the friendliest place, he didn't seem to have any friends. Perhaps the alcohol was for Dutch courage to talk to randoms in the hope of making some? *Girl, stop. Stop finding a story to explain a situation from someone else's book that you haven't even read Jheeze.*

*

I hope you had a good sleep?

Reads the message.

It's cute I suppose. It's been ages since I've received a thoughtful morning message—but it's six am. It's from Luckson.

I click onto his WhatsApp pic to see his selfie. *Yep, that's how I remember him.* In fact, it's exactly how I remember him down to the clothes and location. *The location...* Regent Street. I zoom in, and can see part of *my face* in the background! This dude actually tried to get me in his selfie! All too weird. Too many negative signs.

BLOCKED!

My future husband, only drinks on social occasions…

Chapter Eighteen

Mr Arty

I love the Metro's 'Rush Hour Crush' section, although they need an update page. I want to know if Silver Fox eventually found the girl with the leopard print coat on the 7:34am train from Elmers End. Like, talk about leaving us commuters hanging! But I'm a lover of love—and no longer the romanticised versions, but the real life versions. This column proves that most people have communication issues. A lack of confidence or nerves gets in the way, and that prevents them from talking to the woman or man they are already sharing glances with. Regret: that's what this column's really about. Regret due to a lack of follow-through, and hope that the person in question will hopefully pick up the paper and identify themselves. *Leaving a lot to chance, no?* I even read it in the hope that one day I'll recognise my own description on the page from a secret admirer. I wonder if there is more chance of winning the lottery? After the horoscopes, I don't bother with the rest of the paper. I just close my eyes and try to meditate. You know, clear the mind.

It's September and as far as I'm concerned autumn has come way too early. I'm cold, grouchy and pissed that the train driver has failed to put the heating on. It's just unacceptable—*like this drought I've been in forever.* The Black man drought, let me be specific. The Black man *who wants to be with a Black woman* drought. The Black Man *who finds a modern woman attractive and not a threat* drought, and the Black man *who is everything I am looking for, and is looking for the same thing* drought. My mind, soul and whole being are parched. I'm shrivelling up. OK, so that's really dramatic, but I yearn for stimulating conversations with male energy. Sometimes I just need to hear that bass in the voice and feel the pressure on my chest. Just sometimes. I press play, put my wireless earphones in, and turn up the volume to quieten my mind. It doesn't work—I select my dating app instead. Swiping is also calming.

Hmm, OK, a few messages here. I paste my standard intro in reply, which is a mixture of basic info about me and some engaging questions. This guy Patrick responds straight away—not bad for eight am on a cold Monday morning. He's forty, six foot tall, and a graphic designer. Handsome, would like children, lives in Elephant and Castle. He linked his Instagram to his account, *no idea why people do this, four pictures max is all you're getting from me.* I take a look. He's really arty, his Instagram has really interesting shots, angles, patterns and lines, very abstract. He definitely has a good eye.

We continue speaking via the app until I get to work. He messages me again in the evening, and we exchange messages back and forth over the week. On Sunday he types:

I think you're cool, do you fancy heading over to voice notes, to see it we vibe before the next stage… a phone call? Here's my number, just drop a note when you're ready?

I save his number, then hold the microphone symbol and slide up.

"Hey Patrick, I like this suggestion. Is this a thing I didn't know about until today?"

He records a reply. "Hahah, no, I actually nicked the idea from someone who did it to me. I think it's a great way to get to know someone before committing to a phone call. You have a nice voice. Bit posh for south."

"What do you mean? I'm not sure if I'm meant to be insulted or not."

"No offence meant, hahah. So how long have you been on the app, what's it been like? I know you're gonna ask me too, so may as well tell you in the same voice note. It's about a year now since I started on the apps, and it's been OK, loads of dates, still single, but willing to mingle. Oh God, that sounds cringe. Wait, what I mean to say is, I'm still open and not scared."

I laugh and send a response. "OK, interesting. After a year, why don't you think you've found someone? I started to take online dating seriously around December last year. It's like having a part-time job on top of your actual job. I haven't gone on any dates with anyone I've met on the app yet, though, so I'm happy to take any tips."

"OK, so to answer your first question, we just didn't click. I'm particular, can't explain it. Advice? Well, I'm still learning, but just be yourself is kinda obvious. Well, to you and me perhaps, but not everyone. I mean, I had a date with a girl who clearly wanted to be Beyoncé, it was so strange. Be a fan but also be yourself, damn!"

I hit the button again. "Hahah, OMG, no way! The way you tell a story just cracks me up."

"Look," he says on his next message. "It's clear we get on— how about we skip the phone call and head straight to a date?"

I smile. "Yeah, why not, how about next week Thursday? You can pick, somewhere not too far from both of us."

"Yes ma'am, that date can work. I'll let you know where. Over and out! *KREEEP-PPPP.* By the way, that was meant to be a walkie-talkie sound effect, but you knew that. Bye!"

Haha! He was just so easy to get on with. This could work out well…

Hi Symona,

How are you?

Italian Restaurant—More London—London Bridge, 7:00pm on Thursday 7th September. The bookings in my name. I look forward to seeing you.

Pat

☺

*

Looking around the restaurant, I agree it's a great spot for a first date. The glass windows all around provide a great view of the Thames, which is lit up with twinkling lights. London is so magical at night. We're getting on really well, and it all just feels effortless. "Right, do you have space for dessert?" Patrick asks, looking at the menu.

"I don't think I do, I'm stuffed."

"Well, I'm a cake man—there is always space for dessert," he says, raising his hand to get the waitresses attention. "Can I get the sticky toffee pudding with vanilla ice cream? Just one, with two spoons please, cos I'm watching my figure." The waitress and I both laugh. *This man is a C-H-A-R-M-E-R!*

"Well, I'm a supportive woman, so I will happily help you," I tell him, and he nods his appreciation.

A little while later, he asks, "So, tell me, why are you single?" with an intrigued look on his face.

"I haven't met the right person yet, that meets my requirements."

"Well, what are your requirements?"

"In short? Someone who has confidence, character, commonality, similar values and beliefs. I'm looking for a modern man, someone who gets that I also have ambition and independence."

"But that's standard." He glances up as the waitress brings the dessert and puts it on the table between us.

"Only if you're a modern man. It's important to me that I'm with someone who is."

"Babe, ya found him! I'm right here, pudding."

"Are you talking to the dessert or me?" I ask, laughing.

"KMT. Let's tuck in. I like to eat it when it's still hot. It's not as nice when the ice cream cools it down, ya get me?"

"Jheeze, alright cake connoisseur. You sure you want me to share it?"

"Just eat, before I change my mind."

*

I'm stuffed and I just want to lie on the couch and chill. Instead, I have to prepare myself to brace against the cold. I mean, I just need a driver on standby, already. I'm freezing, but Patrick suggests we take a walk by the river bank. *Ugh.* I agree, though. Can you burn calories just by trying to keep warm?

"Shall we?" he asks, poking his arm out for me to link into. It feels nice, and I don't feel as cold as I thought I would. *His body heat, wine or the food? Or all of the above perhaps.*

We walk slowly by the riverbank. It's only nine thirty, but it feels so quiet, especially for a Thursday night, which is like the new Friday, apparently. We have great conversations, and moments of silence which don't feel awkward at all.

"Damn, he's good," Patrick says, nodding towards a saxo-phonist playing romantic jazz. "Let's go over and give him an audience." We walk over and take in the moment. Every note floats beautifully through the air with the power to warm the cold-hearted. I feel the performer's soul, I feel this Black man's soul whose breath is at one with his instrument.

"Let's take a seat over there," I suggest, because I need to sit down—my legs are shaking and the wine is licking my head in the breeze. *I need to steady myself.* As soon as we sit down, we're transported to a private concert that is worthy of the standing ovation we give when the song comes to the end. Patrick digs deep into his pocket and drops some coins into the saxophonist's case. There's a brief conversation, and then they spud each other. *What's going on?* I ask with my eyes, which Patrick correctly reads, as he walks back over to me on the bench.

"This next tune is for you," he says. "Guess the artist."

As soon as the melody begins, I know it. "It's *There Goes My Baby* by Usher! Don't play with me, you know. Just don't do it. I love this song."

"Wow, that was quick. I love it too. The violin version is also incredible."

"I can imagine," I say looking at him and smiling. Patrick has a warm face, nice smile, and a few faint freckles across his cheeks and nose, which I've only just noticed. Our magic warm bubble bursts when the song comes to an end.

"You're shivering. It's time to get you home," he says.

He leans in and his mouth meets mine. His tongue, teasingly considerate, his kissing style, sensual. That is what I'm left with as we depart, going our separate ways.

*

"Sorry sis, I'm not free at the mo, I'll call you back later, OK?"

"Where are you?"

"I'm at Patrick's."

"Again?"

"Yes, again! Hah. Call you later."

I put my phone down and hug the empty pillow next to me.

It's the end of the month and I've seen Patrick at least six times now. I'm trying not to make my mind run wild, but you know, he definitely has something. Could this arty intellectual be The One?

I love waking up in his bed. It's so big and comfortable. The teal, rustic four-poster bed is an unconventional colour choice, but it works really well. On the left side of the wall he has a huge mirror, the frame of which he has painted yellow, which strangely works—and I just love his black-and-white themed kitchen. He certainly has style and is not scared of colour, patterns... Or experimenting with flavours. Don't get me wrong, he can cook, I just question the mix; like, ginger in a tomato-based sauce doesn't work for me. Neither does a banana smoothie with avocado. *So wrong*.

"Morning babe, do you want some coffee?" I ask, finding him in the second bedroom, which he has turned into a very cool-looking office.

"Erm, yeah sure, thanks," Patrick says without turning around.

"You want breakfast, too?" I ask, hugging him from behind and whispering into his ear, gently brushing his ear lobe with my lips.

"Hmmmm... Babe you can't do that, I'm trying to work," he says roughly, shrugging me off. *Red flag*. Surprised by his reaction, I silently step back in confusion, trying to locate what has irked me. Patrick stops drawing, sighs heavily and turns around before wheeling the office chair towards me whilst holding his hands out. I place my mine in his.

"I didn't mean to snap," he says. "I'm nearly done, I just need to focus a bit more."

I nod, closing the door behind me and heading downstairs to the kitchen.

"Babeeee?" Patrick shouts from upstairs a few minutes later.

"Yeah?" I shout back.

"Seriously, how did you expect me to focus when you're naked?" he asks.

I smile and crack on with making breakfast.

A short while later, I tentatively knock on the door whilst holding the tray with coffee, toast and a bowl of granola covered in yoghurt. The words 'come in' don't arrive, so I take the tray through to the master bedroom and chill in his dressing gown on the chaise lounge. I can't relax. This posh coffee is so good, but I *can't relax. The way he shrugged me off, just felt...* My head is trying to talk to my feelings, and I'm trying to make sense of it but I'm not connecting the dots. I just know there's a red flag.

"What?" I ask, when I eventually look up and notice Patrick is leaning in the doorway smiling at me.

"You know you're hot right?" he asks, taking a seat next to me and placing my legs into his lap.

"Even with my twists sticking out in different directions?" I reply, even though my hair may have nothing to do with being 'hot.' *Jheeze, Syms, you could have just said yes, or thank you.*

"Yes," Patrick tells me. "Look, I'm all here for the prep and transformation. I find it fascinating what you ladies can do with your hair." He pauses. "Did you know carrots were originally purple?" I shake my head, wondering what direction he's about to go in. "Yep, that was their natural colour before the Dutch cultivated orange ones. Supermarkets tried to reintroduce the original colour, but customers weren't buying them. My point is, don't fall for beauty standards set by people who don't look like us, and who cannot accept what grows from your scalp or ground naturally. Yah get me?" he finishes passionately, with a slice of humour. "I love my hair; I actually feel I'm so creative because I'm connected. An antenna, that's what this is," he adds, stretching out a kinky strand.

Journal
8th October 2017

I'm not trying to move in with Patrick. He doesn't believe me, all because I asked if I could leave a few essential things there, like spare knickers, a toothbrush, headscarf, cream and a few hair products. I don't know what the big deal is about. I'll be damned if, at this age, I'm gonna be walking around with a bag that holds everything I need in case I see him. And so arrangements to stay over are planned. Slightly boring but hey, I don't have time to keep buying duplicates of everything.

I haven't invited him to my space yet, because I like my space. I live alone and I'm particular about who comes round. He will eventually, just not yet. What I'm saying is, trust takes a little longer for me to build. I like seeing men in their space, it gives me an insight into how they treat me, their level of cleanliness and creative eye. Plus, it's just so easy for women to go into care mode when they're in our space.

Apart from that… and the detection of slight mean-ness, am I being harsh? Nothing else is a problem. We get on and enjoy similar things.

Last week, I wore heels to work and by the time I got to his, my feet were killing me. I should know better. He saw my discomfort and, without saying a word, massaged my feet as I flaked out on the couch. I didn't even want a foot massage, I hate people touching my feet. I just wanted to take the sadomasochist shoes off—but it turns out a massage was exactly what I needed.

He ran me a nice hot bath with candles all around, and when I came out, he dried me down and then creamed me from head to toe, massaging every part of my body in the candlelit bedroom. I looked at him in appreciation, but 'the look' also came out. You know the one. 'I really appreciate… love you', 'are you the one?' and 'can I have your babies?' I mean, it was all mixed up, I couldn't tell you which one it was. What I do know is, I have no desire to tell him. If you love a man, you have to keep your mouth shut in case he isn't ready. Experience has taught me that. When a man reveals he loves you, then it kinda means he's ready for commitment and you now have license to share your true feelings. It's frustrating. I don't think this is modern man behaviour, but this may be the closest I get.

Journal
22nd October 2017

I'M SO FUCKING MAD!!!!! I don't understand. I just can't make sense of any of this. I feel betrayed in the most voyeuristic way, and I feel helpless and powerless. I haven't eaten in three days; I can't hold anything down. I'm just so angry and stressed out. My stomach is in knots and I just want to scream!

I broke up with Patrick three days ago. We weren't in a relationship, but we were exclusively seeing each other, whilst my radar was still up and dating apps still live. He keeps ringing, but there is nothing he can say or do to fix this.

My face couldn't be seen, but that's not the point. The point is, he never asked for my permission. My body, from different angles, posted on Instagram. My feet, my dimples at the base of my back, my beauty spots on my ankle, my lips, my hands. There was even a shot in between my legs. Who does that? Apparently it was 'an homage to me and my beauty.' He has hundreds of likes on Instagram and some of the comments are just vile, as men express what they want to do to me. He turned me into an object, divided into parts to be ogled. As his numbers grew, what would it have been next? A sex tape? Wait! Has he ever secretly filmed us and now do I need to worry about revenge porn?

Apparently he 'respected me by not revealing my face, which proved he took me into consideration,' from his perspective. What the fuck is that? Wrong and strong, pure ignorance and no respect for my voice or opinion. If he can do that in the name of 'art', what can he do in the name of love? I feel sick to the pit of my stomach. Think about ME, consider ME and my fucking feelings for ONCE. Surely this is not too much to ask for? Over and over again he says sorry, but he still doesn't get it. The trust is broken and beyond that, this is fucking weird behaviour.

I smashed his yellow mirror on my way out. I just saw red and had to do something. The rage came out. He can replace the mirror easily and move on, whilst I have to deal with my internal broken pieces. I really wanted to delete his Instagram account, but somehow within my rage I knew that wasn't a good idea, plus I didn't know his code to unlock his phone. Upskirting is illegal, so I've reported him—full name, Patrick Hanwell—to the police. Fucking bastard, how dare he? BLOCKED.

I feel all sorts of emotions at the moment that make me want to cry or smash things. I will tell the girls, but not just not yet. I need to deal with this. "See the lesson and keep it moving?" If I don't know what I missed, how can I learn from it? This challenge has made me more courageous, but I need to slow down and take stock of a few things.

Chapter Nineteen

Hamilton

26th October 2017

I specifically asked for recommendations for a therapist who is a man, a Black man, as a way to work through any issues I have with male authority. His name is Hamilton, it's my first session and I'm unapologetically vomiting everything out.

"...I mean, are men doing the inner work? I ask because as I get older, my disappointment remains. It's just so tiring. The joke is, my disappointment isn't based on my expectations, it's based on the basic notion that you shouldn't treat people like crap. How the hell did I attract Patrick? I've looked back over everything and there were no signs." I sigh. "I'm just so tired. I've done so much work on myself and this whole situation has just knocked my confidence. I'm thirty-eight and I still don't trust men. I'm trying to remain open, but it's just so disappointing. I believe men at some point will let me down, but I also believe in self-fulfilling prophecies, so I need to watch my mind. I'm angry, really angry. I know this stuff with Patrick is mixed up with Darren and my Dad and I'm trying not to put everything in one pot, but it's difficult because they all have one thing in common: they have never apologised to me. I deserve an apology. I am worthy of an apology, but I have learnt not to hold my breath waiting for one. I just don't have time for this. I've been consciously single for a reason."

"Hmm," Hamilton begins. "From what you've expressed it sounds like being consciously single when you were younger really helped you to find yourself and heal, but now it sounds like it's a shield—a shield protecting you from disappointment."

"Are you implying that I'm still single by choice?"

"I'm expressing an idea for you to look into regarding your beliefs around relationships. A shield is used for protection, and I'm wondering if you are shielding yourself in the label of 'consciously single'?"

Mind blown. "I just need to be an alchemist, to magic all of this old stuff away and bring in newness," I tell him.

He nods. "Therapy is spiritual alchemy, and you're here looking at the parts to transform. You are *already* an alchemist."

Like I said: mind blown.

Chapter Twenty

The Catch Up

Tasha can't be bothered to cook, so we've ordered in. Pizza over Guyanese food is just rude, but I get it—less mess and stress. As usual the prosecco is flowing, which I'm not drinking. I'm old enough and wise enough to know that some drinks have the ability to bring me down if I'm too tired or not in a good place. Baileys is giving me comfort and warmth—it doesn't go with Pizza as Chan has already informed me—*I know*—but I'm good with it. I feel OK, I'm working through things with Hamilton, and I'm in a better place than I was three weeks ago.

"Alright ladies, you have a good evening. Good seeing you all," Tevin, Tasha's husband, says to us all.

"You, too," we all say in unison.

"Babe, I'll see you later. Love you," he says, kissing Tasha on his way out. These two are such a lovely couple. You feel their love as soon as you step into their home, it's just in the air.

"OK, he's gone. Update time," Tasha says with glee.

"I'm sort of seeing someone," Adisa tells us excitedly. "Nothing serious, it's only been a couple of weeks."

"Wow, this is great news. You're beaming. Where has the Adisa I know gone?" asks Tasha.

"Oh, she gone. She was boring."

"OK, girl! So tell us about this man that has you looking giddy," Zaara says, laughing.

Adisa explains she met Fabian, a solicitor, at her workplace. As she walked in, she caught him checking her out. "The level of brazenness was teetering on the edge of rudeness, but I was sold when he flashed a smile, handed me his business card and told me to call him."

"Damn, you would have cussed him back in the day," says Chantel.

Adisa nods in agreement and sips her drink. She goes on to explain that she called him at lunchtime and met him for drinks later that evening in a bar in Clerkenwell.

"Charm collided with an overload of confidence, I liked it. I find that really attractive in a man. I had to leave at eight pm, as I had dinner with an old work colleague that I couldn't cancel—"

"Err... yes you could," interjects Chantel.

"Yeah, you're right. Anyway, we exchanged numbers and I left. I met up with my friend Ella, but I was distracted because he was Whatsapp-ing me throughout. He sent me his address and a picture of his dick and asked me to come over..."

"Bloody hell!" screams Zaara with delight and shock, which vocally reflects our surprise.

"I have never experienced such forwardness. I told Ella, she said I should go, but I didn't want to seem eager. I went to the toilet and stupidly left my phone on the table..."

"Why is that stupid?" asks Zaara.

"Can I finish the story without interruptions please?"

"There's the Adisa I know," Zaara says, chuckling.

"So, when I came back from the toilet, Ella told me my cab was on the way. The bitch ordered a cab to his house because she told me I needed to 'blow out some cobwebs'."

Zaara's eyes are wide, Chan is smiling, my mouth is hanging open and so is Tasha's.

"For once I just thought, why not? I was angry and a little tipsy when I got in the cab, less angry and still tipsy by the time I arrived at his flat in Stoke Newington." She shakes her head and begins to smile. "He greeted me at the door with a bare chest, navy tracksuit bottoms and a firm erection. I nearly choked on my own saliva. Ladies, I was scared…"

"So…" Chantel begins to butt in and is shut down by Adisa.

"No, Chan, can I just finish the story please?" she begs.

"Why are you such a control freak? How do you expect me to remember what I wanted to say when you're done? This is not how normal conversations work, love."

"I know, I know. Look, I'm sorry. It's not even about me being controlling, I know I can be, but I am embarrassed and I just want to spit it all out, so it doesn't long out. Please, I'm nearly done." Chan nods accepting the request. "As I walked in, the drink licked me HARD, and although it was only nine thirty, I just felt frazzled and so hot. He dealt with the issue, including giving me amazing sex. My arse didn't leave until Saturday after-noon. I would still have cobwebs if it wasn't for Ella. He's five years younger than me but seems wise and mature. I'm fine with this arrangement at the moment."

"Which is?" asks Chantel.

"We spend time together," she says.

"So you're fuck buddies then," states Chantel. Adisa's face scrunches up like she has tasted something horrible. "Just call it what it is, hun. Who you tryna dress it up for?"

"Crass..." Adisa says, cutting her eye at Chantel. "We are getting to know each other. Anyway, that's me, nothing else to say."

"Hold on, Hold on..." I say. I have to interrupt because the obvious needs to be addressed "You went from wanting a church man, being against one-night-stands to... to... *this*. There is no judgement at all, I'm just intrigued about how you're feeling about it all."

"Man, I was trying to skirt over it," Adisa says honestly.

"I know, and you wouldn't allow any of us to get away with it, so it's your turn. Spill."

She sighs. "Firstly, he's religious and goes to church. So I haven't strayed from my preference. I have always been against one-night stands, but I never said I was saving myself until I was married. People tend to assume that if you're Christian and single you're celibate. I have chosen not to engage in sex because I haven't met someone I wanted to be intimate with. I'm not being reckless and I'm not harming anyone. I know so many Christians, male and female, who are engaging in intimate acts and do everything but have sex. Am I really that much different to them? Look, I have battled with my own guilt around this. My thoughts and actions go against what I've been taught, but I'm trying to navigate myself, my journey and my own relationship with God. Sexual intimacy, as you've said in the past, Chan, is important. What if I marry someone only to find out we aren't sexually compatible? I mean that is important too. So yeah, that's it."

"Thanks for sharing hun, as Syms said, no judgement," Tasha says warmly.

"Thanks guys. Chan, where you at?" asks Adisa.

"Well, I'm still seeing Seyi, he's met the family…"

"Syms, what's he like?" Adisa enquires. "I didn't get to talk to him properly at your b'day, Chan."

I met Seyi two days before Chan's thirtieth birthday party. He came round to mum's. He was nervous but did well. I like him, actually. Intelligent, grounded, and he adores sis. They seem to get on well and he was so attentive at her birthday. Made sure her glass was always topped up, affectionate but respectful, and it's nice to see her so happy.

"Yeah, he seems alright," I say, not wanting to give him *too* much credit for now.

"Time to change the Facebook status?" Zaara interrupts with excitement.

"Does anyone even bother to change their FB status anymore?" Chan says. "Unless you're now married, I don't think it's necessary anymore."

"For as long as FB has existed, I've never changed my status. How sad is that?" says Adisa.

"I'm in the same boat" I say.

"Anyway, I'm happy," Chan says. "I'm thirty now, getting old, so—"

"Listen, don't even! Old? With your thirty-year old self? Talk to me about this again when you also find five grey stands in your pubic hair overnight. I'm traumatised," Tasha says with a straight face, then cracks a smile.

Zaara raises an eyebrow. "I didn't even think about getting greys there, but of course, it makes sense."

I want to laugh my head off but something tells me not to. I'm glad I don't.

"Seriously though, I got a shock. Although I don't feel forty-one, it reminded me that I'm now closer to menopause and the choice to have a child will soon be gone." Tasha pauses and takes a sip of her drink. "Tevin and I both decided ages ago that we didn't want to have children and I, we, still feel that way, but it just felt weird. My grey hairs, to me, were a visual representation of my eggs dying. I doubt that is factually correct, but it's what came up for me. I'm OK now, but it took me a couple of days to work through it. It's just five grey strands of wisdom, all is well." We all instinctively get up and give her a group hug, staying there for a few moments before sitting back down.

I want to say something to Tasha, but I can't find the words. The tears welling up in my eyes, which I know she can see, are for her, which I hope she receives as empathy, but it's also for me. *This is a lot.* Tasha knows she doesn't want children, I know I do, and although we have different wants, the sense of pending grief due to body changes outside of our control is present for us both. Right now, I'm also experiencing the fear of pending loss due to perceived missed opportunity, not helped by my decision to pause my active search for a partner. My biological clock is still ticking. Her five strands of grey hair just reminded me. *Triggered?*

Yes—but I'm aware this time and I've caught myself faster.

"So whilst we're sharing like this, I've decided to become a vegetarian," announces Adisa. Words we thought would never come out her mouth. We joke about how she'll cope without pepper soup, egusi soup, suya, steaks... every meat and fish based dish—but we stop when she bursts into tears.

"Ugh, I said I wasn't going to cry." She sighs. "Basically, I've found out I have five big fibroids, which explains my heavy periods. I'm having an operation to remove them next month, but I'm worried, because I really don't want to have any scars on my womb-lining wall, or any complications that reduce my chances of having children. I'm asking God to take away my fears. I'm changing my diet to see if it will help—and no more relaxer, too. I'm going to go natural, hence why my hair is in braids. Thanks for listening, nothing needs to be said, I know you love and support me and you're there if I need to talk, which I have done far too much of today. Next person, I beg come through... Zaara?"

Respecting Adisa's wishes, Zaara exhales and updates us. "I have nothing to say really. Been on a couple of dates, and that's it. I feel calmer and I'm actually enjoying going out less. I don't want to get too comfortable in this space, but I feel good right now. It's what I needed, actually."

I want Zaara to keep talking, or someone to ask her a question so that my turn can be delayed, but no one does. I can feel the knots in my stomach, today feels like big reveal day. Zaara looks at me and I take the cue and just get on with it. "Firstly, Adisa, thanks for sharing about Fabian and your fibroids. We're your friends and there's no such thing as talking too much. We are all here for you, please remember that and I hope all will be well. I'm sure it will be as those procedures are so common these days." She nods and mouths "thank you."

I take a deep breath and calmly express, "I'm not seeing Patrick anymore. I broke it off three weeks ago because I found out he was taking shots of parts of my body and posting them on Instagram without my permission."

They're about to lurch into all sorts of questions, judging by their shocked faces, which is understandable—and like Adisa, I just want to say what I'm saying without being interrupted. I hold my hand out to indicate they should wait, and I naturally begin to speak louder, to drown anyone out. "Yes! Yes, I'm angry, upset and hurt…" I begin, before reducing my tone. "I didn't tell any of you because I wanted to just deal with it. Chan, I didn't want to worry you or Mum and I just wanted you to have the best thirtieth birthday without my distraction. I went into auto-pilot mode. The police are handling it, and I'm seeing a counsellor, so I'm in a better place now. I'm just waiting for the court date, and I'll let you know when that is. Upskirting is a crime, and I hope he gets what he deserves. And so, I've slowed down on my dating venture." I swallow a sip of my drink. "I'm still glad I challenged myself and upped my game, so nothing has been lost. I'm just choosing to be in flow for the moment. Which for me means being more grounded, self-assured and trusting my intuition." I see my friends exchange concerned glances. "I'm in a good place, really, so please don't be worried. The universe still has my back and is sending me jokes. I was in a coffee shop the other day and a man asked to take my picture! At least he asked, right? When I asked why, he said he wanted to show his mum. Of course, I asked why again and he said, 'So she can bless and pray over it so you can become my wife!' You just cannot make this up!"

"Man was about to call on different powers," says Zaara, laughing. I'm grateful she does, because the mood feels too heavy and I'm done with feeling angry and upset. I need this laugh.

"Ladies, here's to another year older, another year wiser," I say as I raise my glass of Baileys. "Here's to coming out of comfort zones, being more confident and assertive. Here's to listening to our bodies and intuition. Here's to having clear intentions and being in flow."

"And to courage, faith and health," Adisa adds.

"And to freedom," says Zaara.

Chan chimes in with, "And acceptance!"

Tasha ends with, "And love. Love from a place of self-love first. Cheers, ladies."

"Cheers!"

Chapter Twenty-One

The Call

Journal
12th November 2017

Seeing the girls last night was so good. I'm a reasonably together person, fiery and spontaneous at times, which comes with pros and cons. I don't believe in star signs but I would say Aries is spot on with my character. My no nonsense nature enables me to walk away from things and people that no longer serve me. I love that about me, too. However, I don't like what I've been attracting recently.

Challenging myself is great, but it came from a triggered place, which wasn't good. Asta is in her own lane, as am I. I didn't see Patrick, coming, and even if I'd got to know him over a longer period of time, the outcome may have still been the same, so I'm not gonna beat myself up. I've been celibate for a while, but it was never about the sex. The attention was nice, and for someone who supposedly struggles with male energy, I allowed the ones I'd met recently to control the pace.

Anyway, that's done but it has also made me think of my Dad. 'The relationship with your father can reveal something about your relationships with men' I'm told, and it makes sense. I have always known that Chantel has commitment issues due to being rejected by Dad, and I have trust issues. It's so easy to see now. At first I was apprehensive about having a male counsellor, because I'm used to talking to women, but Hamilton's great. In fact, him being Black is even better, as he's helping me see things through a different lens, which is interesting. I feel like he gets me, so I don't need to over-explain certain things. It's good.

*

After twenty minutes of tossing and turning I decide to give Mum a call. It's ten pm, she'll still be up and it's not too late. She answers after three rings—she always does, which is great, I'm convinced she is attached to it. We talk about general things for the first ten minutes, before I finally attempt to address the reason for the call.

"Mum, I've been going on a few dates recently—"

"Oh, that's good. Anyone you like?" Betsy says, interrupting with delight.

"Yes, but no… What I want to say is that I have trust issues with men, which is why I haven't been actively looking til now. What Dad did to you wasn't right, and I know I shouldn't take it on, but…" I trail off as I start to feel emotional.

"Oh, Syms. Darling, I understand. What your father did and how he handled it impacted us all. However, I would like you to remember that not all men are the same, and just because it happened to me doesn't mean it will happen to you."

"I know. I know it logically, but the fear is there. In counselling I dealt with my anger issues, and only now the fear seems to be coming up, because I've been disappointed by the people I've been seeing recently. Disappointment in the lack of consideration for me." I pause, but not for too long as I don't want Mum to interrupt. "Clearly there is stuff I still need to work out, and I wonder if speaking to Dad will help solve it, so I can have better relationships in general. Does that even make sense, Mum?" I ask, questioning my rationale.

"Syms, I want you to understand that your destiny is not defined or tied to your father's actions. It's the memory of what happened, and you don't necessarily need him to help you in order to move forward. That's giving someone too much power. It's about fifteen years now and still no apology, but I moved on the day I told him to leave. If you want to call your father, call him. I just don't want you to be upset if you don't get the response you are looking for."

"Thanks, Mum. I'm just..." I grab the tissues from my bedside table to wipe away my waterfall tears.

"It's OK, darling, let it out," she says reassuringly.

"I'm just annoyed. Just when I think I've got through one issue, another pops up. When does therapy end?"

"Hahah! It doesn't because a perfect state doesn't exist. Everything happens for a reason. See the lesson and learning and keep it moving. This is my stance, which you don't have to follow—"

"Mum, I recognise that saying," I interrupt.

"Your grandma used to say it all the time. This was her mantra," she says, and I can tell she's smiling before finishing her sentence. "Consciously choose your situations."

I shiver, as chills run up my spine.

"Can you send me a picture of Grandma so I can remember what she looks like, please? No rush though, OK mum?"

"No problem. Will do. Remember, your father loves you, he just has a wrong and strong way of showing it right now. Do not continue to make the ending of our relationship negatively feed yours. I love you. *We* love you."

"Thanks Mum. Love you, too."

I end the call. I feel better, but my brain heads into overdrive. *My Grandma…*

Grandma Cedella, lived in Jamaica and died suddenly when I was twenty years old. Due to the distance and I guess money issues, I only met her five times, but found her to be a kind, loving and warm person—though not to be messed with. She could slap you with her stare and show love and affection through her smile.

Mum's just sent me the picture. *Yes, I remember her.* The eyes, nose, cheekbones and lips are exactly the same as Mum's and although her hair is covered by a colourful headscarf, I remember her long, jet-black hair, which neither Mum or I have. As I zoom out, I remember being in Jamaica like it was yesterday. *There she is,* standing on the veranda of her pink house, oozing regal status through her posture, whilst her hard and short lived life can be seen in her eyes. That woman had stories for days—she was a fantastic storyteller. The one about the mongoose always had me howling. She must have told that tale a hundred times in the time I visited her and yet I don't remember it. I just remember it involved a mongoose. *It's so bad that I don't remember it.* I need to ask Mum.

The mix of alcohol, crying and tiredness is kicking in because my eyelids feel heavy. I have no idea why I resist sleep but that's what's happening right now, I know it. And yet here I am still staring at the photograph, my eyes are fluttering... My phone slips out of my hand. *I surrender*—and as soon as I do, I feel myself spiralling into dreamland...

Pitch black is replaced by warm orange and the sound of someone humming a tune. I travel closer to the sound and see Grandma standing on the veranda looking out from her pink house, exactly as she did in the picture. Her hair is hidden under a green and white patterned headscarf. She's wearing a white top with a flowing pink and lime green flowery skirt. Her clashing, very bright attire is watered down by her calm, grounded and regal presence.

"Hello, darling. Come closer nuh man, let me see my beautiful granddaughter." Grandma is smiling and beckoning me to come closer. I walk up the red polished steps, which ignite my senses, and I greet Grandma. She envelops me in her warm embrace, like patty and coco bread. I feel loved and nourished.

"Come, let's sit," Grandma Cedella says, as she releases me from the embrace and points to a bamboo chair next to her. I take a seat and exhale, the tiredness escaping my body. As I inhale, I breathe in my surroundings—the smell of mangoes and roasted breadfruit—and as I exhale, small particles of anger in the pit of my stomach are released.

"Symona, I'm glad you answered my call to come and visit me. I've always been around you but it's only the last couple of years that I have been speaking to you and you have been listening," she says calmly.

"I really wasn't sure who the voice was, I only just figured it out," I tell her, whilst looking out at her luscious green garden. I set my gaze back to Grandma. "You know Mum misses you, right?"

"Of course I know, granddaughter, but we visit each other often, so it's fine," she says, smiling.

Sorrow slowly takes over my smile. "Grandma, I feel a bit lost and confused at the moment. I'm trying to push myself, but I'm not getting positive outcomes. I'm losing faith that what is for me is still on its way." I begin to well up.

"You are bold, tenacious, courageous and independent. You want to make sure that you are steering your own way. These are all good qualities. However, decisions made from a place of impatience can lead you down a different road. Forcing and rushing doesn't bring what you want closer, it takes you further away. Being over doing. Be in flow with the tide, not against it. Do you understand?" I nod, but Grandma decides to continue. "When you accept where you are, and believe that what is for you hasn't passed you, you sit in faith and gratitude, and not lack. When you went to Barbados, were you looking for anyone?" I shake my head. "Exactly, and everything that came was what you needed."

"The magnetic pull!" I exclaim. "Grandma was that you?"

She smiles and there's a long silence before she answers. I shut my eyes to ease my impatience and like a sponge soak up the sun's rays accompanied by the feather-touch wind. I open my eyes when Grandma begins to speak again, and notice she is holding a mongoose.

"I am your guide and protector. You have many ancestors watching over you, but I'm your chief counsel. You have a destiny and purpose, like everyone on your planet. I guide you and show you signs in numerous ways, but you have free will to make your own decisions. The magnetic pull, as you call it, is an instant attraction which has been formulated lifetimes ago. You feel it because you recognise the energy. Nothing is by chance. Everything is by soul design."

"So you didn't create the magnetic pull between me, Mr Barbados and Mr— I mean, Jaden and Ramiro?" I ask, for extra clarity.

"No. Everything you have experienced was already decided by you. You just forgot when you came to Earth. Your ancestors and I have the ability to see what is ahead, and we only intervene to protect you if it's outside of your soul plan, your destiny."

What Grandma has just said digests with ease. I've been on this spiritual journey since I was sixteen, but there's a lump in my throat. I swallow, but it won't go down. Grandma Cedella moves her chair closer to me and gently rubs my back, which dissolves the lump.

"What is it, granddaughter?" she asks.

I wipe away my tears and speak once my breath steadies. "You said, everything has already been decided by me. But I don't see how I would have chosen to go through all of that. Why would I do that?" I ask, unable to look her in the eye. "The amount of trauma it caused me, I just... I just don't understand, Grandma." I burst in to tears again.

"Sweet pea, you have done so much work on yourself to be where you are now, and I am so proud of you. But you wouldn't be where you are and how you are today, if you hadn't gone through that. There are lessons everywhere, and you must see the blessing. We are sometimes challenged and stretched to grow. This is part of the human condition."

The silence is broken by a cockerel calling.

"Hmm," Grandma begins again. "Humans bury things to ignore them, not realising that is where the gold resides. Digging deep destroys patterns and unlocks doors, because that is where all answers are found. You have opened and walked through many doors, but there is one that you have opened and closed many times over the years, and it remains with you because there is still healing to do. You last looked at this door six years ago, Symona," she says as she points to a door that appears in the distance. I look in the direction she is pointing and see a red door floating above the green grass. "The door is locked, but you already hold the key." I look at her with confusion, so she continues. "The acknowledgement of what you have been avoiding is the key. Identify what it is and you will be able to unlock that door," she says, looking into my eyes. I'm not sure what she sees, but a wave of love overwhelms me that causes my tear ducts to flow again. "I know, darling, I know, but it's time to move forward. I invite you to go and unlock the door, Symona," she says with encouragement. "Of course, you have free will—however, what is not looked at will remain."

"How will I reach the door?" I ask her.

"You will know when you get there."

I walk down the steps and towards the door. By the time I reach it, the sky is jet black, with stars twinkling around me. I turn to Grandma, who is still on her veranda, bathed in the warm orange sun, now standing as she watches me, which brings me comfort. I turn back around and the red door is now floating above me. I instinctively step back, and put my hand on my heart. I close my eyes and whisper a name, before opening them again. Nothing happens. I turn to Grandma for guidance and she slowly nods her head. The door vibrates and lands at my feet. I hesitantly walk towards it. I'm nervous, but calm. I place my hand on the door handle, and it opens. Light instantly floods out, which takes me by surprise. It's blinding, and yet I can see.

"I'm here, Symona." Grandma is now by my side. "There is nothing to fear. The door will not close behind you." She must have felt my fear. "You will be OK. Do you trust me?" I nod. "OK, it's time. Go now. I'll be right here."

I walk in slowly and white light penetrates through my body with such impact that it catches me off guard, making me feel as unstable as a tightrope walker. All I can see around me are vast waves of light. No path, no rooms, no clear direction and no sense of time. The only thing I can do is just trust and continue walking. The further in I go, the more intense the pulsating waves become, which feel like… like Grandma—pure love. I close my eyes to fully bathe in it, whilst still walking. The sensation is like nothing I've ever experienced before. The light gradually becomes less intense, although the feeling remains. I open my eyes and look around. I gasp. Shock, wonder and excitement hit me in different directions. I blink, hoping it's not a mirage, before staring back at the spot. I walk over, as there is only one way to find out. My pace slows down as I approach, until I'm at a standstill. With doubt and hope combined, I tentatively call, "Lucille?"

The little girl with a head full of curls, playing with her toys on the floor, turns around and says, "Mama!" with excitement. A mixture of emotions rise from the pit of my stomach and pour out of my eyes as I watch this little girl—*my* little girl—struggle to stand. In spite of my shock, instinct kicks in and I gently pick her up whilst swaying from side to side. Hearing her heartbeat is music to my ears. Eventually I put her down and sit opposite her crossed legged, to take in the baby girl I thought I would never see. No more than a year old, she looks like me. Similar complexion and features. I look into the pool of her big brown eyes and hear, "I love you, Mama." Surrendering to the surreal, I respond back in the same way, telepathically, whilst lovingly looking into Lucille's eyes.

"I love you too, baby. I always have and always will. I'm just so sorry I couldn't have you. Please forgive me."

"Mama, I know. I wasn't meant to stay. I wanted to feel loved in your womb and then go home. Please don't be upset anymore. It wasn't my time or your time, Mama."

This spirit full of wisdom and delight, my child. I take her into my arms and gently cradle her. She explodes into fits of laughter at being tickled, which makes me laugh too.

"Symona, darling, it's time to go now," calls out Grandma. I don't look behind me because I know she is waiting for me at the door. I don't want to leave Lucille, but I know I have to, so I give her enough hugs and kisses that will last an eternity, before placing her back on the floor amongst her coloured bricks. I walk away and look back until Lucille is almost out of sight.

The intensity of the pulsating waves of light returns, this time causing excruciating pain in my stomach that causes me to close my eyes. In the same moment, a strong wave penetrates my body, causing my eyes to fly back open at the impact. Different coloured blobs of all different shapes and sizes float in front of me. Some are separate and others are connected to each other. I look down and they're coming out of my body, floating out and up into the white space like a large lava lamp. The pain has gone. I stand still, watching the blobs move further and further away like lost children's balloons. I feel at peace. My whole being feels at peace. I breathe in and out deeply, filling my lungs with the best oxygen I have ever taken in. All the blobs disappear, and I continue walking to the exit, which I can now see. I turn back one last time, and I realise it's Lucille. *Lucille* is the source of the light that fills this whole space. Her light, love and energy bathed me before I even saw her.

"Bye, Mama." I hear her as a whisper.

"Bye, baby."

I lunge into Grandma's arms as I step out of the door in floods of tears. She embraces me for a while before leading me back to the veranda and helping me to sit down. As I look out, the red door and surrounding night sky with sparkling stars disappear before my eyes, and the green grass and warm orange sun returns. I open my mouth to speak but the list of questions in my head do not translate to sound. Yet Grandma responds.

"I know darling. Your daughter has been with me since she returned home. Although you had an abortion seventeen years ago, she decided to appear in the way she felt would bring you the most comfort. Your daughter loves you, and as you have seen, she embodies the name you gave her. Lucille. Light. Your light," she says, touching my face.

"But I… I…" I'm struggling to compute all of this.

"With thought comes emotion, feeling and motion. Everything has a reason. Nothing is just because. You made a decision then, which was decided years before then. I know it's hard to believe, but in order to move forward, you must let go. You saw the build up of residue leave your body—it has all gone now. And the void you felt, have always felt, should now be filled. However, you now need to consciously align with your mind, so you do not continue to carry guilt and self-sabotage there."

"What do you mean Grandma?" I ask.

I watch as Grandma puts her right hand out to the sky, pinches her index finger and thumb together and pulls her hand down. Like a magician removing a tablecloth from a table, the landscape before us is replaced with a blanket of calm water. Grandma touches my elbow, instructing me to stand up and I follow her to the front of the veranda. Holding onto the rail, Grandma says, "Watch," whilst placing her right hand on my head and her left hand into the stream of water in front of us.

Reflected in the water's surface, I see a younger version of me crying uncontrollably in the toilet. There's a man behind the door, asking her what's wrong with concern. Grandma creates ripples in the water by moving her hand. Once the water settles, I see the younger me lying in bed, turned away from a man, silently crying. With every motion and stillness of the water, I'm presented with the same scenarios with different men and various times of crying alone. Grandma removes her hand from my head and takes the other hand out of the water. She says, "Thank you Oshun," and the landscape returns.

Lost for words, the tears stream down my face. I feel numb, but words finally come pouring out my mouth. "I took precautions, Grandma. I did everything right, but I didn't know the condom split. I thought God punished me. I was devastated that I was forced to choose, and heartbroken that my boyfriend cheated on me and abandoned me, leaving me to deal with everything by myself. I just, I just…" My words dry up, and I sob into Grandma's bosom, allowing my hot salty tears to speak their own language.

"Lucille knows. We, your ancestors know. You have done a lot of inner work already, but it needs to continue to ensure growth. What you seek is seeking you. Stop being so time obsessed and just be present. Nothing for you will pass you. Everything happens for a reason. See the lesson and learning and keep it moving. Consciously choose your situation. Nothing good ever comes from running in the opposite direction to the wind. And lastly, red flags and sign posts are there for a reason." She takes in a deep breath and exhales. "Symona look at me. I'm so proud of you. This is your home, your spirit is always connected to here and so you can come anytime to visit me and Lucille, if you wish. The door is always open." She kisses the centre of my forehead and steps back, leaving a tingling sensation that spreads to my eyes. "Also, it's important for me to say, my daughter would have understood your reasons. She would have supported you and loved you unconditionally. Please know that." I think I have always known that deep down, but the fear of seeing judgment and disappointment in my mum's eyes was too much of a risk.

"Will you still talk to me?" I ask.

"Only when invited, from now on. If you need to speak to me, just call me. You must go now, granddaughter. I love you."

We tightly embrace, and I begin to walk down the veranda steps and back through the luscious green garden. As I do so, I notice the warm orange sun is replaced by purple rays—coming from me.

*

A banging headache jolts me out of my sleep. It's three am on a Sunday morning. *Ugh!* I feel like I have swallowed a cactus and run a marathon, *what the hell?* The bottle of water that I luckily have by my bed doesn't even hit the sides, but it's better than nothing. I close my eyes and focus on my natural breathing rhythm whilst doing a mindful body check from my feet to my head, to see where the tension lies. I place both hands on my chest, over my heart, and it feels as though it's aching. I focus on the beat and the sound becomes magnified, giving the sensation of *another* heartbeat, sending a quick succession of snap shots. *Lucille! Light. Grandma Cedella. The red door. Sun. Blobs floating in the air. Mongoose.* What? *Did that actually happen?*

Lying in the foetal position, I hug the pillow close to my chest, and call Lucille's name. *It's been years since I've done this.* "Lucille." As soon as her name leaves my mouth, a wave of peace washes over me, and I cry tears of joy, because I feel and know this is a breakthrough. The snapshots return. Red door. Blobs in the sky. Release. Peace. Mongoose. Purple light. Red.

Struggling to sleep, I begin searching through storage boxes. Three boxes later, I eventually find what I'm looking for—my red spiral-bound journal. The memories flood back as soon as I hold it. Full of anxiety, pain, sadness and heartache. *I don't need to go back there.* I jump to the pages in the back of journal and decide to write a new entry.

Dear Lucille,

You came! You allowed me to meet you. Thank you, thank you. I'm so happy and honoured. There will never be enough words to express what I want to say, but please know you have been in my heart for seventeen years. I'm truly sorry. If you want to come through again to have an Earth experience, my door is always open to you. However, I will understand if you want to choose a different Mummy next time round.

My adorable, beautiful child of light, I will love you always.
Your Mother x

I read it over and over again, to ensure I've said everything I want to, and once satisfied, I close the journal for the last time. The red spiral wiring is a struggle to pull out, but I manage it without drawing blood. Once it's removed, I take every page from the book and rip the loose pages up as small as I can, stuffing them into my dressing gown pockets. It's silly o'clock but I don't care—I need to do this now.

I switch on all the lights and step out into my mini, mini, concrete garden. I feel bad putting the pieces of paper in the plant pot, but the plant has already died, like my past, which until now I kept alive. I set the paper alight and watch my words transform and disintegrate into the air.

Peace.

Chapter Twenty-Two

Mr TK Maxx

Work was tough today; in fact, it's been tough the last couple of months, but I'm done. My Christmas break starts now and I don't want to see anything work related until January. I've hardly taken any holiday this year, it's not good because I'm exhausted now, but I hope it pays off. I took on more responsibilities because I'm determined to get a promotion early next year, if that doesn't happen, I'm out. I now have the whole of December off, and I'm looking forward to resting. I wish I was going somewhere hot, but the thought of finding clothes, packing, getting to the airport, dealing with jet lag etc, etc was tiring just thinking about it. I also didn't fancy travelling far on my own. Chan would have been up for coming with me, but I just want to be by myself, be silent and do nothing. The staycation in Brighton for a couple of nights is going to have to do. The water is not blue and neither is the sky, but I'll take it.

I'm exhausted and I just want to get home, and yet I'm walking away from the bus stop and towards Lewisham shopping mall. A few squashed apples and bananas on the ground reveal that market stallers were there, but aren't now. Hair shops, supermarkets and TK Maxx are the only places open. It's cold, dark, and there aren't many people around. I don't need anything, I barely have the energy, but I just want a different scenario to break up my work-home, work-home pattern, which I've been doing for the last couple of months. It's winter, so it's normal, but I've also not really wanted to see anyone or do anything.

Just as I'm approaching the department store, a tall Black man with dreads that reach the middle of his back walks out and stops. Head down and engrossed on his phone, he stops to type. As I walk past him to enter he looks up, our eyes meet, and he smiles. *He's really handsome.* But I'm not interested—and yet I look back. He's still there looking at me, smiling with one eyebrow raised. I walk past the colour-coded bags, which I never do. I'm distracted. Before my mind could even have a discussion with my legs it was too late, because they're walking back to him.

"Hey. I'm Symona. I saw you and thought I would just come over and say hi."

He turns around with a surprised look on his face. "Hi. I'm glad you did. I'm Marcel," he says, holding his hand out, which I shake.

"So getting straight to the point, since I'm on a mission to get something before this shop closes, are you single?" I ask. He nods his response.

"Do you have children?"

He nods again, and then says, "But they are teenagers now."

"Oh, so how old are you?"

"Forty-one, I started young, and you?"

"Thirty-eight and no children yet." He breaks into a smile. "What?" I ask.

"Sorry, I was just admiring you. How are you thirty-eight? You're beautiful."

"Thanks. So are you." *What am I doing?* "Anyway, I need to go now. It was nice meeting you." *I know I'm running away.*

"Can I have your number?" he asks. I hesitate. "OK, how about I give you my number and I'll leave the ball in your court to call me?" he offers as an alternative.

I hand him my phone so he can add his details.

"Nice meeting you," he says, handing the phone back.

"You too. Bye," I say as I walk back into the store.

I'm not interested in men at all at the moment, and yet I approached. *Why?* Why did I do that? My focus is all over the place, and the railings and railings of clothes and shelves of stuff before me adds to the distraction. *Swimwear… I only have bikinis. Perhaps I should get a swimming costume for the spa?* I abandon this thought and head to my happy place—homeware, on the third floor.

All different shapes and sizes, I love a unique-looking picture frame. *Photos… Patrick…* Just like that, I'm triggered. I'm affected, how could I not be? But I've been through worse and survived. In comparison this is a breeze. *Too nonchalant.* Not a breeze, but manageable. My trust issues have been reopened, which I'm working through, as I'm not trying to make this my story. My confidence hasn't gone anywhere, which is good to see, but why did I feel the need to go over and talk to that guy when I had no intention of anything coming from it? I also have no intention of buying anything, so this is all pointless.

The warmth of the shop is immediately replaced by an even

colder, darker and later evening. I'm annoyed at myself, as it didn't need to be this way. I should have just gone straight home, but it is what it is. The bus arrives within three minutes of me arriving at the bus stop, just like the app predicted, along with the answer to my question. *Control.* I approached Marcel to feel in control.

Marcel—deleted.

*

It's so strange seeing the sea and having the heating on, but Brighton was everything I needed. Two nights in a beautiful room with a beautiful view, great spa facilities, not too far from home, the best fish and chips and peace.

My phone pings, notifying me of all the messages I've received whilst my phone's been off for two days. *I daren't look at emails, I'm not doing it.* The last unopened message is from someone on Facebook Messenger. *Who's that?* I stare at the art-filtered picture in disbelief, because I thought my Facebook account was like Fort Knox. *Clearly not. How did he find me?* I open the message.

Facebook
2nd December 2017

Hi Symona, I realised when I left you that I wanted to see you again, but of course didn't have your number. Whilst I hoped you would call, I didn't want to leave it to you. So I went on Facebook. To be honest you weren't hard to find,

**especially as we have one mutual friend and you came up as
a suggested friend. However, I totally get it looks stalker-ish. I
assure you, I'm not a stalker.
I would love to hear from you.**

Marcel ☺

Facebook
4th December 2017

**Hi Marcel, I'm glad you cleared this up without me having to
ask. I don't believe you're a stalker, so no need to worry. How
are you?
Symona.**

We exchange messages over the next couple of days and decide to
meet up on the weekend. I actually like the fact that he searched
for me… and I don't. I wouldn't have bothered, but that's just
me. If I hadn't have gone to the shopping mall, I wouldn't have
met him. Would I have still bumped into him if I used the other
entrance? I took his number and deleted it, I closed the lines of
communication, and he found me again. What are the chances
of that? *A sign?* My intention is to see what he's about, that's it—
because I'm intrigued.

*

He looks content, staring out of the window to the beautiful view, which is spoilt by the dishwater colour of the River Thames. It disappointedly looks nothing like the vibrant blue in the opening credits of EastEnders. I'm running a little late, as I forgot about the walk from Greenwich overground, but it's all good. Marcel is looking in a different direction so cannot see me walking at a brisk pace whilst I touch up my foundation and re-apply my lipstick, *thank God*. The walk feels like an eternity, I eventually arrive.

"Hey, I'm sorry I'm a little late."

He stands up to greet me and gives me a little hug. "Ah no worries, at all. It's good to see you," he says, smiling.

I love this winter look on men. Polo neck, blue jeans and boots, simple yet classy. The aftershave he's wearing, lovely—teeth, not so much. *Don't be shallow, teeth can be fixed.*

"You look lovely, and this restaurant is a great choice," he says, looking around at the ship-inspired restaurant wrapped in 360 degree views.

"Thank you. So do you. I know eleven in the morning is a strange time for a date, but as this is more of a meet-up, I thought I'd make it casual."

"It's all good, I was off today anyway so it worked well for me. I'm going to start Christmas shopping after, to get it out the way. So, have work bugged you yet?"

"Don't know, haven't looked. Hah! Whatever it is, they are capable enough to sort it out. I've always been really hands-on, and that doesn't help anyone. So I'm all about delegation and creating boundaries now, and they have to get used it. To be fair it's also the quiet period, so it's a great time to let go. I enjoyed my staycation in Brighton."

"Nice," he replied.

"When were you last on holiday?" I ask.

"Erm… Must have been six years ago, we went to Antigua."

"Who's we?"

"The family—myself, children and wife," he says.

"You have a wife?" I ask, looking at his hand for a ring. "You said you were single."

"I'm married, but we've been separated for two and half years, which is why I'm not wearing a ring."

"OK… How long have you been married for?"

"Eleven years, but I've known her since we were eighteen years old."

"What! So why have you separated now? And how old are your children?" I know I'm asking a lot of questions, but now's the time.

"I guess we want different things now. My daughter is twenty-one and my son is seventeen."

"I get it. So are you actively looking to date? I only ask since that's a long relationship, and you probably only know who you are as a husband and a father. It's time for 'you time', don't you think?"

"I hear you, but not really. I'm just going with the flow. "

Red flag. I'm not satisfied with the answer. After being with someone for that long you're either gonna go wild with the new sense of freedom, or get into another relationship as soon as possible because you don't know how to be independent.

"So why are you still single?" he asks me. "I mean, you're

attractive, intelligent, ambitious, funny…?"

"I have no idea, but it is what it is. I just haven't met the guy yet."

"How has dating been?"

"It's a rollercoaster ride, and I feel I've had to learn new skills."

"Huh?" he says in confusion.

"Hahah, you know—how to flirt, how to communicate on apps. My confidence has definitely increased."

"I couldn't believe it when you approached me. I was well impressed," he says, smiling.

"Really?"

"Yeah! Men like compliments, too."

"So be honest, if I didn't approach you, would you have come over to talk to me?"

He shakes his head. "No, because I'm shy anyway, and I'm out of practice. I've got no game."

I totally understand where he's at, and it looks like he needs to level up, like I have. *Understand the gaps in capability and fill them.*

There's something about him that I like. It was a good non-date that turned into a date. The conversation flowed. Coffee was exchanged for cocktails, and then a light lunch. We may have still been there if I didn't already have plans to meet Chan at the BFI. I've just updated her.

"Five hours, Syms! How?" Chan asks animatedly.

"I know. I know. I planned to leave after an hour, but he's so easy to talk too. I feel like I have always known him. He also goes to the same gym as me, but I have never seen him. How mad is that?" Before I allow Chan to answer I continue. "We have a lot in common. He's spiritual, vegetarian, has read *In the Meantime*, too."

"Really? Jheeze, you two sound like twins."

"And that is where the similarities end. He is so attractive, but I don't really like his teeth. And he doesn't seem worldly enough—"

"What do you mean?" Chantel interrupts.

"He was baffled as to why I went to Singapore because he said Black people don't go there. Like, *what*? That is a limited view. What else does he think we don't do? The comment irked me. But the deal breaker is that he doesn't want kids. I mean he doesn't want any *more* kids. He saw the disappointment in my face and immediately said he would reconsider, but I told him not to try and fool me, or himself. The strength in his voice was undeniable, Chan. He was sure."

"Hmm. I'm sorry," expresses Chantel.

"No, don't be. Men in my age group are likely to already have kids and potentially not want anymore. It's a harsh reality."

"So it's done then. You aren't gonna try and change his mind?"

"Who has time for that? I can't change a man's mind and I don't want to," I stress.

"Teeth can be changed though. That can be sorted out."

"Again, that's not my job to tell him. He should already know and want to do that for himself. I get what you are saying though, but—"

She interrupts again. "OK, so you need to decide. You either put this down to an encounter and leave it at that, or you develop a strict friendship with no extras. Just make sure you don't block your blessings."

"What do you know about blocking blessings?" I ask, surprise evident in my voice.

"My counsellor is great. I'm just trying to do things differently, Syms. The space needs to be clear for your blessings to come through. I'm not trying to patronise you, I know you know this, I'm just reminding you. Don't fill up your time and attention with maybes."

"Look at my sis and the thirty-year old wisdom she's dropping. Yes! Anyway, enough about me, how are things going with you and Seyi?"

"Really good, that's it. No drama."

"You don't have to tell me, but what issues are you working on with your counsellor?"

She sighs. "Commitment and rejection, as it's always been. I can see my progress but every now and then, rejection fears pop up. Seyi and I are great, but I often think it's too good to be true. So, I'm working on that."

"Well done, sis. Proud of you," I say.

"Changing the subject for a minute. How are you feeling about court for the Patrick case next month? It's come around fast."

I agree. "I know, right! I feel OK. I just want it done now. Not a great way to start the New Year but it's fine. Thanks for booking time off work. I appreciate it."

"It's all good, sis. Everything will be OK".

"I hope so. More drinks, or home? You decide."

"Home," she says.

"Where has my sister gone, who are you?" I ask, laughing.

"She's still here, just a more grounded version."

Chapter Twenty-Three

Reflections

Journal
1st January 2018

I'm at home, not because it's cold and I don't want to pay extortionate prices for rave tickets and ride in triple-the-price taxis (even though I don't). I'm home because I want to be. No other reason than that.

I would love to exchange my flat for a celeb-style LA abode, find love and live in the sun all year round, but it's not meant to be. The Holiday is on again—the predicable New Year's Eve feel-good film, which causes me mild depression as, year after year, it reminds me that my situation hasn't changed. I'm still single. But today, this year, I'm enjoying this movie like it's the first time I'm watching it. (I've seen it seven times).

It's been an interesting year: one of adventure and courage, insight and discovery, breakthroughs and healing, and I wouldn't change any of it. My phone is popping off, which means it's probably 2018 now. Happy New Year!

May I be clear on my intentions, present to the flow, sensitive to my intuition and guided by my ancestors. May nothing for me pass me, and may the people not for me fall away.

I have many questions I don't have the answers to, but I trust they will come.

Chapter Twenty-Four

In Flow

I hate the stair machine with a passion, but it made sense for me to try and love it once I found out it's better than the treadmill for burning calories. Now that I kind of like it, I can't get on it—because of *New Year, New Me* the gym is annoyingly packed. But experience tells me that by the third week of January it will be back to normal. *I cannot wait.*

"Hey, did you jog for your whole thirty-minute workout?"

"Oh, hey Marcel!" I say out of breath and wiping the sweat from my brow. "Yeah, why?"

"I can only last fifteen minutes. I get bored going nowhere," he says, laughing.

"Tell me about it. But the stairs are worse."

"Yeah, I'm not doing that. Hah! Do you want to train together?" he asks.

I hesitate because I'm a get in, work hard, and get out kind of gym-goer. I don't chat or make friends—in fact, I'm sure people think I'm stoosh, but I don't care. I'm focused. I don't know what he's like. "Yeah, sure," I say. *I'm about to find out.*

Journal
7th January 2018

I actually enjoyed the spontaneous session with Marcel yesterday. He would make a really good Personal Trainer—he looks like one and sounds like one, but he's a plumber. My legs and arms are killing me because he worked me hard. They say couples who train together, stay together, and I can most definitely see how that could work—and how it could go wrong. I was really proud of myself. No resistance at all to his instructions, but I think that's down to how he communicates. I have never been a fan of personal trainers who bark orders. My Dad never shouted at me for anything, so I don't see why I should have to take it from someone whom I'm paying to help me get fit. Everyone is different and there are different styles for different people.

Marcel's been going to that gym for over ten years, like me, and in all that time, I've never seen him. First day in the gym after the Christmas break and boom! How? He looked good, and he has a lovely way about him. He seems really caring and attentive. He's in the friend zone—with severe boundaries.

✳

I'm running, I'm in the zone, and I love the feeling. It feels like my mind, body and spirit are aligned and working together. I feel driven, focused and fit, which is why I come to the gym three times a week minimum. The time is carved in and unmoveable, and it's doing wonders for my legs, bum, tum and general well-being. My phone pings. I'm running too fast to look at it, plus

I'm in the zone and it can wait.

I enjoy looking in the mirror and wiping the sweat of my face and chest. It makes me feel accomplished. I head to a different machine, and I see that Marcel is on an exercise bike behind me, having what looks like a pretty smooth ride. He gestures to me to look at my phone. I open the message that I heard come through, which I can now see was from him.

Hey Syms, you're doing a great job, get it, get it, get it! Your bum looks great from this angle by the way.

"Perving on me, I see?" I say with sass.

"No, pure appreciation. How you doing?" he asks.

"I'm good, but I have no idea what you are doing. This looks too easy."

"This is my warm down, hun, don't worry, I'm not slacking."

We end up training together again, and have a mini argument over dumbbells. He's trying to correct my technique, but there's nothing wrong with it. I'm doing the same thing my former personal trainer taught me. It's actually *his* technique that is wrong, but he's having none of it, so we have just agreed to disagree. Now he's watching me do my sets "all wrong". Haha. He's so easy to be around. Funny. Gorgeous. Nice temperament. All positives, just one glitch… He doesn't want kids. Which is fine, we're not together. Plus, I have bigger fish to fry right now. *I just need to get through this month.*

Journal
30th January 2018

Dear Grandma Cedella, please let justice be served today.
And so it is.
Love Syms x

*

"Tea or prosecco?" Chantel asks teasingly. "I know, silly question." Rocco greets us excitedly as soon as we walk into her flat, and it's just what I need.

"Thank you so much for coming with me, sis."

"You don't need to keep thanking me, you know. This is standard sister support," she says as she pops the bottle. Taking a seat at the breakfast bar, my sister raises her glass and toasts my success, in her style. "Here's to the fuckwit getting a taste of his own medicine." Our glasses clink and we knock back the bubbly stuff. Relief rises from our shoulders like the steam on New York pavements, and mine finally sink to their normal position.

"He just didn't get it. He does now," I say. *I really hope he does.*

Hey Ladies,
I'll get straight to the point. Patrick was found guilty. Over two years he must complete a 35-day programme, 30 days' rehabilitation activity and 60 hours of unpaid work. He also has to join the Sex Offenders' Register for five years. I'm sure

251

he gets how serious this is now. I'm happy with the result.
Thanks for your support and words of encouragement. Syms
x

I press send and quickly speak to Grandma in my mind. *Grandma Cedella, I call upon you to protect me from Patrick Hanwell. Please shield me from any harm he may plan against me, and may our paths never cross again. I release all anger. I know I'm loved, blessed, and protected. Thank you for being around me.*

January is over as fast as it arrives, and I'm glad. The year can now begin.

*

I walk to the gym, but then continue walking to the bus stop on Lee High Road. *I just don't have the energy today.* I glance into the barbershop on the corner just before I cross the road—and Marcel glances back. "What the fuck?" he mouths in confusion, looking just as shocked as I am. I watch as he gets up from the tired looking black leather sofa that's screaming to be laid to rest, and comes outside to meet me.

"This is so weird," he says, holding his phone in his hand. "I was just messaging you, look." I look at the half-written message and don't know what to say. We chat for a while until his barber knocks the window and gestures to him.

"OK! Syms, I have to go. I'll call you later."

Interference, that's what this feels like, because we keep randomly bumping into each other. I feel like a pawn in a game of chess. *Grandma, are you playing games?* I don't hear an answer because I already know the answer. *She doesn't interfere.* So what does this all mean? Right now, Marcel and I are friends. We get along so well, and due to my belief that he needs to remain single, I haven't entertained the idea that we could be something else to each other. Even though I'm really attracted to him. He doesn't want any more children, and I'm not trying to catch feelings for someone who doesn't want that. But I'm paying attention and feel I can flow a bit more… I'm not sure, but I'm going to do it.

Flow.

Journal
14th February 2018

Marcel doesn't celebrate Valentine's Day, but he wants to do something on a different day.

He sends me good morning messages every day, and signs off with the rose emoji. It's cute. But I don't want to get used to these things— these things that produce emotions and feelings.

Journal
17th February 2018

Considerate men exist. You matter. You are needed. You are necessary. I see you.

*

**Hey ladies, So, I ended up in A&E over the weekend. I had to cancel plans. I'm OK now, thankfully.
Marcel looked after me.**

"Hey, just seen your message. You better explain yourself. A&E! Why? Hope you are OK now. And Marcel? I thought you were just friends? I beg, don't get blindsided, Syms," Adisa says in a rush, instantly making me regret answering the call.

"Hey hun. My left calf muscle swelled up, which reminded me of my DVT scare years ago in Barbados on the same leg, so got it checked out. For precaution, they gave me an injection—via the largest syringe needle I have ever seen—through the side of my little muffin top, which the doctor then told me I had to do myself over the next three days, to thin out my blood in case there's a blood clot."

"I can barely pluck my eyebrows without my eyes watering, let alone basically stabbing myself. What the hell?" she says in distress.

"I know, but it's all good, it has to be done. Luckily I'm not scared of needles."

I hear her sigh. "So update on Marcel then, please."

"He'd bought cinema tickets to see Black Panther, but since I was still in A&E I had to cancel—"

"Can you just jump to the part that explains how Marcel ended up looking after you, please?" Adisa says impatiently.

"Damn, OK! He picked me up from the hospital and we went to Shoreditch. We found a bar and even with my swollen leg, I danced like I was back in Corks Wine Bar."

"Hahah, so you found a corner to crub in and your hair was sweated out?"

"EXACTLY!"

"I miss those days! Anyway, go on," she says rushing me.

"When he kissed me, my stomach did somersaults. I haven't felt that feeling in a long time. I asked him to book a hotel room, because sometimes spontaneous is good and I wanted to be in a neutral space."

"Wow! Tell me more."

"Hahah. All you need to know is he's good. Caring, considerate, attentive, sensual. I really enjoyed spending time with him. He nearly passed out when he saw the needle for the next injection, though!" I laugh again.

"So what next?" Adisa asks.

"I'm not sure. I have more questions than answers at the moment." *Am I willing to forgo children for love?* is the main one, which I don't share. "All I know is, I'm attracted to him, I enjoy his company and... I don't know."

"I'm glad you had a good time, and I'm glad you're OK. Just be careful, Syms."

"I will. Night, hun."

I end the call, thinking about what she said. *Be careful.* Careful not to catch feelings, be blindsided or waste time. Do men worry about having to be careful?

*

I'm thirty-nine next month, and the weeks are rushing by to get me there. That's how it seems, at least. I've been seeing Marcel practically every week, and I have to admit I'm getting too comfortable in the flow of no intentions, which I need to address.

"How was your day, Syms?" Marcel asks as soon as I pick up the phone.

"Good. I've just finished doing a deep condition on my hair, blow dried it, trimmed it… and then decided to chop it all off," I reply, trying not to give the lie away.

"WHAT? No, no, no. You cut your hair? So how is it now?"

"Really low. Like really low. Not bald though."

"Babe, why? I saw you on Saturday and your hair was so nice in the twist out."

"Don't know, just decided to," I say nonchalantly.

"Send me a pic, now. I'm sure it looks nice as you have a nice face and decent head shape but send me a pic now, please."

"Babe I'm joking. I just trimmed it! HAHAHAH."

"That's not funny, Symona. How would you like it if I told you I cut my dreads?"

I wouldn't like it at all. In fact it would be a deal breaker, *another one*. His dreads are as long as Tasha's and just as beautiful, and I love the smell of the shea butter he makes and uses on them. It's unique to him.

"So, I wanna discuss a few things, because the nature of who we are to each other has changed since we had sex," I tell him, getting serious. "From how we met to now, I just would not have guessed it. I love your company, we get on—on so many different levels—but we are on completely different books, at opposite ends of the spectrum. I'm trying to experience everything you already have, whilst you're finding yourself. I just think we need to set or realign our intentions."

"I hear you hun, and I agree with everything you said," Marcel replies. "I also enjoy being with you, and I want to be with you. You would make a great mother, and I wish I could give that to you because you deserve it, but I can't at the sacrifice of what I want for myself."

"Would you consider adoption?" I ask.

"No. I don't want any more kids at all, which includes, IVF, adoption and fostering." He sounds more certain, and I feel as though all of my options are taken away. Is this it? Do I forego having children to have love? Is this really my story? The best godmother and future aunty in the world is a nice title to have, but is it enough? These are the new questions that I am faced with, and I need to find the answers.

Journal
20th March 2018

**SYMONA, IT'S TIME TO GET REAL**. Do you still want children? Be specific. Do you still want children that you birth? Do you have time to have two children that you birth? (Hmm yes, if I have twins. They run in my family, so it's possible.) Can you afford twins? Can you afford more than one child? Would you be happy being a step-mum? Would you consider adopting? How would you feel if none of these options materialised?

Time isn't on my side, and so I can't keep going with the flow. The *longer it takes to meet someone, the shorter my opportunity to have kids becomes. No one is perfect, no situation is perfect, but being with Marcel is a big compromise, if I do want a child. Flags ignored at the start of a relationship always becomes the reason for the end of a relationship.*

Potential love with no child, or remain single, hoping that I match with a man who wants the same things as me? So many questions, not many answers, and a whole lot of uncertainty. I don't want to make this a thing, but it's a thing. A very big thing, and I know nothing new can come into a space that is already occupied.

*

I wake up with a head full of dreams that for once I don't write down or check the meaning of, because my internal battle whilst awake is clear. My dreams are just playing them out in my sleep. I could do with working from home today. I just need a slower morning that doesn't involve any form of travel, but I'm going to go in—and late, at this rate.

As soon as I get on the bus to Lewisham, I know I've made the wrong decision. The traffic and number of kids tell me I'm closer to nine am than I need to be, which isn't good, but stressing isn't going to change my circumstances. *Solution!* I'll get off at Lee and catch the train from there.

I look up from my phone because I sense someone is staring at me. *I'm right.* I smile at the little boy with the big blue eyes and blonde hair, and he smiles back before pretending to go shy, as kids do.

"Jonny, turn around," his mother says, noticing he is all up in my boat. "Sorry, love," she says to me.

"No need to apologise, it's fine," I tell her as she turns back round, leaving her son—roughly two or three years old—to stare. It wasn't an 'I haven't seen Black people before' stare, *which I have seen a few times.* It was an 'I remember you' stare. *He one hundred per cent recognises my spirit, for sure.* He shows me his book, and I decide to engage. "Zahra's Journey. Do you like that book?" I ask. He smiles and nods. "What insect is Zahra?"

"She's a butterfly," he says, stretching his hands out wide.

"That's right! And can you tell me her colours?

"Yes! Erm, red… black… blue, and lellow" he says proud of himself. It's so cute when children can't pronounce yellow.

My stop is coming up, so I ring the bell, get up and wave to Jonny and say, "Byeee," silently. He waves back smiling. As I step of the bus I hear, "Bye Mum! Bye."

"This isn't our stop Jonny, come on face the front please."

Whilst I want to doubt my ears, I can't. I heard it, and I know he was talking to me. I'm not freaked out because something similar has happened before, at Asta's sister's wedding, over eleven years ago. Her name was Nia, she was about two years old. Sign post then, and sign post now.

As I wait on the platform for my train I search the meaning for butterfly.

To see a butterfly in your dream signifies you are following the right path, transforming and listening to your intuition. It may also refer to your need to settle down.

I wasn't dreaming but it applies. *You can't make this up, even though it sounds it.*

I open my messages and type.

Morning Marcel, fancy meeting up after work?

Sure

He replies.

The day has just begun and I'm already exhausted.

*

"Not much happened, babe, just work," Marcel says, looking at me in a deadpan way.

Not sure how to start, I start anyway, knowing once my mouth is moving my brain will kick in at some point. "So, I've been thinking about us."

"OK," he says nervously.

"We get on really well on all levels, and we've both been transparent from the start, which is really great. Whilst in flow, we have coasted into a relationship, which both of us just accepted. The problem with coasting is there's no direction, and I cannot afford to just drift, not at this age. The reality is, your mind isn't going to change. I know and respect it, but by being with you, I'm closing my mind to the possibility of having children. I was happy to go with the flow because I was happy to avoid committing to a decision around children. Trust issues and fear, based on past stuff, are the reasons for the avoidance, and so I have never allowed myself to really soak into the idea. I own it. I think you are a great person, Marcel, but I have to stop seeing you."

He looks at me for a moment before speaking. "I didn't think I would meet anyone again after my separation. I met you and thought you were amazing. You *are* amazing. The way you think and the way you are showed me a different way to be in relationships. Your communication and listening skills are exceptional... and it's a shame."

"I felt your love and thoughtfulness, our connection is real and how we met was not a coincidence, but it's time. Nothing is lost. I've also gained."

"Do you want to keep in touch?"

I sigh, it wasn't meant to come out as loud as it did. "I think it's best not to, to be honest. I'm always going to be attracted to you. A clear break would be best for me, which I would like you to respect."

"Sure. OK. Well... Symona Brown, it's been nice knowing you."

He holds me tightly in an embrace. I'm upset, I know he is too. I'm going to miss this, all of it. His kisses, being caressed, his morning messages, seeing him. But it has to be done. Consciously choose your situations.

Chapter Twenty-Five

The Early Birthday Present

I hated having periods when I was younger. The cramps, accidents and flow were all one big inconvenience. Now, I just see it as a gift. Each month I am gifted with another chance to have a child. *Oh, how the tables have turned!*

I saw it as an inconvenience today though, even though I knew it wouldn't affect the scan. It just so happened that my period decided to stay longer and cross paths with my egg count check. Having to explain to Dr Shah and female nurse, Marie, before pulling my tampon out and wrapping it in tissue, was a lot. That was before having a wand, which reminded me of a giant dildo with lube on it, inserted into me and gently swished about.

They put me at ease. Lying on my back with my head turned right to the screen, I could see the doctor circling things in my empty womb that I couldn't otherwise see. I imagined what it would be like to have a living thing with its own heartbeat pumping away in there, but I didn't have to imagine too hard. The memory of seventeen years ago hasn't faded, but that was then, and this is now. The quiet, airy vaginal ultrasound was filled with noise from the thoughts in my head about the worst-case scenario, whilst battling with hope that everything was OK.

I prayed the results would reveal my egg count was way above four, and that my uterine structure was normal and with no fibroids. That is all I wished for whilst lying there for the ten minutes or so. I got dressed, put in a fresh tampon and prepared my mind for the results.

The doctor's explanations feel rushed and clinical. The diagram he's drawing upside down informs me he has done this and perfected this over the years, but it doesn't make what he's saying make any more sense, and the nurse sitting directly behind me makes me feel even more uneasy. Some doctors need to learn how to talk in layman's terms, because I don't know the medical terminology for my bits—especially the bits that I haven't seen since biology class with Mr Baker. And *warmth*. Give me some warmth! *I'm a single woman coming to you to see if I can still have children This is a big deal for me, which you aren't acknowledging!* I want to say this so badly, but I remain silent, on the verge of tears I don't allow to fall.

I muster up the courage to ask another question, because every answer I've had so far ends with "OK?" at the end, which lands to my ears as "OK? Are we done now?"

The appointment is forty-five minutes long and I have paid £300, so no, I'm not about to be rushed out, even though I heard what I wanted to hear.

"Egg count in total is eight, which is normal. Your womb is in good condition. You have one fibroid, no more than 2.5 centimetres long, and nowhere near the wall lining. Nothing to worry about. OK?" Adisa pops into my head.

"So, if I choose to have my eggs frozen, how much is the rent?" I ask. His face tells me he doesn't like the word 'rent', but that's what it is. They collect the eggs, which they store until you're ready to use them, and in the meantime you pay for storage space. He explains the process and I have already decided it's not for me. That's how I feel now, anyway.

Tasha and my sister offered to come with me to the appointment for support, but I wanted to do it alone. I burst into tears as soon as I leave; relief, gratitude and a different type of anxiousness pouring out of my eyes. The egg count is an approximation, as it can change month by month, so the result isn't set. Nevertheless, I'm glad I went and I have an idea of where I'm at. Mum began her menopause at forty-seven, so that is the rough timeline I have based on genetics. Moving towards forty, further away from an abundance of healthy eggs and towards menopause. *Just wow. This feels surreal real.* And still, for my sanity, I choose to be grateful. I wonder how many people book themselves into a fertility clinic for an egg count check as an early birthday present?

Chapter Twenty-Six

New Beginning

The Cayman Islands have to be some of the prettiest islands I have seen, and also some of the most soulless. There's a gloss, like shiny new veneers that make a smile seem fake because they're too big and bright for the mouth they live in. The place also lacks a strong Caribbean identity—it feels like a mash up of Jamaica and Barbados with country music flung in, which confuses my ears every time I turn the radio on. However, I'm grateful that I get to spend my thirty-ninth birthday week here. I wanted a different experience, and thanks to Zaara's friend Xena, I'm staying with her for free. How kind.

One evening, dressed in black looking like midnight ninjas, we arrive at The Rum Point Club, an hour away from Seven Mile Beach. I'm nervous as I've never kayaked before. I wanted to take the speed boat, but Xena insisted on kayaking as it's an eco-friendly method of transport, kinder to the coral reefs. I knew I couldn't argue with that, so refrained from telling her that I was scared of falling out and worried about how I would get back in.

We're going on the bioluminescent tour, which basically is when the water magically sparkles. The internet version of my description which explains how creatures in the water cause the phenomenon makes my skin crawl, so I prefer my basic one.

We find our rhythm in the kayak and we're soon gliding across the water like pros. With each stroke of the oars, I felt more at ease. The moon looks close enough for us to touch it and be transported to another dimension, whilst the waves are the deepest blue-black I have ever seen, rising, falling and twinkling as it catches the moon's light for as far as my eyes can see, with no land in sight. I have a few mini freak-out moments and question what I should do if I see a shark's fin. I have to shut my eyes and just focus on breathing until those images are drowned out. When I open them, I felt a sense of peace and being at one with the universe.

Ten minutes—*an eternity*—later, we arrive at the bay, and I'm mesmerised by the shimmery water that sparkles and comes alive with every swish and swirl with my hand and oar. I put both hands into the water, cup them together and lift them out, glittery water trickling through the gaps like a mini waterfall back into the sea. This must be the closest feeling to being in *Avatar*. I attempt to spell out my name with my oar, and take so much pleasure watching any shape I created shine before disappearing. I just hope I always remembers this moment, because this place is truly something.

We stay for a while before beginning the journey back to shore. Xena and I have a chat about life and where we're at, before peace overcomes us and we are silent within our own thoughts. *I haven't experienced this kind of visual and silent peace before. It's so beautiful.* The clouds are grouping together though, and we agree rain will soon come. I can see Grandma in my mind's eye. Before now, I have only ever seen her when I'm asleep. The warm rays in her world envelop me from inside—I can feel her love. My thoughts are interrupted by numerous flashes of lighting in all different directions. Surreal and magical, I feel vulnerable underneath the forks and jags of electricity above us. There's nowhere to hide.

"Symona, I'm here with you and there is nothing to fear. Do not let distraction take you off your path." I hear my Grandma say.

Every flash slashes the images of past memories and feelings that no longer serve me.

Dean. Sean. Abortion. Dad. Anger. Aaron. Guilt. Stephen. Regret. Conor. Prejudice. Patrick. Betrayal. Slashed and disintegrated. *Spiritual alchemy.* New space created for new memories, alongside the remains of past good. Grandma smiles and disappears as soon as my foot touches the dry land.

Changes and challenges are necessary for growth. Any moment can be a new beginning. Welcome thirty-nine—and I look forward to meeting you, forty.

ChapterTwenty-Seven

Broken Chords

The sound of my rolling suitcase on the pavement doesn't give me the same feeling of joy when I return from holiday, it never does—and it certainly doesn't today. There is nothing worse than returning from the land of pure sun and shine to be greeted with rain. April showers could have just held off until I got home, *damn*. Instant holiday blues and back to reality.

Suitcase unpacked and stored away and holiday clothes shoved in the washing machine, did I even go away? Yes, I did, as proven by my 500 emails. *Why?* I get on with it, so that I'm on top of everything by the time I walk into work tomorrow morning. The first email I go to is the summary report sent to me by Sarah, the most senior person in my team. All updates are there, nice, clean and clear, no waffle—just as I taught her. I reach point six and I literally cannot believe it. *How the hell has Jenny been promoted to a higher position than me?* It makes no sense when she has less experience.

"Hey Angela, how are you?"

"Hi Symona, I'm good, but how are you?"

"Yeah, I'm good, Cayman was amazing, and—" she interrupts me.

"Syms, you're calling me because you have just found out about Jenny, right?"

"Mmhmm," I manage to say.

"So, how are you feeling about it? I know it's a silly question."

"Angela, I didn't think feeling numb and rage at the same time was possible. Everyone knows deals happen on the golf course and in bars, through lines of coke. Things haven't changed. I've never been about that life, hence why I'm not in those circles and here we are. I'm overlooked again. I'm done. So done. Knowing your stuff and working hard doesn't always get you places, and eight years means nothing. We've all been sold a lie. It's who you know, that's it. Network. After everything I've done and continue to do, I still don't get what I deserve. How is that possible?"

"I get all of it, and I'm so sorry. It goes without saying that I didn't know. I found out via email at the same time as everyone else."

"I know. I've just found out, it's fresh. Let's speak tomorrow when I'm in, OK?"

"Sure, hun. Get some rest."

"Thanks, will do. Bye Angela."

Journal
17th April 2018

Relationships have been my main focus in the last two years, and rightfully so. I have worked through a lot of things, and now I have to turn my attention back to my relationship with work, because this cannot continue. I'm livid. I've given so much for little return.

It's an unfair and unhealthy relationship. I wouldn't accept this substandard treatment from a man, so why with work? 'That's life' is not a worthy reason. Office politics and racism is ruining my ability to thrive and I'm done with allowing them to affect my growth, well-being and financial wealth.

Journal
18th April 2018

My strong email to my manager and HR ensured an informal meeting was arranged immediately. I brought with me a bag full of receipts, which included all my achievements in the last eight years, my up to date CV—and Jenny's CV from when I hired her under three years ago. Do not play with me! And lastly my appraisal, where said manager promised me a promotion in January. Four months into the New Year and nothing. I requested to see the job description for Jenny's role: surprise, surprise. Nada. My grievance is based on discrimination, there's no other way to view it. As the most senior and only person of colour in my division, it's crystal clear. I've left them to get back to me in regards to telling me how they are going to rectify it before I go down the formal route. I'm hoping they'll do right by me, even with their lack of integrity highlighted in fluorescent lights. As we know, hope is a waiting game, which I don't have time for.

*

I've been summoned to my favourite hidden restaurant in Blackheath by Chantel. The maître d' escorts me upstairs and…

"Surpriseeeeeeee!"

I had a feeling. The ladies are here, including Angela.

"Why didn't you tell us?" Chan screams.

"Because I haven't signed the contract yet," I say looking at Angela, smiling.

"It's a done deal anyway, and you deserve it. Hello Account Director! Woop, woop, woop!"

"Ah, thanks guys. It's taken two months to get here, but I'm pleased. Even though it was informal, I was prepared to go further. I got an employment lawyer for guidance and I was prepared to go all the way. Eight years, to resign and start again? No, I wasn't prepared to go out like that. It's not my dad's company, but I have contributed to its success—"

"Yes sis, so proud of you," Chan excitedly interrupts.

"—and so I've also set up a company called Sym-phony PR. I have been consulting outside of work hours. There's no conflict of interest Angela, you know me," I say, laughing as I look over at her. "Two months in and it's doing well," Everyone excitedly claps.

"Oh, I'm here for all of this!" shouts Zaara.

"Business woman come through! I'm so proud of you," says Adisa, clicking her fingers.

"Come on, get your glasses up. Here's to new beginnings, boss moves and knowing your worth. Congratulations, Syms, and we wish you all the best with Sym-phony PR," announces Tasha. "Cheers!"

"Thanks everyone," I tell them. "Thank you for your continuous support, it means so much. Learn from the lessons and keep it moving. Cheers!"

Chapter Twenty-Eight

Emerge

2nd January 2019

The last six months of last year were mental, in a good way. After my promotion was announced it's been all go, go, go. Meeting new clients and doing so much more travel, which I love. New Year's was spent in Barcelona with the girls, which was incredible. There was no way I was going to have another year of staying at home. Sym-phony is going well and I just feel so good—grounded and self-assured.

Every year since my thirtieth birthday I've bought myself a ring. My collection varies in colour and style. Although diamonds represent my birthstone for the month of April, I've refused to buy myself a diamond ring for obvious reasons. However, I'm nearly forty and I'm tired of waiting. I saw a ring with three 18-carat diamonds in a row set on a gold band, and it looked like it already belonged to me, so I bought it. My extra-early fortieth birthday present to myself. It goes without saying that I've put it on my wedding finger, you know, just to see what it looks like.

Last night, when we got back from Spain, I felt so inspired. Using pictures and words closely matching my desires, I created a brand new vision board and placed it at the side of my bed so it's the first thing I see when I wake up and the last thing before I switch the light off at night.

At the top right hand corner of the board is the word EMERGE, which is my word for the year. This is the first time I've assigned a word, and I feel this captures it all. The mantra I've written that goes with it is:

May I step into all that I am, to be the best version of myself. May I trust that solutions will always be found, and may my partner, my destined match, come out of hiding and emerge.

At the centre is a picture I found of a pregnant Black woman, with a Black man lovingly holding her from behind. Next to it is a picture of a Black woman and Black man holding their baby, both consumed with joy at their new addition to their family.

These are the key things for this year   being surrounded by health, wealth, joy and symphony. I look forward to emerging further into my potential, presence, power, and into my ability to pivot, change, and walk away when necessary.

Chapter Twenty-Nine

Charlie?

Journal
15th April 2019

My birthday yesterday was everything I wanted it to be. Surrounded by twenty-one people whom I love dearly, in a plush private room, with waiters and a vibe we controlled. Good music, good food, good people. It was exactly how I wanted it. I have officially joined The 40 Club. Like every other birthday before, I feel exactly the same, in spite of the rising numbers. The anxiety and sleepless nights leading up to this big day has, at times, been unreal and it's just come and gone, like it was no big deal at all. The cheek of it! Lol.

I caused myself to have a mini mid-life crisis due to triggers—comparison, opinions and pressure from myself and others. It's all valid, I felt what I felt which I'm glad I acknowledged, because I've worked through a lot of stuff. The learning doesn't stop, as Mum has always said, much to my disappointment, but I get it, she's right. I can see how much I've changed in three years, let alone the past ten or twenty years. The biggest lesson? You can't rush what isn't ready, and buried trauma doesn't go away, it just sits and controls silently.

I didn't want to look at the past, because I thought I would be relieving the pain again and again, but you know what, it's nowhere near the same. Talking about it has helped me to work it out, out of me. My counsellors past and present—Debbie and Hamilton respectively and, of course, Grandma—and journaling, have been pivotal in the process. Spirituality from a place of ancestral understanding is what I'm interested in. My experiences with Grandma are both dreams and not dreams at the same time. So much of our knowledge and ways have been lost and labelled as bad. I'm connected to God and my ancestors—how can that be bad?

My focus was on finding a man. I was looking for a particular car, when all along, I had the keys. I found and unlocked myself and I'm in a better place for it. A better place to fully receive what comes my way. The man and subsequent baby haven't arrived… yet, but I feel grateful. Grateful for all I do have. I let go of fear and choose love, trusting in what's already written. Trusting that what I'm seeking, is also seeking me. Nothing for me will pass me. I'm looking forward to this chapter.

Journal
18th April 2019

I really didn't want to work my birthday week but I had to, because it's just so busy. Tomorrow is the start of the long bank holiday weekend, so it's all good. I don't really want to go to this immersive play Xena has invited me too, but I will, because she has just moved back to London from Grand Cayman. Zaara and Chan are also joining. I'll be fine once I get there, plus I don't plan to do anything over the long bank holiday weekend besides resting.

*

I arrive just after six-thirty pm at the venue in Holborn, hot and a little dehydrated as I had two G&T's with my team a couple of hours before, in the local pub, as we finish work at three pm the day before all long Bank Holiday weekends. I see Zaara straight away in the queue.

"Hey hun, how are you?" she asks. Without waiting for me to respond, she says, "I am so flipping hot, I feel like I'm melting."

"Me and you both hun," I say with no energy. "It's been a long week and I'm already frazzled. I love the sun but this is just clammy hot."

"We just need a sea breeze and a sandy beach." Zaara says, laughing. Her hair is out and her brown afro with copper ends looks just gorgeous.

"All this is yours?" I ask, pointing to her hair. She nods. "Why the hell do you cover it up so often, it's gorgeous!" I say, gushing.

"That's *because* I cover it up. Protection, girl. I'm all about the protection."

We check each other out and both agree that we've opted for the minimal-dress-up look. In other words, we found something in our wardrobe that was passable.

The event is set in Harlem in the seventies. The music genre is funk and Soul Train—think James Brown. As it's immersive, everyone is invited to dress up—however, I'm pleased so many other people have opted for the minimalist look, too.

"Thankfully there's no fake afro in sight," I comment to Zaara.

"Oh yeah," Zaara says, scanning the queue. "There is nothing more cringe than seeing a white middle-aged man or woman wearing fake dreads or a fake afro, attempting to take the theme seriously whilst taking the piss out of us. But they seem to have listened."

"What do you mean?" I ask with a confused look.

"Didn't you see the email that stressed our hair is not a costume, so unless you have a natural afro, no afro wigs allowed."

"Oh, that's great," I say, pleasantly surprised. I loosen the bow on burnt orange shirt that I regret wearing and flap my arms to get some breeze. It doesn't help. I just need to be still and take it, but I'm so hot. My black culottes are pulling in the heat, and my open-toed platform shoes that looked comfortable, aren't. I know I have two hours, max.

I hate dress up—*the second reason why I didn't really want to come.* This event is just about bearable because the dress code isn't too restrictive, unlike the numerous fancy dress parties I've turned down over the years. It's not my thing. Every workplace I have ever worked at knows this, and yet the pressure to join in on work 'themed' summer and Christmas parties is so annoyingly intense. I've always done the bare minimum, just to shut people up.

One year the theme was 'come as an artist or as a famous painting' for a summer party. I went as Frida Kahlo and was accused of wanting to look pretty as I didn't do a mono brow. My accuser was right, though. I was doing it for participation and not for the tacky prize and pictures that would come back to haunt me. The creative bunch went all out that year. Valletta went as a tin of shit as homage to the work by Piero Manzoni. She made it from scratch, and thankfully she won. Imagine losing to someone who has put in less effort? *Hmm. Work-life.*

Angels and Devils, I must say, was the only time I made an effort. I went to this Christmas party as Cruella De Vil. I was so proud of the effort I put in. Donald Trump showed up, the Pope (with a devil's tail poking out) and Kaonashi from Spirited Away, which was a winner. That level of detail I will never be able to compete with, so I don't. I stay in my lane, knowing a prize will not be coming my way and I'm alright with that. Though let me be clear, if a sabbatical for three months was offered as a prize, cash in the hundreds, or a ten-day all-inclusive holiday somewhere more than six hours away, then it is safe to say that *'Let the games begin, biatches'* would be my fight slogan. The love for dressing up would be dug up from the deepest part of my dormant spirit and rise like a phoenix bursting through the hatred of this type of 'fun', shattering my can't-be-arsed mantra. But since that's not going to happen...

Zaara interrupts my thoughts to tell me that Xena and Chan will be here soon. Now at the front of the queue, we enter the building and are transported to the seventies. First stop—the ladies. We're just leaving the bathroom when Chan and Xena, who also have the same idea, arrive.

"It's so good to see you! Group hug," Xena says, and we all oblige.

A guy, who has really made an effort with his brown suede costume comes over. Approximately six feet tall, rich dark brown skin with a kissed-by-the-sun glow and big, brown eyes that are warmly intense. *I'm guessing he's Ghanaian?* He greets us in an American accent.

"Hey ladies, I'm Charlie from Harlem. Welcome."

We all say 'hi' in-sync, and I introduce each of us, *I don't know why.* "This is Xena, Chan, Zaara, and I'm Symona," I say, smiling at him.

He looks at me and asks, "So, did you all just get here?" I nod. "Let me tell you what happens. You're going to grab a drink at the bar, and then head over there to the club manager," he says pointing to someone on the left-hand corner of the room, "and he will tell you your table number."

"OK, thanks Charlie," I say, as we begin to walk over. Charlie touches my elbow and I stop to look at him.

"Symona, you have a really beautiful smile."

"Oh, thank you" I pause and look at him with suspicion before asking "Are you on script or off script right now?"

"I'm so off script right now," he says smiling. "You are a beautiful woman."

"Thank you." I say smiling whilst choosing to pay more attention to this man in front of me. He has big kind eyes that I can read. I see a thought, which I choose to ignore. I turn back and see my friends are heading towards the closed, big brown double doors next to a sign that says *dining room* in gold italic writing.

"Let me walk you over," Charlie says. Once we catch up, he

asks Xena if they know their table number.

"Yes, we are on table 60," she says.

Charlie walks past us and opens the door to where the music is coming from. "All the tables have numbers, table 60 is just over there. Have a good evening, ladies," he says, addressing us all. "Symona, I'm going to come and find you later OK?" he says to me. I smile and nod my response.

"Well, look who has an admirer!" comments Xena, followed by nods of agreement from Zaara and Chan.

"Behave yourselves," I say with a semi-straight face, in an attempt to shut down the beginnings of a teasing conversation. The band starts, and I catch myself discreetly searching the room for Charlie. *There is something about him*. He looked younger than me, but his whole approach was smooth.

The play is happening around us. 'Supper Boogie' is an interesting concept: an immersive theatre experience with audience participation, a live band and three-course dinner. However, by the time we get to the mains, we're confused about the mish mash. We chat between songs and somehow manage to pick up the storyline along the way.

"Hey ladies, I'm just checking if everything's OK?" Charlie asks, coming over.

I wipe my forehead and neck. "It's really hot in here, and we have been waiting a long time for our drinks…"

"OK, no problem, let me look into that for you now, because I'm on shortly." He adjusts his head mic.

"Thank you."

"Fancy joining the Soul Train?" he asks, looking at me. I

politely let him down. "No problem." He shrugs and heads off to find the nearest waiter.

"Girl, if you didn't know before, you should definitely know now—you have an admirer!" says Chan, backed up by the others.

As the drinks arrive, I excuse myself and go to the bathroom, the only place with an air con breeze. As I walk back to the table, I feel a different energy, and I look around to try and detect where it's coming from. I notice there are a few handsome men in small groups, looking dapper in their seventies attire, fitting in well with the décor and the massive disco ball hanging from the ceiling. *Must be that.*

I take my seat and notice Charlie interacting with a female audience member from across the room, whom he leads to the centre of the dance floor. *Of course he's selected her, Symona — they're of a similar age and she is gorgeous.* The Soul Train does look like fun, but it's just too hot. Everyone's using whatever makeshift fan they can find to fan themselves.

"Come on ladies, let's just get up and dance for a bit. It's mad hot, but let's shake a quick leg," I suggest, standing up and hoping everyone will follow. Everyone agrees but Xena, who remains at the table. I spot Charlie at the same time he sees me. *He's coming over.* We dance together whilst speaking about surface level things. *He's actually gorgeous.* I try not to sweat more than I already am.

"So, I have rehearsals first thing tomorrow so I've got to leave now—well, after I get changed," Charlie says, before pausing and continuing. "Can I have your number? I would like to see you again."

I'm unsure, but say yes, based on his whole approach and my intrigue about him.

"Actually, can I give you mine? My phone is in the dressing room," he says, beaming.

"Oh, my phone is at the table, erm hold on. Chan, can I borrow your phone, please?"

She unlocks it and hands it straight to Charlie, grinning.

"OK, it was nice to meet you, and I look forward to speaking to you soon," he says, handing Chan's phone back to me.

"Likewise," I say, smiling and pressing save on his entry.

"*You know he likes you, you know he likes you, ugh, ugh, ugh!* Come on, dance with me," Chan says, singing and throwing some tired shapes as I give her phone back to her.

I give up when I glance down and see my tired lifeless two-step. My feet are killing me, I'm still hot and I decide to call it a night.

*

The next day, I call Charlie at five pm, but he doesn't answer so I leave a message.

"Hey, it's Symona, from last night. Call me back when you're free."

He calls back, I miss it. I call him back, he misses it. At seven pm, his name flashes up on my phone.

"Hey Symona, this is Charlie! Sorry we keep missing each other. How are you? Did you enjoy the show?"

"Hey Charlie. It was really good, but it was just too hot. I

guess the air con decided to break down on opening night, huh?"
I say breezily.

"That's exactly what happened," he tells me, laughing. "All
the actors struggled too, but it should be sorted for the next show
on Monday."

"Cool. Well, I just want to say... how you approached me
last night was so good. I never get approached like that from men
here. How long are you in London for?"

"Oh, thanks. I'm here for the duration of the show."

"So, what part of America are you from?" I ask, intrigued.
There's a slight pause.

"I'm an actor from Finsbury Park, Symona," he says, breaking
into a North London accent and laughing.

"OMG, I feel like an idiot now, I was so convinced!" I say,
laughing too.

"Nah, don't worry about it, I feel good knowing my accent
was believable."

"But it wasn't just the accent, it was also the approach and the
gentle persistence..."

Our chat is effortless and the conversation is rich. *There's a
lot of commonality, which is nice. I have never met a man who likes
going to the theatre, and here's Mister Theatre himself.* This is great,
I can suggest going to see plays without moaning, and we can
review and discuss afterwards.

"So, are you religious or anything?" he asks casually.

"No, I'm spiritual. I believe that 'We are spiritual beings—'"

"'—Having a human experience'! Me too," he chimes in,
finishing the sentence.

Yes. The checklist now has a few ticks. Confident, emotionally intelligent, funny, engaging, well-spoken and spiritual.

After thirty minutes of chatting, the question I'm dreading comes.

"So how old are you?" he asks.

"Guess," I playfully respond, knowing I'm gonna get burnt.

"Erm… twenty-eight?" he volunteers.

"Higher."

"Thirty-two?" he questions with doubt.

"No, try again."

"Thirty-three?" he questions, with a tone that indicates he doesn't want to offend. I decide to cut to the chase because the longer I drag it out, the more dramatic it all becomes.

"No, I've literally just turned forty. It was my birthday four days ago," I say as breezily as possible, in the hope it takes the shock factor out. *Who am I trying to kid?*

"FORTY!" he exclaims, shocked. "You don't look forty. I thought you were twenty-eight like me".

"Oh my God, twenty-eight! You're nearer to my sister's age. Wow. I don't date younger men, I'm a transparent ageist. I mean, you seem cool and wise, but I'm not a cougar. Perhaps we can be friends?" I say, owning my slight renkness.

"I have enough friends, I don't need anymore," he tells me, causing my mouth to hang open. "Look, I know you're an ageist, but how about we meet anyway for a coffee or something, since we do get on? Plus, I have dated older women before. No pressure, of course," he adds, with such maturity. There's a long silence, which I don't know how to fill. He senses it and chips in.

"So, right now you're on the bench because you're not sure if you want to join my team, and that's OK. I invite you to sit on the subs bench, observe, and then make a decision at some point, as you can't sit on the sidelines forever. How does that sound?"

I'm stunned into further silence. Without missing a beat, he says, "Tomorrow, seven pm. Meet me outside Liverpool Street Station?"

I try not to smile but, I know he can hear it within my response. "See you then. Bye."

I hang up and freak out. I have no idea what is going on right now. *Why does he have to be twenty-eight?* He sounds more like my age group, why can't he just be my age? I don't think I'm asking for too much. I wonder how we'll look together? Will it be obvious? Oh man, the Judgement. Will people think we are brother and sister over partners? What will my sister, mum and friends say? *OK, stop. Just stop. Breathe... This is not about anyone else. Are you really going to let other people's opinions determine what you do next? Are you really going to give them that much power? Come on love, you are a big woman.*

So, what do you wear on a date with a twenty-eight-year-old? I decide to start figuring it out now. I look at the array of clothes arranged by colours before me and attempt to put combinations together in my mind. My phone pings—it's Charlie.

Hey Symona, I forgot to say—I will be at rehearsals all day before I meet you. Don't dress-up, just be comfy-casual. Thanks for the chat, and I look forward to seeing you tomorrow.

Yes! I'm loving the consideration. He has just saved me from outfit stress. Jeans, top, Converse and a jacket it is. I'm a bit nervous but I'm also looking forward to it, based on that effortless one-hour call.

I message the Supper Boogie Group to inform Xena, Zaara and Chan of Charlie's age and that I'm going on a date with him, and I'm really surprised by the response. Each person sends a meme back to represent their shock, but all agree I should go for it.

He has a lovely way about him
writes Zaara.

I just loved his confidence. He was into you, Syms. You should give him a chance. Plus, who cares that he's younger
says Chantel.

We're all struggling with our own age group, just enjoy
states Xena.

I'm thankful for their support because this is definitely outside of my comfort zone. I'm gonna update Adisa and Tash when there's something to tell.

Journal

Whilst there are concerns due to Charlie's age, I have no doubts about him as a person. Isn't that weird? I feel like I am being nudged forward towards him by a gentle breeze at the base of my back. Really hard to explain. I wonder if Grandma Cedella is doing something. Hmm, but she said she doesn't interfere with what is already written…

*

The next day, I arrive at Liverpool Street Station and Charlie's already there, waiting. I'm a *little nervous*. I walk directly into his eyeline so he sees me coming. He smiles as he stands up to greet me.

"Hi," he says with open arms. I hug him. *He smells good.*

"How did rehearsals go today?" I ask.

"Really good. I'm directing a play which opens in a week's time, so we are just polishing and ensuring it's tight. Thanks for asking." He quickly packs away the scripts he was looking at back into his bag. "Do you like Thai?" he asks, checking he's got everything.

As he's talking, I notice his full lips, and teeth that are straighter than mine. His chiselled symmetrical face that is accentuated by his big eyes and long, jet-black eyelashes. *I need to apply at least three coats of mascara to achieve that length.* His eyes are what I remember from the other night. Deer-like, striking yet warm.

"…Symona, does that sound OK?"

"Oh! Yeah, sure. I love Thai."

We leave the station and head towards the restaurant. It's really crowded, so our pace is set by the masses of people all around. "So, your age shocked me so much that I forgot to ask you what your real name is," I say, laughing. "I can't keep calling you Charlie."

"Oh yeah, I completely forgot! My name is Kwesi, as I was born on a Sunday, but everyone calls me Remi."

"Remi, I like it. Is that your stage name?" I ask seriously.

"No, and yes. It's my middle name, which I use. I don't know many Remi's and so it helps me to stand out in the profession I'm in."

Out of nowhere, a guy throws a stationary Boris bike into our path. Remi pushes me out of the way and the bike misses me as a result.

"Thank you," I eventually say. It happened so fast my reaction was delayed. "People always seem to act dumb when it gets a bit warm."

"I know, right! Let's walk the back way to avoid all of this. Link my arm so I can navigate us." *Hmm.* I like. I do so, and we weave in and out of people who seem to be lost, high or lacking a general sense of direction. *Drunk people look so strange from a sober lens.*

A man holding a pile of large flattened boxes, which he's struggling to carry, walks in front of us then suddenly stops and turns around, nearly whacking me with the boxes. Remi drags me away to avoid contact. "What the hell is going on?" I ask with confusion all over my face.

"I don't know hun, but the energy here is all off. I think we'll be fine once we get off the main road." I agree, and so we walk to the traffic lights and wait for them to change. From the corner of my eye I see a man dash into the road. It's the man with the flattened boxes again. He has dropped his keys and is struggling with the boxes to pick them up. Distracted in his own world, he narrowly misses getting hit by a bus. We both watch in total disbelief as he casually walks to the other side of the road, totally oblivious to the danger he just put himself in.

"Don't you think this is starting to feel like Final Destination?" I ask, because it totally does and it's starting to freak me out. He agrees with me and we quicken our pace. *I could have sounded mad, but he gets it, which is great.*

We arrive at the Thai restaurant, and as soon as we step in, it feels like a different world. The big Buddha, lit tea light candles and the smell of incense burning, feel like the calm away from the chaos outside. It's perfect. We sit at one of the corners of a square sharing table, order and continue to chat, before we're joined by three men in their late thirties on the other side of the table. They say "hey" before looking at the menu. *They're definitely not Londoners.* I'd guess American. A few minutes later, our conversation is interrupted.

"Excuse me guys, have you been here before?" says Mr USA1. We nod.

"OK, in America we don't have this layout, you know where you share the table with other people and you can talk to them," he tells us with a smudge of excitement.

"Although we share the same table, we're not obliged to chat. This is the UK; we don't really talk." I know I sound rude, but I'm trying to create boundaries because I know what's going to happen—this first date is going to get hijacked.

And it does. Slavery, Trump, *Get Out*, Basketball, and this guy's Harvard education.

Don't get me wrong. The topics are interesting, *but OMG, shut up already!* Now I know why his other two friends are quiet—they know they can't get a word in edgeways, so don't bother.

"You know Black spaces are important, because we need to be able to just talk without constantly explaining ourselves to white people. It's so draining."

"The Black space in itself is important…" As soon as those words leave my mouth I know I've made a mistake. I've been sucked in and there's nowhere back. "…I prefer to move away from always interlocking my voice and experience with the need for white people to hear me and understand me…." *I'm still talking and I can hear my passion coming out.* I'm in my element right now. "In a country where I often feel disconnected, it's important that we understand ourselves and each other." *I love these conversations.*

"So are you two dating?" Mr USA1 asks. Of course he asks—I made him comfortable enough to ask. He hasn't even acknowledged what I've just said.

Remi and I answer at the same time.

"No," I say.

"Yes," says Remi. *Awkward!*

"We're getting to know each other," I clarify, trying to clean it up.

Remi excuses himself to go to the bathroom, and it's then that I realise saying 'yes' was his way of asserting power, which I completely missed.

"Why do you ask?" I query Mr USA1 spontaneously, as I'm

intrigued.

"Oh, it's just that you shared food," he says.

"So?" I ask. Never in my life have I been bright enough to ask complete strangers invasive questions. I would have just made assumptions based on my observations. Which he would have seen if he shut his mouth for long enough.

Remi comes back to the table to a delivery of brandy shots. Big Mouth bought a round, and we all back the drink. They ask for their bill, and whilst waiting, we take a group shot and exchange Instagram accounts. Why? Well, he's already intruded and nothing about this evening has been normal, so why not. They pay for their food, wish us a good night, and leave.

The calm returns.

"Do you feel the difference?" Remi asks.

"Yes! Bloody hell, he was a lot!"

"But hun, you entertained all of it," he says. "Did you fancy him? The guy with all the questions?"

"No, I didn't fancy any of them. Did I look or sound like I did?"

"You are naturally friendly, which is a great quality but it can be read in the wrong way. I think that's why he asked whether we were dating. I said 'yes' as a hint for him to back off," he says. *Knew it!* "But we gave different answers," he says, slightly smirking whilst shaking his head.

"I'm so sorry. I didn't realise. I think I got caught up in the debate. I love a debate".

"I can see that. It's OK, it's not a biggie, but I wonder if you would have done the same thing if I was your age?"

BOOM! No is the firm answer to his question. There is no way I would've behaved like that if he was my age or older. Even though I'm here with him, his age is a problem and it's showing up in my behaviour. If this was the other way round, I doubt very much Remi would be struggling as I am. Older men dating younger women is normalised.

"I'm sorry. I didn't mean to be disrespectful," I say,

"It's OK. Let's get the bill."

As we're waiting for it to come, Remi receives an Instagram notification from Mr USA1, who has liked one of his pictures. Remi looks at his account, and we can see the guy is married to a white woman who looks like she is about to give birth in a hot minute. We are both so surprised. "No wonder his friends were so quiet— he chats shit," Remi says.

"Do you believe people can be pro-Black and marry outside their race?" I ask.

"I mean there are layers that both people are gonna have to unravel but, yes. Love who you love and do the work."

I nod in agreement. He pays the bill and I order a taxi. There's a slight awkwardness, which I choose to sit on and not call out. He waits with me until my car arrives, and when it does, he opens the car door for me. "Thank you for a lovely evening. I'm sorry I allowed it to be hijacked. I'll message you when I get in, OK?" He nods and waves me off.

Three minutes into the journey, my driver narrowly misses a speeding car. Fifteen minutes later, he avoids another potential accident from a car in front of us swerving and abruptly breaking. My driver overtakes the car, and once clear, he parks up and alerts the police before starting the journey again. I have no idea what is going on. The whole evening has been surreal, intense and life feels… fragile.

Grandma Cedella, please continue to watch over me as I make this journey home. Please protect our path, this driver and this car so no harm comes this way. Thank you in advance.

I make it home in one piece and give thanks. I message Remi and tell him about the drama on the way home. He replies:

Today was energetically off, fancy trying again next week Saturday?

Yes, that would be nice
I type back.

I like his temperament. He dealt with everything really well, but he shouldn't have had to. If I do continue seeing him, I have to get over his age real quick and judge him purely based on how he shows up, and our connection.

*

The following Saturday, we meet outside Brondesbury Station and head to The Kiln Theatre to see *The Half God of Rainfall* by Inua Ellams, which I'm really looking forward to. Remi doesn't know what we're seeing yet, but I'm sure he'll like it. He looks good and I'm looking forward to spending some time with him. We've spoken a couple of times during the week, so this feels like a continuation with no gaps.

I collect the tickets, and I'm pleased he's already familiar with Inua's work. We grab a drink and take a seat on the coloured pouffes in the cafe. Remi sits down and adjusts his position, which involves moving closer to me. *He seems more assertive today.* I'm distracted as he grabs my hand and places it on his outstretched psalm.

"You have massive hands," I say, walking into the next obvious response.

"Yeah, I have big hands *and* big feet," he says, smiling. I laugh and look at both his hands.

"How come your hands are so soft?"

"I'm an actor, darling," he says playfully in a posh voice. The bell rings, signalling it's time to head into the theatre, as we both stand up he looks at me and says, "It's really good seeing you. Thanks for getting the tickets, I know it's gonna be great."

I nod, and he places his arm around me as we enter the theatre to find our seats.

The lights dim and the play begins. The two actors set the pace and we're rapidly transported into their mythical world. Remi leans over and whispers that he knows both actors. "I attended an acting workshop, and they're both brilliant." I focus for the first thirty minutes, and then my mind starts to wander onto Remi. I look at him and he looks back. I lean in and ask whether he is OK. He nods and asks me the same question. I nod and he smiles back, putting his arm over my shoulder, which I lean into. *This feels nice.* He has a manly quality about him that I didn't expect from a twenty-eight year old.

Remi interlocks my fingers with his. The black stage cracks and light floods through. The sound of thunder travels around the stage, which strangely intensifies the tingling sensation I'm feeling in my hand. The energy eventually dies down.

The play ends, and everyone stands up to give a standing ovation before we head out to the bar area. As soon as we step out, I bump into not one, not two, but three friends I know, who all know each other. *Can I just get comfortable with this age thing, without seeing the world first please?* I think silently before introducing Remi to my friends—Bea, Rich and Jess. We discuss the play before naturally splitting off to have separate conversations.

"So, are you on a date? Is that your man?" asks Bea with wide eyes.

"Yeah, we're on a date and can't get no peace," I say, laughing.

"He's gorgeous. Seems really warm and into you."

"How do you know that? You have only just seen us," I ask, confused.

"Energy doesn't lie, babes. I can see it from here, even though he is over there chatting to Jess," Bea says. I look over and admire how Remi's handling this situation. *Wise, mature, grounded, good looking, and a master at creating energy surges through the body. Who is he?*

Rich comes over, and Bea decides to get a drink.

"So how long have you been dating for?" he asks, like a big brother.

"This is the second date," I say.

"Really? I thought you were going to say at least three months. You guys seem so comfortable. I like him, you know. Seems like a decent guy," he says, whilst looking at Remi talking to his girlfriend. "You look well, Syms. I can see he is a little younger than you but don't watch that, you don't even look your age, so don't sweat it, OK? I know how you think already." Rich has no idea how much I needed to hear those words.

I join Jess and Remi and ask if he's ready to leave. He says yes, and we both say our goodbyes. "I like him," whispers Jess in my ear as she hugs me.

"You enjoy that man," says Bea, and I laugh out loud.

We walk back to the station arm in arm and I'm feeling somewhat reassured. Reassured that I don't look like a cougar.

"Fancy dinner?" Remi asks as we look at the train map to decide our best route home. I nod and we decide to go to Shepherd's Bush. The train comes as soon as we arrive on the platform. There's no seats, so we stand opposite each other, holding the orange railings above. We discuss the play, my friends, and that energy he caused.

"I don't know what you are talking about," he says, rocking back and forth with the train, smiling.

"Yes you do—the energy thing you did when you held my hand."

"You are making me sound like I have super powers. Are you getting me confused with the play?" he says, laughing. He steps forward and gives me a hug, whispering into my ear, "If I can do that, imagine what else I can do?"

Even how he did that excites me. He steps back out of my

space to look at the reaction he's created. My poker face is my response, which he sees right through.

We arrive in Shepherd's Bush in no time, and we're quickly seated in the Italian restaurant. I'm so glad Remi suggested another date, because today has been so much better than our first. In spite of our age difference, we have a lot in common. A lot more than just being spiritual and vegetarian.

"And so—" He keeps smiling when I'm talking. "What?" I ask.

"I'm just looking at you. You're beautiful," he says, smiling.

"What makes me beautiful?" I ask, totally milking it.

"Your lips, smile, your kookiness and opinions. I also love your hair when it's out like that. Of course, I'm still getting to know you, but I like what I see so far."

"I feel the same way."

"Is that all I get?" he teases.

"I think you're really mature for your age. I actually still can't believe you're twenty-eight. It actually messes with my mind. You're well read, ambitious, emotionally intelligent and make great points. You have a lovely smile and great teeth, but I think your eyes are your most striking feature. They say a lot even when you aren't saying anything."

"Oh yeah? What am I thinking then?" he asks, knowing he's causing me internal stress.

I look, and I think I see something but I'm not sure.

"Yep, go on, tell me?" he says pushing me.

I pick up my make-up bag, excuse myself and head to the bathroom. *How is this twenty-eight-year old making me feel confused*? No answers come. I touch up my make-up and head back.

"Are you OK?" he asks.

"Yeah, I just needed…"

"Time to avoid the question?" he suggests, interrupting my flow. I burst into laughter, because I cannot believe the level of this man's confidence. "In all seriousness. I'm really enjoying your company and I would love you to come back to mine. No, not to do anything but chill. What do you think?" he asks breezily.

I'm not surprised, as that's what I saw in his eyes. "I'm enjoying your company too, but let me think about it a bit more." His age is at the forefront of my mind and it is causing a mish-mash of feelings and confusion.

"No pressure, it's just a question. Although, wanna decide by the time we finish dessert?" he asks, smiling.

I nod to the timeline, even though I'm forty and shouldn't need one. I finish my chocolate cake and look at the patient man in front of me. "So, I would love to spend more time with you, but I'm on my period and I'd prefer to be in my own space."

"I understand, but I'm not trying to have sex with you. I'm just offering space to chill if you didn't want to go straight home. If you need things to feel more comfortable, Westfield is right there," he says, looking out of the window, "but there's no pressure at all."

This guy is good. I don't want to like a younger guy, I really don't!

"OK, let's get the bill," I say.

He insists on paying, and we leave and walk over to the mall, which takes less than two minutes. I try not to beat myself up but

I do, as I've spent nearly an hour pondering what to do, wasting time, only to make the decision and realise it wasn't even a big deal. *He must think you have confidence issues. Sort it out, Syms.*

We head to H&M and just before we walk in, he tells me he needs to go to Primark and will meet me outside H&M in fifteen minutes. I head upstairs to the lingerie section and scan the lacy underwear before remembering it's not that kind of chill. I put the three items in my hand down and head to the sensible pyjama section. I pick up a white, long-sleeved top, grey thin tracksuit bottoms and a pack of knickers. I pay and wait for him outside, and he shortly returns with a massive Primark bag.

"You did an actual shop?" I say, comparing bags.

He laughs. "I actually went in for one thing and saw all the things I needed, so thought I may as well get them now."

"Makes sense."

Looking like a couple who've just shopped together, we head to the Underground and make our way to Finsbury Park, where Remi has just moved into a flat in a converted house with a rooftop garden. He warns me that it's not yet perfect and not to judge him.

"We're here," he says after we've walked roughly ten minutes from the station. He lets us in and switches on the lights. Spacious, high ceilings and minimalist, because he's literally just moved in. I take off my shoes.

"Hold on," he says, stopping me from walking any further. "I bought you these." He pulls a pair of blue and white fluffy slippers out of his bag and puts them on the floor. "I don't want you getting splinters in your feet, the carpet should be laid next week."

"Oh hun, that is so kind of you. Thank you so much for thinking about me."

"I had to guess your size because your phone died. They're a six?" he says squishing his face up.

"I'm a seven but, they're perfect," I say, even though my heels are hanging of the end a bit, because it doesn't matter, I'm touched by his consideration.

He shows me around the flat, which feels as big as a whole house. Everything is done except for the carpet in the front room and staircase, whilst the second bedroom just needs additional furniture, and additional extra touches like art, picture frames and so on. *It's a nice place with potential.*

"Take a seat and relax. Do you want a cup of tea?"

I ask for peppermint, and he puts some music on whilst I wait.

Neat, considerate, funny, charming and caring. *All great qualities.*

"Symona, can you come here for a sec? I'm in the bathroom." I put down my tea and head to the bathroom. "I've run you a bath, I hope you don't mind. I know how long it took for you to make your decision," he says, rolling his eyes and smiling, "but I want you to feel comfortable." *Who is he? Grandma, who is he? Seriously.*

"Your bag is here, a fresh towel is there, the green toothbrush is yours, and so are the peach shower gloves. Take your time," he tells me,

"Thank you hun, appreciate it."

He heads out and closes the door.

I stand and look at the candles he has lit around the bath. The plants on top of the mirrored cabinet, and the big cream mirror that has the words *BEAUTIFUL* etched into the glass. *Oh, I'm in trouble.*

The temperature of the water is perfect. I step in, lay back and relax. Remi increases the volume of the music so I can clearly hear the soothing sounds of a range of neo soul artists. I could have stayed in the bath for a lot longer, but I don't want to take the piss. As I get out and watch the water drain away, I hear Grandma Cedella loud and clear. *"Judge him by what he does, what he says and how he treats you, and not his number."* I take a deep breath and exhale. "I'll try," I whisper.

I feel lightheaded as soon as I get out of the bath. This happens sometimes when either the bath is too hot, or I get out too quickly. I think this time it's the latter, coupled with being on my period. The window is wide open but I can't feel any air. If I don't lie down soon, I'm going to pass out. I wrap myself in the big beige towel, open the bathroom door and quickly head to the master bedroom, where I flop onto the bed. The music is still loud, so I know Remi can't hear me. The room is spinning, I'm beginning to sweat, and I cannot muster up the energy to open a window. It's cooler here than the bathroom, so I know I'll be OK in a minute. I just need to close my eyes, concentrate on breathing slowly and wait for the feeling to subside.

After a few minutes, the light-headedness dissipates and my

thoughts begin to filter through. *Sigh! This is just embarrassing. I beg, please don't let Remi find me like this, spread eagled, looking like I'm about to make snow angels on top of the bedsheets. I'm meant to be... No, I __am__ a together woman, who has a good job, my own business, a wealth of experience and yet... I feel blindsided, blindsided by this man who's a lot younger than me.*

Some time passes, perhaps 10 minutes or so and I feel a lot better. I slowly get up and realise the childlike position I was just in, makes me realise I haven't felt *carefree, fun or creative in a while. Hmm.* I head back to the bathroom, where the steam has evaporated. I look in the cupboard, and I'm greeted with my favourite brand of coconut oil. I smother my skin and wipe away the excess before getting my new sleepwear out of the bag.

I pick up the trio of knickers I'd bought, and notice the security tag is still on them, grouping them together. *FFS, why?* Do they normally tag knickers? I pull the security tag but nothing budges. The grey bottoms also have the tag. The cashier just had two jobs to do, take my money and take the security tags off the clothes, it's not that hard. I have no choice but to get Remi involved.

"Remi, by any chance do you have some scissors?" I call out.

"Yeah but haven't seen them since the move, why?"

"So, the cashier forgot to take the security tags off my clothes..." *I feel like a child who can't open a jar and needs help!*

"I'm coming," he says, then appears in the bathroom doorway. He looks at me, and I try and hide my embarrassment.

"You sure you didn't steal them, hun?" he asks, bursting into laughter.

"No," I say in a serious tone, "but now is the time to show me your other powers." I laugh eventually, too. He pulls at the material on the knickers and the tag breaks free with a massive rip at the side. "I'm sorry, I tried to not rip too much material. You can still wear them. I can't do anything about the trousers I'm afraid. You're gonna just have to walk around here looking like a criminal," he says laughing before leaving.

I shut the door and place a sanitary towel for added protection on my new ripped knickers. Feeling fresh and unsexy I head back to the front room, where Remi is sitting down with a bowl of freshly fried plantain and two glasses of apple juice.

"How was your bath?" he asks, looking at me.

"It was lovely, thank you. I really needed that. How do you like my stolen wear?" I say, posing.

"You look beautiful. I may need to arrest you. Come and sit down. I thought you might want a snack." He nods at the bowl on the table. "Seems like ages since we ate."

"You call plantain a snack?" I say, laughing.

"Why are you laughing? It's the best snack. Plus it's plan-tain not plan-tin."

"Listen, we don't say mount-tain and foun-tain, so why would plantain be plan-tain? Look, I am not about to get into plantain pronunciation wars. I'm saying it the Jamaican way, you're saying it the Ghanaian way, neither one of us is wrong. How about that?"

He leans over and kisses me. I didn't expect it. His soft full lips are gentle and considerate, as is his tongue…

"So did you agree with what I said then?" I ask as I pull away.

"What do you think?" He smiles. "What's your love language?" he asks, changing the subject.

I look at him whilst trying to hide my wonder. How does this twenty-eight-year old man know about love languages? "Have you read the book?"

"Of course I have," he tells me confidently. "It's vital information for the success of any relationship, as we all show and give love in different ways."

I couldn't hide it, so I just said it. "I'm impressed. I have never met a man who has read the book. My love languages, in order, are Physical Touch—I liked to be kissed, hugged and caressed. Quality Time—everyone is busy, so making time to see someone is important to me. Relationship time needs to be carved out like how I carve out gym time or meetings. Acts of Service—less about gifts and more about the little things, like making dinner, running me a bath, rubbing my feet etc. And finally, Words of Affirmation—I don't need to be told I'm beautiful for validation, I like to be told because it's nice to hear. I want a man to tell me how he feels about me. What about you?"

"Mine are the same as yours, for the same reasons actually, which is great. I've given you all of your five love languages. But I think I could do a bit more on the physical touch. Fancy a massage?"

Who is he? "I would love one."

Chapter Thirty

Timing

The sun streaming through the blinds wakes me up. I roll over to my right. Remi's back is to me and the covers are pushed down to his waist. How did this young man persuade me to end up here? *He got skills*, I give him that. I move in closer to spoon him, laying my hand across his chest, my pelvic area resting against his pert bum.

He stirs. "Morning." He changes position, manoeuvring me to lay on his chest, and plays with my hair *that I didn't twist last night*. "What three things are you grateful for today?" he asks breezily. "This is my morning ritual, so you may as well join me."

"Erm, I'm grateful for my health, your amazing bed, and you. You made me feel really comfortable, and your massage was great. Thank you."

"No worries at all. I'm grateful to have watched an amazing play. It was a good date choice, thank you. I'm grateful for this new home, even though it's not a home yet, and I am grateful that I have a beautiful woman in my bed." He kisses my forehead and cheek.

I straddle him and kiss him passionately. "You know you're a handsome man, right?" He raises an eyebrow. "Seriously, you are—but you have to know it for yourself," I say, before rolling over and heading to the bathroom.

On my return I linger in the bedroom doorway and announce that I'm going to leave now. "OK, but let's have breakfast first."

I nod and head back into the bathroom. Feeling uber-comfortable, I leave the bathroom door open and step into the glass walk-in shower. The hot water running off my skin, feels good, and he makes me feel good, *but his age.*

"Can I come in?" he says, knocking on the open door. "I need to pee."

"Of course you can, hun."

He walks over to the toilet behind me, and I continue to rinse the shower gel off my body. I look down and realise he must be able to see my tampon string from behind, before deciding I don't care. *It's just a string, men need to learn to deal with women's cycles.*

Remi flushes the toilet, washes his hands and begins to head out the door. He stops and asks, "Coffee and eggs on brown toast with veggie sausages?" I look at him standing there, naked.

"That would be amazing, thank you," I say, beaming.

He nods and leaves the bathroom.

I head to the kitchen, after coconut oil saves my life again. From the doorway I watch him scrambling eggs and ask if I can help. "Yeah, you can help yourself by putting on the slippers I brought you," he says, raising an eyebrow. I fetch them from the bathroom and return wearing them.

"I'm nearly done," he tells me. "Take a seat and put some

music on, please." His tone within the instruction lands well to my ears. In fact, it lands so well that it turns me on. I open the Spotify app and select my playlist entitled Symona's Still Single, *obvs*. It's my feel-good playlist, which has an array of songs I love that I've compiled over the years. I press play, and Musiq Soulchild blares throughout the flat. I take a look at Remi's bookcase, and I'm impressed by the vast array of topics, from Egyptology, spirituality and vegan food to wealth management, *How to Love a Black Woman*, tantric sex, and seduction techniques. *This man is not ramping. Sienna is the only person I've met with a similar collection.* I pull the seduction book out and read the back.

Remi places the breakfast he's made onto the coffee table and calls me over. I turn the music down, grab a cushion and choose to sit on the floor, facing him. "Thank you for making breakfast. I'll wash-up."

"No, need, hun. You're my guest," he says, smiling as we tuck into our food.

"You have a very interesting selection of books."

"Thanks. I have more in storage, I just had to bring things over bit by bit." We discuss our favourite books, genres, authors and music, giving reasons why. The conversation flows nicely.

"What are you doing today?" he asks, closing his knife and fork.

"Nothing, apart from prepping for the week ahead."

"So why are you leaving so early? Are you trying to runaway? You can stay and chill if you want."

I look at him, smiling. He looks back. There is a silent moment of thoughts exchanging before I pull away from his gaze.

"Oh-oh, you're in trouble," he says, smiling and clearing the plates.

"I don't know what you're talking about," I retort with my rubbish poker face, sipping my coffee. "Thanks for the offer, but I should head back." I get up to put the cup in the sink.

"No worries at all. You can leave your stolen goods here if you want, they will be clean and ready for you when you come back," he says, walking up to me and hugging me from behind.

"When I come back, yeah? How come you're so sure?" I turn around to look at him.

"Well, you're yet to try the good stuff," he says suggestively.

"What? Your 100% pure vegetarian sausage?" I ask, laughing my head off.

"Get your mind out of the gutter," he tells me with a straight face. "I'm talking about my cooking, actually. You haven't sampled my amazing dinners." He leans in for a kiss. When our lips part, he steps to the side and says, "OK, well I will let you go. Thanks for visiting my mini, very mini chateau. You are welcome back anytime."

I smile and walk into the front room to collect my bag, and then to the hall to put on my shoes.

"Remember to let me know when you're ready to come off the subs bench," Remi says, winking at me as he comes over and zips up my patterned jacket.

"Oh, so I'm still good enough to be on your team then?" I enquire teasingly.

"Yeah, I think so, but I'm only really going to know once you start playing the game with me. You know, showing your full potential." *Damn.*

"Oh really?" I raise my eyebrow as I open the door.

"Yes, really. Make sure you call me when you get in."

"Will do. Thanks again for your hospitality. Bye."

The walk back to Finsbury Park station is exactly what I needed. The fresh air feels great, I feel great, and the feeling continues until I reached the Underground.

What are you doing? Syms? He is twelve years younger than you. If you didn't think Mr TK Maxx was on the same page as you and he was forty-one, why would you think a twenty-eight-year old would be? This makes no sense. You are wasting time you don't have. Grandma's words cut through, *"Judge him by what he does, what he says and how he treats you and not his number."*

I try and heed her advice.

*

It's been a month since I met Remi, and we're getting on really well, speaking every day and seeing him once a week, sometimes at the weekend, and sometimes after work. The Victoria line is everything—my commute to work is only twenty minutes door to door from his flat, as opposed to fifty minutes and two trains from mine, making it too easy to head back to his house during the week. I've done it twice now. He's given me a bottom drawer and made me feel really welcome with his open invitations. However, I've realised I have a problem with taking up space. I often decline his offers to come round and would rather leave early than stay later, even if I'm enjoying myself. No man has ever asked me to leave because I've outstayed my welcome, so I'm not sure where this has come from.

What I know for sure is that the gifting of the bottom drawer is one of the kindest gestures a man can offer to a woman who he's getting to know. It is the true representation of 'You are welcome, I want you to stay and I want you to be comfortable.' It's not something a woman can suggest, it has to happen naturally when he's ready. It's the potential flicker of an openness to commitment. *Well, that's how I see it anyway.*

Going to bed and waking up with someone is what I've missed. Remi's cooking skills are on point, and so are those massages. After my other encounters with men, I told Remi I didn't want to rush into anything, and he was absolutely fine with it. "I don't just lie down with anyone. I'm also still getting to know you." Is this what a discerning, modern man looks like?

Later that evening, I receive an email from Remi that renders me speechless.

Date: 18th May 2019
Subject: Table 60 Travel Ltd

Dear Miss Brown,

I hope you are well.

We are grateful to have you as our only member.

I'm writing to you on behalf of Remi, who has asked me to check your availability for the 30th-31st May to attend a Hotel and Spa break in Surrey. I understand that it was a milestone birthday last month. Congratulations! He would like to honour and celebrate you on those suggested dates, as he was unable to attend your actual day (as he hadn't met you yet). He would also like to acknowledge that it is one month today since you both met.

Please kindly R.S.V.P to confirm acceptance of this invitation, confirming those dates work for you. Alternative dates can be provided if needed.
I look forward to hearing from you.

Yours faithfully,
Charlie

This man is really something. I type out a reply.

Dear Charlie,
It's so good to hear from you, I hope you are well.
Please tell Remi that I would love to attend, and both dates work well.
I look forward to hearing from you in due course with more information.
Kindest,
Symona x

I call Remi as soon as I've sent the email.

"Babe, I'm so surprised," I say before he's even had a chance to say hello. He laughs. "No seriously, it's such a lovely thing you've done. You really didn't have to—"

"I know," he says, interjecting.

"But I am glad you did," I finish. "So thoughtful. I'm looking forward to it."

"Me too. Did you get the Table 60 reference? Did you see what I did there?" he says, chuckling.

"Yeah, I thought it was great. The detail, the words, loved it. Thank you so much."

"You deserve it, hun. Your birthday sounded amazing but I wanted to celebrate you. I know you think forty is a big deal, especially in relation to my age, but babe you look great. You can easily pass for much younger. Plus out of the two of us, I act older than you," he adds, laughing.

"Hahah. I'm actually your age and you are mine," I say, laughing my head off. "Anyway, it was just a quick call to say thank you. I appreciate you."

"You are welcome, hun. I appreciate you, too. Goodnight."

I update the Supper Boogie group by simply saying:

Ladies, he is taking me away to a spa hotel for post-birthday celebrations. Who is this 28-year-old? Answers via meme, welcome.

I press send and head to bed.

*

The weeks fly by, and the day of the hotel and spa trip arrives.

I'm excited—and on time, which surprises Remi, who is standing waiting for me under the big four-faced clock in Waterloo station. He has a weekend bag, whilst I have a small suitcase. He greets me and asks why I'm carrying a suitcase. "It's a hotel with a spa, which means I also need my swimwear, shampoo, conditioner, and my hair dryer with the afro pick attachment, because I cannot guarantee that their hairdryer will fit my attachment, and—"

"Jheeze, I forgot. Yep, I get it. All good. Let's go," he says grabbing my hand and walking towards the platform and onto the waiting train.

One hour and fifteen minutes later, we arrive at Haslemere Station, jump into a taxi and head to the hotel. Arriving at the grade II-listed Tudor building, we make our way to reception, where we are greeted by Fred, who should be a stand-up comedian with all the jokes he cracks. He checks us in and hands us the key. We head to our room, and Remi opens the door, allowing me to walk in first. *I'm impressed.* The white-tiled bathroom is big and contemporary. The roll top bath with silver feet looks inviting, although I'll scrub it myself to ensure it's clean, whilst the bedroom screams luxury. Somehow the bold floral wallpaper works, along with the silver cushions that add to the overall opulent feel. The lattice windows produce a view of acres and acres of rich, green uninterrupted land. "This is beautiful, hun. Thank you so much," I say, turning to Remi, who's standing by the dressing table on the other side of the room.

"You are welcome babe. Happy post-40th birthday," he says,

stepping to one side to reveal the bottle of champagne and two flute glasses. He pops the bottle and we both chill on the chaise lounge by the window. *Again—who is this man?!*

We relax and chat for about thirty minutes before I suggest we explore the grounds. The restaurant and spa are within separate buildings, but the decor and overall Tudor feel remains throughout the property. The land surrounding the buildings is the selling point. There's a marquee beside a lake with a fountain in the middle of it which would make the perfect setting for a wedding. We take a seat on the white benches nearby, and the subject of marriage comes up.

"Is marriage on your list?" Remi asks me.

"It used to be. I'm not so sure now. Every woman thinks about the white dress, bridesmaids and walking down the aisle, but now it just seems like a lot of money for one day, one moment. I think I would prefer to put that money towards a house."

"I get that," he says, "but what do you think about marriage as an institution, especially as you are spiritual?"

"Yeah, I've decided I'm not really down with the forever thing. I read somewhere that our cells change every seven years. If that's happening internally, what does that look like in feeling, thought and behaviour? We are in a constant flow of change, and yet I'm expected to believe our love for someone remains and doesn't deplete with time? Unless I find my destined soul mate, I'm not sure how this is gonna be sustained, outside of doing the things to keep the flame alive. I don't want to feel pressured to stay with someone I no longer love because a piece of paper binds us." *I have seen too many friends' parents in this scenario.*

They're together, but distant because the love died between them a long time ago. "Yes, you can divorce, but... I don't know, I think I want a less expensive sense of freedom. My mum and dad weren't married, that may also have something to do with my thinking." I pause before continuing. "I'll probably have a blessing, create my own vows and then devise a contract that both parties can renew if we want to spend, say, a further three years together," I say seriously.

"So it's like a business contract?"

"I guess so. It's all one big business anyway. If I have only one life, I don't want to be tied to someone I don't want to be with. We are coming together as two separate people to build and experience things together, and we both should be able to leave without having a massive dent in our pocket. What you built and what you have before you met me is yours. When our rolling contract ends, we divide the assets we built, created and accumulated together. That's how I would do it. But I still want a ring and some sort of celebration where I get to wear a banging dress! What are your thoughts?"

"To be honest, I agree with everything you said. I'm loving the rolling contract idea," Remi says, looking at me at me seriously.

I take a breath. "Fancy exploring the forest? Dinner is at seven pm, so I think we have enough time before the sun sets. Then we can go back, freshen up and head out to eat. What do you think?"

"Yep, sounds good," he says.

We walk around the forest for a while, then decide to turn back when we reach a field of horses.

"Have you ever had sex in a forest?" Remi asks.

"No, not a forest, but yes, outside. Why do you look surprised?"

"Because you don't look like the type of person who would have sex outside in a forest."

"What is that meant to mean?" I ask, frowning.

"Oh shit, look, it's not bad. I just can't imagine you wanting to have sex out here on leaves, with bugs around."

"Damn straight! You're right," I say, laughing.

"Phew, I thought I offended you."

"Not at all, your judgement about me is correct." I tell him, opening the white gate that leads back to the hotel grounds.

"Men can have sex anywhere, you don't need to lie on anything, so I get why it's appealing and risqué for you lot."

"Err, major assumptions you are reeling off there."

"Am I lying though?" I say, challenging.

He thinks for a moment. "Not really."

I cut my eye at him and he bursts out laughing.

*

We have a fantastic view of the grounds from our round table. I'm famished, so I hope food soon arrives.

"I needed this break and didn't even realise it. I'm still a bit shocked that I am here, to be honest," I tell Remi. "I just didn't expect this."

"I know, and that's why I really wanted to do something.

You're independent, you give a lot to others, and I just wanted to make sure you felt special," he says, reaching across the table and holding out his hand for me to place within his. "The joke is, I don't even think I'm doing anything special," he tells me nonchalantly. "But it does make me wonder what the hell men your age are doing. Seriously, Symona, I don't get why you're single."

"If I knew the answer to that question, I wouldn't be. To be fair, I was single for a long time by choice, and now I'm actively looking and being more open. Perhaps I missed the age and timeframe to catch a man? I really couldn't tell you. What I do know is, I'm happy with who I am now, and that is something."

He smiles before removing his hand from mine to make way for the waitress to place our starters on the table. A bowl of olives, beetroot and lentil salad, and mushroom and garlic pate, which we share and demolish in no time.

"I was so hungry," I say, spreading the pate onto the last piece of bread.

"Well we didn't have lunch, we have walked loads and drank loads… we can always get a side of fries if the mains don't fill us up."

"Hmm, I'm hoping the apple crumble I'm planning on for dessert does the job it's meant to do."

Our mains arrive, and the disappointment is real. Remi orders a big bowl of fries straight away, whilst I try and hold in my laughter.

"I don't like it when people play around with food. Make a main a *main*—AKA bigger than the starter. I want the food to take up the whole circumference of the plate with no gaps. I shouldn't be able to see gaps!" he says with passion. The volume of my laughter tells me it's time to switch to water.

Eventually, Remi fixes me with a serious look. "So, I think we get on, would you agree?"

"Yes…" I say, apprehensive of what's coming next.

"OK, so I think, this is a good time to talk about what we want and where we are heading."

"Sure," I reply, noticing how magical everything looks with the help of simple fairy lights.

"So, I would like you to choose what you want out of four options. One: we call it a day. Two: we become fuck buddies. Three: we get to know each other more and see each other exclusively, or four: we get to know each other and see other people."

Impressed with the transparent question I answer straight away. "I think you're great, and although I need to work the age thing out, I would like option three."

"What was that option again? Just so I'm clear."

"You set the options. How have you already forgotten?" I ask, laughing.

"Because I was also thinking at the same time I set the question. Can you just tell me, please?" he says, sounding a bit stressed.

"Option three means I'm off the subs bench and joining your team. I would like to see you exclusively," I say, taking a sip of wine before remembering it should be water.

"Ah, that's good. I want the same thing. That means no more dating apps."

"I know it means that. But are you sure? We are twelve years apart!"

"It will be eleven years by the time my birthday comes around in November."

"Not much of a difference, hun," I tell, matter-of-factly.

"Syms, I have dated older women before, you already know this. The last woman I dated was thirty-five years old. Do you really believe you being five years older than that is a massive gap? Because it really isn't. I know you're an ageist and you're worried about looking like a cougar, but you don't—and I'm no one's toy boy. So you're gonna have to figure it out." I smile and look down. "What?" he says with confusion.

"I like it when you go all serious," I reply, smiling. He laughs, shakes his head and finishes his meal in silence, every so often glancing at me with his deer-like eyes.

The restaurant begins to empty out, and we soon become the last guests. The waiters work around us, setting up for breakfast in the morning. A young waiter, who must be new as he has looked unsure about everything throughout the night, brings over our desserts—apple crumble and custard, and chocolate cake and vanilla ice cream. He places it on the table and announces he will be back shortly with the spoons. He returns with five different types of spoons laid out on a white plate—teaspoon, table spoon, soup spoon, serving spoon and long spoon. As he places the plate on the table, he says, "I didn't know what spoon to bring, so I brought you the selection to save myself from going back into the kitchen if I was wrong." It took everything for us both not to burst out laughing. We say thank you and watch him go behind the bar looking very happy with himself.

"I literally cannot cope," I say, trying not to erupt into floods of tears. "I have so much to say but I can't. I will, however, give him points for initiative." I cast my hand above the array of silver spoons. "But none of these spoons are a dessert spoon!" I exclaim, finally giving in and unleashing my loud, drunken laugh.

"It's insane," Remi says, shaking his head. "I thought everyone knew what a dessert spoon was. I guess this isn't his fault. The establishment should have trained him."

"Really? Isn't that the parents' job?"

"I'm just baffled. The real question right now is… what spoon are you going to use?" Remi says, laughing. I'm now struggling to breathe as I watch him select the serving spoon. "Why? Hahah, why the serving spoon?"

"It's time to go! Choose the biggest spoon and eat up!"

I'm now bending over laughing, trying my hardest not to slip off my chair. He selects the tablespoon for me, as clearly I'm taking too long. "It's the next biggest spoon. Eat up!" he says again, placing it in my bowl whilst shoving cake into his mouth.

*

"My stomach is killing me."

"And mine is growling because I'm still hungry," Remi says. "I might need to order a takeaway."

"What the hell is wrong with you? Where do you put it all?"

"I'm still a growing lad… apparently," he says with attitude.

"Oh, there it is. I was wondering when that would show up?"

I say smiling.

"What?" he asks, in confusion.

"Your Scorpio sting."

He smiles sheepishly as he knows exactly what I'm talking about.

I put some music on and we both navigate around each other as we get ready for bed. Then I crawl into Remi's arms and he places the cover over me. He kisses me passionately, slowly travelling over to my cheek, down my neck to my breasts, and then further down. He stops when he reaches his destination. I gasp, look at him and close my eyes...

When I eventually catch my breath, I say, "Thank you."

"You always say thank you afterwards, have you noticed that?" he asks. "And you really don't have too." He pulls himself up and we lie side by side.

"I know. You have given me something and I'm saying thanks. It's manners and a compliment combined."

"You're cute," he says, looking at me. I smile, then sit up and reach over to the bedside table and dig my hand in the coconut oil that I packed. I ask Remi to turn over, then spread it across his broad shoulders, moving my hands up and down his body, focusing on knots before moving to another part of his smooth back, then concentrating on his arms, buttocks, firm thighs, and then his feet, trying to remember how reflexologists do it. He moans when I gently rub his arches. *Yes.*

"Turn back over," I firmly instruct. He does as he is told, and this time I decide to work from his feet upwards. Travelling up his thighs, I brush his manhood before focusing on his chest and arms, replacing my hands with my lips when I work up his neck.

Eventually, I straddle him and stroke his penis. Leaning forward, I kiss him—and in one quick move he flips me over so I'm underneath him and in the perfect position for missionary. *Impressed.*

"Do you want to have sex?" he asks, looking at me. I nod, and he reaches for a condom and puts it on. He manoeuvres himself and positions the tip at my entrance. He kisses and caresses my face and asks, "Do you give me permission to enter?" I nod and he gently eases himself in. I hold him tighter so he feels closer, and we eventually climax together.

He kisses my cheeks and looks at me closely, asking if I'm OK after he tastes tears.

"I'm OK, I just need a minute." He nods and slowly pulls out, removing the condom.

"Can I check it?" I ask, and he hands me the condom for inspection. Satisfied, I give it back and he puts it in the bin in the bathroom.

He spoons me when he climbs back into bed, covering me with his body and planting numerous kisses on my cheek. "Talk to me," he whispers.

I roll over to face him. "I'm not sad, I just got emotional because it felt so good. It's been a long time since I have given myself permission to really enjoy sex, to give and receive in equal measure, and it felt nice. My tears are happy tears, don't worry. Regarding the condom checking, it's something I do for peace of mind and now it's a habit."

Remi holds me for a few moments without saying a word.

"Thanks for telling me, hun. Sounds like you've been through a lot and have had a breakthrough. It's all good," he says intuitively.

"Yeah, I have." *I really have.*

"I'm listening, if you want to tell me," he says with empathy.

I pause… and begin.

*

The sound of metal clanking on wood wakes me up abruptly.

"Sorry, hun, I didn't mean to wake you," Remi says, picking up a fork from the floor. "But actually I was about to wake you up anyway because breakfast, my darling, is served." I prop myself up, and he lays the tray of food on my lap.

"Morning, hun," I say. "This is lovely." He grabs his own tray from off the trolley and sits on top of the bed, facing me. Whilst eating breakfast, we discuss last night, the food, spoons, sex, and options.

"So, we are really doing option number three, yeah?" he asks to triple-check.

"Yes, we are, if that's what you still also want?"

"Yep. I want Symona Brown all to myself, because she's great."

"Cheers to option three."

"Amen to that," he says, clinking my mug with his. "Check out is at eleven. It's eight thirty now—fancy a walk to take in the last bits of this pure oxygen before we head back to polluted London?"

I smile. "Sure."

*

We arrive back at Waterloo Station at 12:45pm. I hug Remi and thank him for arranging a lovely break. We embrace, and part ways. As I ride the escalator to the Overground, my phone vibrates.

"Missing me already, huh?" I ask, upon answering my phone.

"Nah, I'm just hungry. Fancy joining me for lunch?" he asks cheekily.

"Yeah, why not. Meet you by the Underground barriers?" I suggest.

"Yeah, go on then."

We greet like we've just seen each other for the first time.

"You're in trouble," I say, looking into his eyes.

"I know," he says tapping his Oyster card and walking through the barriers. "Lets go to Dalston."

"Dalston? I thought you were thinking of somewhere more central. How convenient that you're suggesting somewhere near to where you live. You tryna get me to stay over again?" I ask, raising an eyebrow.

"I don't know what you're talking about," he says, smiling. "I just want guaranteed good food made with love that fills my plate and that place is in Dalston and made by the hands of a vegan chef, Atreka, who I also want you to meet. Plus, do you have a pet?" I shake my head. "So what are you rushing home for?" he says, grabbing my hand.

I'm not used this at all. He's allowing me to take up space, which feels nice and uncomfortable at the same time. I like being around him. In the past I've questioned whether I've moved too fast, or been too cautious, but with Remi it feels like the fast pace is the right pace. However, his next question still comes as a surprise.

"Syms, will you be my girlfriend?"

I look at him. "When you say girlfriend, what do you mean? I'm too old for girlfriend and boyfriend titles.

"I would like you to be my girlfriend, my partner, where we come together to build together."

"Damn! You sure you don't need more time?" I ask.

"I may be younger, but I know what I want. I'm not tryna be the type of guy that's willing to sit back and let the catch of the day swim by."

"Is that so?" I say, hugging him. He nods. "Well, a catch knows a catch, so yeah, I will be your partner."

"Great. We'll chat about it later, when you come back to mine—about our expectations, plans, etc." I look at him, confused. "As you know, relationships take work, so I have a few things that I like to do to ensure complacency doesn't occur," he tells me. "Like date nights. They are necessary." *Nothing like Marcel.* This man is all about intention.

We walk out of Dalston Junction station hand-in-hand, and see a drunk, homeless-looking Black man is accosting people as they walk by. He looks at us, and we brace ourselves for the onslaught—which doesn't come. Instead he gives Remi some words of wisdom.

"You got a good woman there. Marry her, she is worthy. Don't mess up like I did. When you find a good woman, you do right by her." Remi nods and we walk on, after which, the cussing and slurred words from the drunk man continue behind us.

"He was transfixed by you, Syms. I wonder what he saw?"

"I'm not sure, but what I do know is sometimes those with mental health issues can see things that everyone else misses. Crazy isn't always crazy and random isn't always random."

He looks at me. "Elaborate, please."

I briefly mention how I met Jaden, Ramiro and Marcel. "So, I believe there are messages and signs around us all the time, and I try and pay attention."

"Symona, I want to tell you something," Remi says seriously. "When I first saw you at Supper Boogie, I couldn't miss you because you walked in surrounded by a purple light."

"Huh?"

"It was like there was a spotlight on you, shining on you, that made me pay attention. I can't explain it more than that. It just so happens that I also thought you were stunning. My point is, I think I was meant to meet you, and my ancestors made sure I saw you. My version of the magnetic pull, I guess."

"Are you joking?"

"No, I promise."

"Wow," is all I can manage, because whilst my head can compute it, it just feels surreal.

I'm reminded again that this world is a magical place, an eco-system full of sign posts. I've had my own fair share of experiences, to hear someone else's, in-relation to me, feels... I can't find the word. Erm... I feel honoured.

Lifting your head above the noisy distractions, and paying attention to the iceberg below the waterline is necessary. If we view thoughts as substance, because thoughts become things, and alchemy is about changing one substance to another substance, then we should also master how to be alchemists in terms of changing our negative thoughts to positive ones. I accepted my fate after Marcel, whilst still being open and positive.

Three years ago, I couldn't see how what I wanted was going to show up or even when it was going to come, and look, now he's here. God, universal or ancestral timing, however you refer to it, exists and it defies the man-made 24-hour clock system. There is time to breathe. *Timing. Time. My time. Is this my time?*

Chapter Thirty-One

Surprise

I'm outside Baker Street Station and cannot wait to see Remi's face when he finds out what date night is tonight. Always on time, he arrives at seven pm on the dot, and his first reaction upon seeing my hair is just what I wanted.

"Babe, your hair!" he exclaims as he looks at my instant ponytail. "This looks great. Very Sade-esque, I love it," he says, greeting me with a kiss.

"Thanks, hun. You look and smell good, as always," I say, admiring him back. "It starts at seven thirty, and we still need to find the venue, so let's walk."

"Is it a play?" he asks.

"I'm not telling you. What's the point in telling you now, when you have firmed it for five days?"

"True," he says, holding my hand.

As soon I see the queue of Black people, I know we've arrived, but I check the address to make sure.

"So it's not a play, but it's something that appeals to only Black people?" Remi questions.

"I didn't say whether it was a play or not. I just told you that

328

I'm not telling you what it is, and that hasn't changed," I say, turning my head away from him and putting my nose in the air.

"OMG, you are loving this. In fact, so am I, because I'm completely baffled." We inch further forward in the queue. For a while, Remi is strangely silent and so I ask if he's OK. "Yes babe, I'm good. I'm just trying to see if I can overhear what people are talking about to give me clues."

"Really? How about you just chillax yourself and wait and see? We will be inside in a minute and all will be revealed. Pretend you are meditating or something, or just use mindfulness to be present, hun." He kisses his teeth. I love that he's struggling with the suspense.

As soon as we walk inside, I pray there are no posters on the wall or anything that gives it away. We've come this far, and it will be a shame for the surprise to be ruined now. I can't see anything. He pipes up again.

"So, this may or may not be a play, but what is interesting is that they are giving free wine on entry. Never seen that happen before at a play, unless it's press night. Oh, and look," he says, pointing to a banner with a picture of a Black woman on a pole.

"Yeah, that might be just a banner advertising what else they do here. This place seems to be one of those spaces that caters for a range of events, don't you think?" I say, looking around, and he grudgingly agrees.

I flash my online ticket on my phone, and then we head straight into the theatre space. The front row seats are reserved, and we walk past them and sit on the fourth row back, which is slightly raised, giving a clear view of the stage. I can hear Remi's brain ticking over. "Go, on, Sherlock, tell me your thoughts?"

"Well, there is one chair on the stage, so I am thinking this is a one man or woman show. The lighting is dim, so not sure what that's saying. The lights are also on us, so that makes me think that this is not a play or whatever, where you passively watch, because both worlds are meeting. The audience is a good mix of couples, different age groups, but I would guess ages around thirty-five to sixty-five. There are also a few ladies here with their girlfriends," he says, bringing to life his theory, knowledge and experience.

I try not to laugh, even though I'm impressed with his observation, but I wonder why he hasn't said anything about the music. So I ask, and his response informs me that he still has no idea.

"Hmm, haven't really thought about it. I just thought they were catering to their audience. We love R'n'B," he says. I nod in agreement but wonder how the famous suggestive song by Colour Me Badd that's playing over the speakers isn't a dead give-away. Shit, he was born in 1990, one year before the song came out. *Oh dear! Hah.*

The house lights are switched off and the music goes down. I silently congratulate myself, because he still has no clue. A spot-light at the back of the stage reveals the silhouette of a woman. Remi looks at me, but I ignore him.

"Good evening, London," says the seductive American voice that bellows out. "Are you ready for Flexie Lexi?"

The crowd cheers. Blackout. Seductive music begins and a spotlight follows the woman with long, flowing braids, wearing a barely-there orange lingerie set and six inch stilettos to centre stage. Her body is shapely, toned, and her skin is a rich shade of brown. She stands there in all her glory and allows the light to shine on her for a few moments. Remi looks at me with his mouth open. I look at him and say, "Happy date night, hun. Black Burlesque, baby!" He squeezes my hand.

"Oh my God, you smashed it!"

"Hey, ya'll," the women on the stage greets us through her head mic. "I'm Flexie Lexi from Miami, and tonight imma show you what Black Burlesque looks like. Are you ready for that?" The crowd cheers. "Well, that's great, but first let me tell you about boundaries. You all brave people in the front row—tonight your man is mine. Imma borrow him, just for tonight, and hopefully you guys will be inspired to go home and play. You see, I'm not tryna break up a happy home, I'm tryna inject some more spice into your relationships, and make you women more comfortable with your bodies. We are formidable human beings, and we need to own our sensual sides more. So tonight, we're gonna play. Whose down?" The audience cheers, and I'm thankful we aren't sitting anywhere near the front row.

For forty minutes we watch this woman break out into different routines, involving one chair, the floor and a few men, without breaking a sweat. Her level of fitness is incredible. The house lights switch on and she informs us that it's time for audience participation. I drop my eyes, because eye contact is a trap in these places. Two volunteers head to the stage, whilst a further four are picked at random. *It's not us, phew!*

Dog collar, handcuffs, whips and blindfolds are distributed, and the volunteers have to dance with their items. "Nerve-wracking for them, great entertainment for us watching," I whisper to Remi.

"I know, right? But if they just owned their sexiness more they would look so much better. Body shape doesn't even come into it. When a woman feels sexy, she *becomes* sexy. These ladies don't believe they're sexy," he expresses with passion, which makes me laugh, but he's not lying. He continues, "You've seen my seduction book, that's where I learnt this." *I remember that book, which I think I need to read.* Flexie Lexi knows how to tease and move her hips. *If she did classes straight after her show, I would attend.*

In no time, the audience members return to their seats, and the house lights swing up again. This time, Flexie Lexi specifically asks for a couple to join her. There is silence, so she throws a warning. "Don't let me come up these steps and select someone, I know you London folk don't like that so… Come on, work it out. One couple is all I need. Yes! You, sir, thank you, come on down."

"Come on, Syms," Remi says, standing up.

"OMG, you volunteered us?!" The daggers I'm throwing at him with my stare are real.

"Come on, hun, she was struggling up there." *I don't get why WE had to help her.* I resign to my fate and take off my black cardigan before we head to the stage. The audience cheers loudly. *How is this happening? My worst nightmare!*

"Hey guys, take a seat. So how long have you guys been together?"

"Officially? One month," says Remi.

"Is that all? Well let's test the strength of your relationship, then." The audience lets out a harmonious *ohhhhhhhhhh* in shock. I look out and can see a few women have their hands over their mouth. Flexie Lexi walks over to the speakers and selects a song. Remi looks at me, and for the first time sees what I had on underneath the cardigan. His eyes widen, and I smile. His reaction was my desired intention. *Lace, works every time.*

Flexie Lexi walks back and puts the 'test' to work straight away by straddling Remi and gyrating on him. She places his head in her bosom, turns back and looks at me. My face hasn't changed—in fact, a few women in the audience look more vex than me, *not sure why.* She gets up and moves seductively before bending over and slowly skimming her way up her legs as she slowly comes back up to standing position. She claps her bum cheeks whilst looking at me. I watch Remi struggle with where to look. He's sweating—and I'm sweating, because I'm on stage under these hot lights with all these people looking at me, at us.

Although he's hot under the collar, which is cute to see, Remi's handling it well. Flexie Lexi turns her attention to me now and… just wow. This woman can move. Light as a feather and yet so strong. She moves seductively, giving me a private dance, but I only have eyes for my man, who is watching us closely. Her form, her confidence, her oozing sensuality is what's so appealing. My hair piece and lace make me feel sexy, but I would love to learn this level of self-assurance.

She finishes her dance, and Remi kisses me and takes my hand as we leave the stage to loud applause. He receives a few pats on the back from men who give him comments such as, "Man, you done well," and "Mate, you held that down," as we return to our seats. We settle back in as passive audience members. Remi leans over to me and whispers, "You look hot. When did you buy that lacy number?"

"Ages ago, babe," I reply breezily.

"I want to see more of that," he says, kissing me whilst placing my hand into his lap. "You did that, not her" he tells me, smiling.

At the end of the show, Flexi Lexie receives a standing ovation, but there was never any doubt this would be the case. Remi receives more compliments from men and women who were impressed by how he conducted himself. A group of women approach me just as we're about to step out of the venue. "Hey, I just wanted to say you did great. I think I was more vex than you and he ain't even my man?"

"Oh, hahah. I didn't see anything to get vex about, she was clear from the start, and I'm secure in my relationship, so it's all good. In fact, I give her props. I need to learn to whine like that. Have a good evening ladies."

From nowhere, Remi pushes me against the wall outside and passionately begins to kiss me. He whispers, "You took me by surprise tonight. There are no words to express how much, I loved that, and just how shocked I was. Thank you. As much as I want to take you straight home, your outfit is too sexy. Let's find a bar."

We find a nice place on Marylebone High Street, and sip on lychee Martinis and Jamaican mules as we enjoy our surroundings. Remi is still beaming. "I just never thought you would have been up for something like that. It's a nice surprise. Not sure if I can top it. Plus, I never even knew there were Black burlesque dancers."

"Neither did I, and that is the main reason why I wanted to come. My girl came from *Miami*. Where do Black women here go to feel sensual and sexy? Where do we go to learn?"

"Ebony porn?" he says, half-joking.

"What I liked about Flexie Lexi is that she was in control all the time. It wasn't even about the man, it was about how her moves made men and women feel. That is what made it hot."

"You're right. Like that lace. It just feels like you came out of your comfort zone today."

"Yeah, I did. I think the type of event gave me permission to. I know it's only lace but... Anyway, it made me feel good. I just need to give myself permission to feel good."

"Yes, you do," he says, looking at me for a few minutes too long.

"What?" I ask shyly.

"Nothing," he says, reaching for his phone. My phone pings, and the message is from Remi.

Drink up right now, I'm taking you home to fuck you.

*

Journal
3rd July 2019

I went to a morning appointment at the hospital with Mum today, and as soon as she finished, I decided to come straight home to catch up on work. I arrived at Lewisham station and decided to walk home to get some fresh air and exercise. I walked past the gym I no longer go to and headed towards Lee High Road. I recognised his walk, build, long dreads and that gym bag immediately. It was Marcel. I've not bumped into him for almost a year. I know he wanted to speak to me, but I just kept it moving. A wave was my only acknowledgment.

So much has changed in a year. I thought back then Marcel was a catch, but I may have found my Bluefin tuna now.

*

Remi messages me at lunchtime and asks me to meet him after work for dinner in Kings Cross. Whilst we talk every day, I haven't stayed over in two weeks because I've been working out of the London Bridge office, which is closer to where I live, and on the past two weekends I've been catching up with my sister and girlfriends. It's worked out well, as he has also been really busy. I'm looking forward to seeing him.

I arrive at the restaurant in the 'new' Kings Cross—the swanky bit at the back, above the canal—and he's already waiting there. We greet, order quickly, and settle into our conversation, which always begins with a quick highlight of the day, best bits only, which he proposed and I adopted. It's too easy to bring the work rant home. What he actually said was, "nine to five should be nine to five, but it's not, because people bring work and their work stress home, which impedes on our time. So, say it if you must, I'm here to support you, but ten minutes max and the rant has to be over. Otherwise, I become an unofficial employee who isn't paid, and home becomes your big fat water-cooler moment. That's not happening."

Love it.

"Work has been busy, but good busy, Serita and Ade are settling in well. I get the feeling that other senior members think I hired them both because they're Black, but I didn't. They were the best on paper and in the interview. You have a whole company of white people, yet I'm under scrutiny because I bring the numbers up from two to four? It's a joke. But it's all good. They'll flourish, because I'll create the right conditions for growth." Remi nods.

"Also I may have a new client under Sym-phony, I'll know by next week for sure."

"You are loving working for yourself, aren't you?"

"I really am. I hope to fully transition over, so this becomes my main and only job in the next three years. This is the building time. How was your day, hun?"

"So good to hear. Yeah, it's been really good. Directing wise, the creative team are now all on board and I have a better idea about the direction of the whole play, and what I'm looking for in terms of casting. I'm on track."

"Ah, that's brilliant."

"I have a casting next week in Birmingham, so I'm also looking forward to that. I was thinking..." he says seriously. "You know you can come round to my place anytime, right?"

"I know," I say warmly.

"Mine is nearer to your workplace, and I'm just saying, if

you want to stay over more days in the week, feel free to. It makes sense."

I look at him. "Are you sure? I don't want to impede on your space."

"Syms, you need to let go of this space thing. I want you to impede on it, even though you're *not* impeding, which is why I want you in my space. I love it when you're around, and I would like you around more, and that's why I got you these."

He lays a set of keys on the table. *What?* I'm pleasantly surprised. I lean over to kiss him. "You are an incredibly giving, thoughtful and loving person, and I'm glad you're in my life."

"You're in trouble," he says, teasingly.

"So are you," I tease back, shaking my new set of keys in front of him.

"Seriously, Syms. I love you."

"I love you, too," I reply, without hesitation.

*

I decide to go home after dinner to gather some clothes, since I'll be spending more time with Remi during the week. On the journey home, I cannot stop smiling as I float in and out of wonder. How has any of this happened? One year later, and everything has changed and continues to change. *Surreal.*

I update the Supper Boogie girls group, and Adisa and Tasha, via voice note.

"Hey ladies, guess who ain't single no more? Are you all free this Saturday so I can tell you one time? Let me know. Woop

Woop!"

I head to the profile section on Facebook and eventually find the relationship button. I stare at the word *single*, which has been the setting ever since I joined Facebook—and decide to leave it as is. This has been a journey. Changing my status for all to see was never really the goal. I just wanted to make sure I was doing enough, putting myself first, addressing my issues and clearing out my rubbish, so that I could be the best version of me. The cherry on the top is that Remi emerged, he came through. Being single gave me the space to work on me. I'm not mad, the time was necessary.

The sun blazes through the train window, and I close my eyes to take in the warm orange sunrays without squinting. Straight away, Grandma Cedella appears in her luscious green garden, smiling at me. I take a deep breath and exhale. Grandma points to something in the distance. I look, and see a blue door.

I open my eyes and make a call. The phone rings…

"Hello, Dad."

Acknowledgement

To Valerie Brandes, thank you for seeing my potential. I'm so proud and honoured to be part of the groundbreaking #Twentyin2020 cohort. Thank you to the Jacaranda team and Uzo Njoku for the perfect book cover.

To Sareeta Domingo my editorial consultant, Symona has been beautifully shaped and It's down to your exceptional editorial notes. I cannot thank you enough.

To Dorothy Koomson, my unofficial mentor, your encouraging words and no nonsense attitude was exactly what I needed. Thank you.

Wendi Bekoe, you saw it all years before everyone else. To every Facebook friend who entertained my dating trials and tribulation posts, thank you. I wouldn't have even known I was onto something had it not been for your comments and engagement. Male friends, that also includes you, as you were just as intrigued. Shout out to Inua Ellams, Emil Socialize and BREIS who believed in me from the get-go.

This book was always going to be written, but it wouldn't have happened in this timeline if it wasn't for you Foluke Akinlose,

MBE. You sent me the competition details and I took the challenge. Thank you.

Thank you to my amazing friends who are true cheerleaders. Special thanks goes out to Caroline King and Zena Tuitt, you were the first people to read the first five pages of my first draft, the book has changed so much since then but your reactions gave me life. Lisa Anderson and Freya Berry, thank you for always checking in and reminding me of my vision on my off days. Ola Oyepitan and Patricia Conceicao thanks for always being there. Natalie Reid and Moniqueca West, the surprise gifts you sent were so thoughtful. Agnes Njoh, thank you for the fun times, stories for days. Selma Nicholls and Natalie Maddix, I'm as proud of you as you are of me, keep doing your thing your way. Natasha Stewart I miss you, but know you are always around (RIEP). I'm really blessed to have you all in my life.

Edison Agbandje and Mairead Armstrong you will never know how your words have impacted me. I thank you from the bottom of my heart for the teaching and insights.

To Ryan Coogler, thank you for your version of *Black Panther*, which gave me the courage to talk about ancestors in my work.

Thank you to writers and artists such as Terry McMillian, J. California Cooper (RIEP), India Arie, Jill Scott and Musiq Soulchild, whose books I got lost in and music I immersed in. Paul C. Brunson, thank you for sharing your insights around

Black love and relationships.

Iyanla Vanzant, your book came to me at the right time and I hope this book serves others in a similar way.

To my partner, Kwame Asiedu, thank you for your love, consideration and patience. You joined my rollercoaster ride with no complaints. You are appreciated and loved.

To my mum, my biggest champion, thank you for everything you've done and continue to do. What you have achieved is inspiring. I'm just copying you, but in my own way. To my awesome brother and family, I love you dearly.

To my ancestors, thanks for your guidance all along.

To my younger self: I thank you for looking out for me. For paying attention, listening to the signs and doing the self-work to ensure that I'm owning and accepting who I am, to be all that I am.

To you, the reader, thank you for reading my book. Regardless of your relationship status I hope it resonates in some way.

To you, Black single woman, I see you and hope I've captured some of your feelings. You aren't alone. Love exists for us too. Please remember x

About the Author

Lisa Bent is a writer of Jamaican descent from South London. Her work examines the inner self work required to heal and thrive. Her degree in Counselling influences her writing style and she champions the continuous journey of self-exploration. In 2015, after six years, she concluded the award-nominated blog Deeper Than Twitter. She has contributed to *Precious Online*, *The Tribe* and the *KOL Social Magazine*. *Symona's Still Single* is her first novel. Follow her on Twitter and Instagram @iamlisabent and find her at www.lisabent.com.